W9-CMJ-946

The Consuming Fire

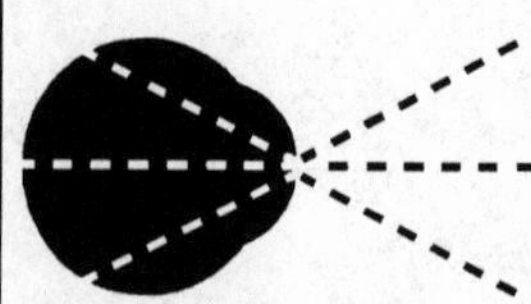

This Large Print Book carries the Seal of Approval of N.A.V.H.

THE INTERDEPENDENCY SERIES

The Consuming Fire

John Scalzi

THORNDIKE PRESS
A part of Gale, a Cengage Company

Farmington Hills, Mich • San Francisco • New York • Waterville, Maine
Meriden, Conn • Mason, Ohio • Chicago

The Interdependency Series.
Thorndike Press, a part of Gale, a Cengage Company.

This is a work of fiction. All of the characters, organizations, and events portrayed in this novel are either products of the author's imagination or are used fictitiously.
Thorndike Press® Large Print Basic.
The text of this Large Print edition is unabridged.
Other aspects of the book may vary from the original edition.
Set in 16 pt. Plantin.

**LIBRARY OF CONGRESS CIP DATA ON FILE.
CATALOGUING IN PUBLICATION FOR THIS BOOK
IS AVAILABLE FROM THE LIBRARY OF CONGRESS**

ISBN-13: 978-1-4328-6147-6 (hardcover)

Published in 2019 by arrangement with Macmillan Publishing Group, LLC/Tor/Forge

Printed in Mexico
1 2 3 4 5 6 7 23 22 21 20 19

To Meg Frank and Jesi Lipp

Prologue

Years later Lenson Ornill would reflect on the irony that his time as a religious man would be bracketed by a single and particular word.

"Well, fuck," Gonre Ornill said, to her husband, Tans, on the bridge of their spaceship, the *We Never Agreed to This.*

Tans looked up from his own workstation, where he had been instructing their son, Lenson, age eleven, on some of the finer points of shipwide energy management. "What is it?" he said.

"You know that imperial ship that wasn't following us?"

"Yeah."

"It's following us now."

Lenson watched his father frown, wipe the energy management screen from his own workstation and call up the navigation screen. On the screen was a representation of all the ship traffic between the outpost of

Kumasi and the Flow shoal that would take the *Agreed* to Yogyakarta, their next destination, after five weeks of travel. Most of the ships were commercial and trade concerns, like the *Agreed.* Two of them were Imperial Navy ships. One of those, the *Oliveer Bransid,* had just plotted a course that would intercept the *Agreed* in roughly six hours, right before it hit the shoal.

"I thought we were paid up," Tans said to his wife.

"We *are* paid up," Gonre said.

Tans motioned to his workscreen, as if to say, *Well, obviously not.*

Gonre shook her head. "We're paid up," she repeated.

"There's a new naval commander," Genaro Partridge, comms officer, said. She was part of the bridge crew of the *Agreed.* "I heard Samhir talking about it in mess. He says he was warned about him when we were loading in the cargo."

"You're telling us about this now?" Tans said to Partridge.

"Sorry. We were talking at mess. I thought Samhir told you."

"I meant to tell you," Samhir Ghan, the ship's purser, said three minutes later, when he appeared on the bridge, in a hurry. Lenson, looking at Ghan's slightly breathless form, knew his father had a reputation for being a genial captain, until he wasn't. Ghan was in danger of making his father not genial. "Sorry. We got busy in cargo."

"Tell me now," Tans said.

"The new naval commander is named Witt. A real grasping prick by all indications. Was transferred out of a job at Hub because he slept with the wrong person's spouse and is trying to get back there by 'cleaning house' here. Which means he's messing with established practices to look like he's being effective."

Tans frowned at this. Lenson, at eleven, didn't know the particulars of his parents' business, but he knew enough to know that much of it was predicated on "good relations" with the various local and imperial law enforcement people of the systems the *Agreed* traveled to. This entailed "established practices," which Lenson had only recently discovered meant giving certain people money and other desirable things in ways that were understood to be not entirely legal.

Lenson was neutral on all of this — he was young enough to believe that everything his parents did was by definition correct, and also to be bored with the fiddly details of their line of work — but it did seem like a long way to go around things.

"Who told you this?" Gonre asked Ghan.

"Cybel Takkat," Ghan said. "My opposite on the *Phenom.*" Lenson knew Ghan was referring to the ship *That's a Phenomenal View,* with whom they had shared a cargo hold at the Kumasi mercantile station. Smaller ships like the *Agreed* and the *Phenom* would frequently co-rent cargo space on the station to save money. Occasionally during the load in and load out things would get rushed and certain bits of inventory that started off on one ship would accidentally end up on another. Now that Lenson thought of it, he suspected this required some "established practices" as well. "She mentioned that one of her payments got waved off by one of her usuals in the navy here. He said he was being watched too closely by Witt's people now."

"We could have used this information sooner," Gonre said.

"Sorry," Ghan repeated. "I meant to tell you. I thought Cybel was just talking about how graft was being cracked down on, and we'd have to be less obvious about it from here on out. I didn't think she was saying that the navy was going to be chasing us to the Flow shoal."

Tans looked over to Partridge. "Any word

from that naval ship?"

"They're not hailing us, no," Partridge said. "They're just moving to intercept."

"We're not at full power," Gonre said to her husband. "We could run for it."

Tans shook his head. "Not yet." He tapped his workscreen to signify the *Bransid.* "That's a big ship. Lots of mass. It's slower to accelerate but faster under speed than we are. If we break and run now they'll catch up to us before we make it to the shoal."

"If they catch us with this particular cargo, we're all fucked," Ghan said, then remembered to whom he was asserting this fact. "Uh, sir."

Tans nodded absentmindedly at this and danced his fingers across his workstation keyboard. Lenson looked and saw his father was making calculations for the *Agreed* and for the *Bransid.* He couldn't follow the details but Tans made a small grunt of satisfaction, and then looked up at him. "Do you know what I'm doing?" he asked Lenson.

"No," Lenson said.

"Guess."

"Trying to get away from the other ship."

"Right," Tans said. "But do you know how? I already said if we accelerated now, they'd catch us."

"I don't know," Lenson said.

"Come on, work with me, Len."

Lenson thought about it. "You're waiting," he finally said, and hoped that his father wouldn't ask for any more detail than that, because frankly Lenson had no idea what would come after that.

"Yes!" Tans said. "There's a point in time after which if we accelerate under full engines, the navy ship won't catch us before we make the Flow shoal, even under their full power. And that time is" — he looked over to Gonre — "four hours, sixteen minutes from now."

"As long as the *Bransid* doesn't start accelerating before then," Gonre said.

"Yes."

"And as long as our own engines are able to handle the load of full acceleration for the three hours it will take us to hit the shoal."

"Yes."

"And as long as our push fields stay active so we're not compressed into jelly by the constant high-g acceleration."

"Yes," Tans said, testily.

"And as long as they don't try to shove a missile into our tailpipe."

"For fuck's sake, Gonre," Tans said.

"Let's not be too impressed with ourselves

yet, is what I'm saying," Gonre concluded. She turned to her son. "And you, go back to your cabin. The rest of us are going to be busy until we hit the shoal."

"There's nothing to do in my cabin," Lenson complained.

"Sure there is. It's called studying."

Lenson groaned at this and trudged back to his cabin, which, despite being roughly the size of a broom closet, was the second-most luxurious accommodation on the ship, after his parents' cabin, which was the size of two broom closets. In his cabin, Lenson activated his tablet and, rather than study, watched cartoons for a couple of hours until suddenly the cartoons wiped themselves out and educational materials appeared on his screen. Lenson groaned again, annoyed that his mother, who was supposed to be busy, had time to check on what he was looking at. Reluctantly he started reading his religion lesson, on Rachela, the Prophet, first leader and the first emperox of the Interdependency.

Lenson was not a very great student in a general sense but found the religion lessons of his study particularly boring. Neither he nor his parents were in any way religious, or followed the tenets of the Church of the Interdependency any more than they followed any other church. They weren't opposed to the church, or any other religion — Lenson knew some of the crew members of the *Agreed* followed their own personal faiths and his parents didn't care about it one way or the other — but the Ornills themselves left it alone and had passed their rather neutral apathy on the matter to their son.

The most you could say about the Ornill family's lack of religion was that when it came to which religion they weren't participating in, they weren't participating in the Church of the Interdependency most of all. For his part, Lenson knew other religions existed but knew so little about them that it couldn't be said he rejected or ignored them. They weren't even on the table.

The Church of the Interdependency, on the other hand, he knew at least a little about. One of the advantages of being the official religion of the Interdependency was that information about it was required reading in the study materials every child in the empire was obliged to have as part of their education. You learned about the C of I, and of the Prophet-Emperox Rachela, whether you believed or not, and whether you cared or not.

Well, that and the Ornills celebrated Emperox's Day, pinned to Rachela's standard calendar birthday, like everyone did, as an excuse for sleeping in, trading gifts and eating like a pig.

Lenson's studies at the moment were not talking about Emperox's Day, or gifts, or stuffing one's self, unfortunately for him. They were discussing Rachela's prophecies, the set of future-seeing pronouncements that galvanized the disparate systems that housed human settlements into the single empire known as the Interdependency and which helped to establish the economic, legal and social systems that the Interdependency still worked from, more than a millennium later.

All of which, Lenson decided, were boring as heck. Not only because the study materials, crafted for readers between the standard ages of ten and twelve, did not go into the prophecies or their impact in any substantive manner, preferring simple declarative sentences that took the material as a pedagogical fact rather than a matter of interpretation and debate (which to be fair, Lenson, again, not a very great student, would not have been an engaged participant in). It was also because of an inchoate feeling that Lenson had while reading about the prophecies, something that he couldn't have put into words even if he had tried.

But had he tried, what they would have boiled down to would have been, *Hey, you know what, basing an entire system of social, political and economic control on the vague, all-too-easily misinterpreted words of a single person claiming divine inspiration is probably not actually all that smart, now, is it.*

This was because Lenson, like his parents before him, was a mostly practical sort, not personally given over to matters spiritual, teleological or eschatological, and indeed all of the above offered up a muted sense of disquiet, the intellectual version of biting into a piece of pie and having a taste there you can't quite pin down but you know is not meant for that particular pie, and throws the whole thing off from being delicious to being a thing in your mouth that you're not entirely sure you want to be there but it would be rude to spit it out so you just swallow it, cover the rest of the pie with a napkin, and just try to get on with your day.

Reading the prophecies gave Lenson this same maddeningly unpin-downable sense of intellectual dissatisfaction on top of his boredom, so he did the only logical thing he could about it: He fell asleep, tablet in hand. This was an excellent plan, until suddenly the *Agreed* rocked violently, spilling Lenson from his bunk, and a roaring wind tore through his cabin, sucking the air from it for several seconds until the cabin door slammed shut.

Lenson lay on the floor, confused, gasping for breath, wondering what happened, and listening to several high-pitched whistling sounds in his cabin. His door had slammed shut but the seal was not perfect; likewise while the air vents in his room had sealed when air begun rushing through them in the wrong direction, there were tiny places where air snuck around the seal.

As a child who had lived on a spacecraft all his life, Lenson did not need to be told what those whistling sounds meant. He went to his door and pushed it completely shut, sealing it. That meant the only place his cabin was bleeding air was through the vents. The vent seals, unfortunately, were out of his reach, inside the walls of the ship.

His tablet pinged and Lenson answered it to find his mother on the other end. After the several seconds of weeping relief she had that her son was alive, she filled him in on what had happened.

"Motherfuckers shot at us," she said, and it was the first time Lenson had ever heard his mother use that particular profanity.

"They couldn't catch up to us and we weren't responding to their hails, so just before we entered the Flow they launched three missiles at us. Our defenses stopped them, but one detonated too close, and parts of the missile ruptured the hull near you. We've sealed off those areas, but we have a problem."

"What is it?" Lenson asked.

"We're in the Flow now," Gonre said. "That means we have to be careful not to disturb the bubble of space-time around the ship. If we disturb it too much, and we rupture it, that could mean trouble for the whole ship."

Lenson knew his mother was underselling the danger. The Flow was like a river that spaceships traveled between star systems, that could take the ships back and forth faster than if they traveled in normal space, where they could only go as fast as the speed of light. But while the Flow was like a river, it wasn't a river — it was an extra-dimensional whatever-it-was that if you were ever exposed to it directly, you would just *disappear.* Ships traveling in the Flow had to make an energy bubble that trapped a bit of space-time with them so they could still exist inside the Flow, and if the bubble popped, so did everything inside it.

"So we just have to be careful on our way to you, and in fixing the ship," Gonre said.

"Mom, I'm losing air," Lenson said.

Lenson watched his mother do a very good job of not losing it. "How much?" she asked.

"Only a little now. I lost a lot at first, but then the door closed and I sealed it. But there's still air going out of the vent."

Gonre turned away her tablet for a moment to yell at someone on the bridge. Then she turned back to her son. "We're going to get that fixed first," she said, "and get some more air to you."

"How long will that take?" Lenson asked.

"Not long," Gonre promised. "Can you be brave until then?"

"Sure," Lenson said.

But after two hours and the air growing noticeably thinner, Lenson stopped being brave and began to cry a little. After three hours he had a full-blown panic attack and it took everything Tans Ornill could do over the tablet connection to keep his son from hyperventilating away the dwindling supplies of his oxygen.

After four hours, and for the first time in his life, Lenson prayed to the Prophet Rachela.

After five hours, she came to visit.

Lenson looked up at the smiling visage of the Prophet, who had a serene, calm smile that didn't quite reach her eyes, keeping in the best traditions of religious iconography through the ages, in which the gods, goddesses and prophets could manage, at best, a disinterested upturning of the lips. Nevertheless Lenson was quieted and warmed by it.

"I'm scared," Lenson admitted to the Prophet. She just smiled more at him, radiating comfort that was more reassuring than any words from her could be. It said to him, or so he believed (and in this particular moment, why should he doubt it?) that she came because he prayed to her, that she came just for him, and that her presence here was proof that he, Lenson Ornill, would survive, and not just survive, but was destined for great things.

It was there, lying quiet in his cabin, gazing up at the Prophet and blinking so very slowly, that Lenson Ornill dedicated his life to the Church of the Interdependency.

The Prophet smiled down at him some more, as if accepting his gift of himself to her church.

Just then the vents clattered as they opened up, flooding the cabin with air. Lenson Ornill, gulping sweet oxygen and in the throes of religious ecstasy, passed out.

"That sounds like textbook hypoxia to me," Tans Ornill told his son in the ship's small infirmary, later that evening. Tans had been the first to enter Lenson's cabin, his immediate terror assuaged when he heard his son snoring. When Lenson woke up in the infirmary, he had immediately told his parents of his miraculous visitor. "You were short of oxygen and you'd been reading about the Prophet just before the attack. So it makes sense you might hallucinate her."

Lenson looked up at his father and his mother, both hovering over his infirmary cot, both so immensely relieved that their son was alive, and realized that they would never appreciate nor understand the experience of his visitation, and (rather maturely, he thought, at the time) decided to let them off the hook, nodded in apparent agreement with his father, and then let them both change the subject to that bastard Witt, upon whom they vowed certain revenge, and who would, Lenson learned much later, somehow find himself on the wrong side of an airlock roughly a year after the *Agreed* was attacked. The rumor was that Witt had once again slept with the wrong someone else's spouse, but Lenson thought other factors might have been in play, which his parents may or may not have been involved with.

By the time Lenson had finally heard about Witt's untimely encounter with the cold, dark vacuum of space, however, he was no longer on the *Agreed;* he was a student at the University of Xi'an's seminary school, the preeminent school for the Church of the Interdependency. Lenson's unconventional upbringing on a spaceship made him an object of some curiosity to his fellow seminarians, but only at first; what marked him further as an object of curiosity was his vision of the Prophet.

"Sounds like hypoxia," Ned Khlee, one of his first-year flatmates, told him in a late-night bull session, taking a swig of frado, a mildly psychotropic liqueur, and passing it on to Lenson.

"It wasn't hypoxia," Lenson said, taking the frado and passing it immediately to his right.

"I mean, you *were* hypoxic, right?" Sura Jimn, his other flatmate said, taking the bottle. "Your ship had a gash in it. Air was sucked out into space. Your cabin was leaking air for hours."

"Yes," Lenson admitted. "But I don't think that was why I saw her."

"Pretty sure it was," Khlee said. He

reached across Lenson to take back the frado from Jimn.

"So neither of you ever had a vision of Rachela? Ever?" Lenson asked, discomfited.

"Nope," said Khlee. "I hallucinated a lizard once, but I was very high at the time."

"It's not the same thing," Lenson said.

"It's kind of the same thing," Khlee said, and took another swig from the bottle. "A couple hits of this, and I might see it again."

Lenson decided that it probably wouldn't be a good thing to confide in his flatmates any more on this particular matter. Nor, as it would turn out, would he be confiding in most of his seminary mates. His fellow seminarians were generally kind, nice, moderate and compassionate individuals, all of whom had a practical, realistic streak in them, none of whom had ever experienced an ecstatic, religious fervor in their life, either for Rachela or for anyone else.

"The Church of the Independency is a largely *practical* religion," the Reverend Huna Prin, Lenson's curriculum advisor, told him in an early meeting, when Lenson decided he needed guidance on the matter and Prin seemed to him the one person obliged to address his issues without undue judgment. "It doesn't really lend itself to mysticism, either in its tenets or its daily application. It's closer to something like Confucianism than Christianity in its root."

"But Rachela herself had visions," Lenson protested, holding up the paperback of Kowal's *The Annotated Prophecies of Rachela I* he'd happened to be carrying about and waving it at his advisor.

"Yes she did," Prin agreed. "And of course one of the great discussions within the church is about the nature of those visions. Were they visions, actual communications with the divine, or 'visions' " — Lenson sensed the quotation marks around the world — "meant as parables to help a divided humanity understand the need for a new ethical system that focused on co-operation and interdependency on a much greater scale than ever existed before?"

"Over the history of the church these debates raged," Lenson said, nodding, echoing a primary text he'd read when he was much younger, imagining the brilliant early theologians going after each other in a high-stakes battle for the soul of the church.

"Well, *raged* is probably overstating it," Prin said. "I think at the Fifth Ecclesiastical Diet Bishop Chen threw a cup of tea at Bishop Gianni, but that was less about the fundamental nature of the visions than the fact Gianni kept interrupting Chen, and she was sick of it. On the whole the early debates were orderly and concerned about the practical issues of how to present the visions. The early bishops were well aware that charismatic religions have a tendency to breed schisms and divisions, which is against the fundamental concept of interdependency."

"Surely there are others who have had visions like mine," Lenson said to Prin, and in later memories of the conversation he remembered the pleading nature of the question to his advisor.

"The history of the church records occasional priests and bishops who claimed religious visions, and used them as justification for attempted schisms," Prin allowed. "The church has an inquiry process for it, which any priest or bishop who claims the visions must undergo."

"What happens?"

"If I recall correctly usually the priests claiming visions are referred to medical attention for previously undiagnosed mental health issues, treated and returned to service, or retired if the issues persist."

Lenson frowned. "So the church declares them crazy."

" 'Crazy' is a loaded term. I think it's better said that the church realizes as a practical matter that visions usually aren't actually divinely inspired but the result of other, less dramatic phenomena. Better to address that than to let the condition persist and possibly risk a schism."

"But I had a vision and my mental health is fine."

Prin shrugged. "Sounds like hypoxia to me."

Lenson brushed this aside. "What happens if an emperox claims to have visions?" he asked. "They're the actual head of the church. Do *they* go up against an inquiry?"

"I don't know," Prim admitted. "It hasn't happened since Rachela."

"Never," Lenson said, skeptically.

"After their investiture the emperoxs don't tend to bother with the church much," Prin said. "They have other things to worry about. And so do you, Lenson."

"So you think I should just chalk up my vision to lack of oxygen."

"I think you should view your vision as a gift," Prin said, holding up her hand to calm her advisee. "However it came to you, it inspired you to a life of service in the church, and that's a blessing to you and has the potential to be a blessing to the church. It's already been life changing to you, Lenson. Are you happy with the path it's put you on?"

"Yes," Lenson said, meaning it.

"Then there you are," Prin said. "In that sense it doesn't matter whether it was divinely inspired or the result of a temporary lack of oxygen. What matters is that in the aftermath — and while you did have enough oxygen — you decided to make the church your vocation. So let's you and I make the most of that, shall we?"

Lenson decided to make the most of it, and plunged into his seminary studies. Some of his early elective classes delved into the mysticism of the Church of the Interdependency, but ironically they were taught in a dry and unengaging style; the church's approach to what otherwise might be forbidden or apostate writings was not to avoid them but to smother the romance out of them with volumes of commentary apparently designed to put the reader to sleep. Lenson read all he could stand and found his interest draining away, slowly at first and more rapidly as time went on.

Two things were happening to Lenson. The first was, simply, that the day-to-day needs of his seminary and pastoral education were taking an upper hand. The amount of time and interest he could give over to the more esoteric aspects of the church —

as little as that eventually turned out to be — was shrinking as he managed the more prosaic topics of service and community engagement and did his time in Xi'an and Hub watching and helping priests and church lay employees tend to their duties, duties that he would one day assume. It was more difficult to stay engaged with the esoterica of one's religion when one was helping stock candles for services.

The second was that Lenson's own fundamental, practical nature, passed down to him from his parents through nature and nurture and never fully tamped down even at the height of his religious conversion, slowly and surely reasserted itself, aided rather than dissuaded by the Church of the Interdependency's mundane aspects. Lenson found that the routine and quiet systems of control the church offered appealed to him and that he moved well within them. Over the course of his years at the seminary he transformed himself in the eyes of his professors and fellow students from an object of curiosity to a model seminarian, one who was marked for his potential for an upward path in the church.

Lenson let himself be carried along in this wave of approbation and affection, in his first postings after his ordination to Bremen (where his parents, after carefully waiting out certain statutes of limitations, had retired, comfortably), and then to his later postings back at Hub, and eventually to Xi'an itself, where in the fullness of time he was made a bishop, with a portfolio for maintaining church services to the poorest of the citizens of the Interdependency — a post that put a premium on the practical rather than the purely spiritual side of the church.

As Lenson, now Bishop Ornill, moved further up and deeper into the Church of the Interdependency, the more the instigating event of his joining the church, the vision of the Prophet Rachela, was demoted in his memory. From a galvanizing moment of conversion, it eventually became a quiet source of faith, then an odd event that had led to a life choice, then a story for close friends in the church, then an anecdote for parishioners and finally a punch line at cocktail parties, where it was dutifully trotted out for new acquaintances when another bishop asked him to recount it.

"It sounds like a beautiful moment," one young woman said to him, at such a party.

"It was probably hypoxia," he replied in a charmingly deprecating manner.

In some small corner of his mind, Lenson

was aware that it was a shame that his sole moment of religious ecstasy had over time been rationalized down to the residue of a malfunctioning metabolic process, by himself no less than by others. But his response to that small corner was, he thought, a good one: that in place of one misattributed moment of mysticism, he had accrued a lifetime of practical service in a church that served as one of the cornerstones of the most successful and in many ways the most enduring of all human civilizations. The cynical would say that the church, so well integrated as it was into the imperial system, was just another lever of control, but Lenson was also aware that the cynical could afford the luxury of their cynicism because of the stability of the system they mocked.

In short, there was almost nothing mystical about Lenson's religion, or in these later days, to his faith. But it did not mean his faith was lessened. In fact his faith was stronger than it ever was. But it was not faith in the Prophet Rachela. It was faith in the church that sprang from her, a practical church, designed to endure through centuries and to help the empire that grew up with it endure as well. He believed in the Church of the Interdependency, and its mission, and his mission, within the warm and solid and fundamentally mundane confines of its rule. He was at peace with his practical faith.

It was this Bishop Lenson Ornill who, with all the other bishops of the Church of the Interdependency as could be assembled within the allotted time, sat in the pews of Xi'an Cathedral awaiting Emperox Grayland II, the titular head of the Church of the Interdependency, who had, unusually, decided to address the principals of her church as the cardinal of Xi'an and Hub — which is to say, as the actual head of the Church of the Interdependency — rather than in her more prosaic guise of emperox.

This raised eyebrows, since no other emperox in living memory had chosen to do so. The last who had, Erint III, has done so over three hundred standard years previously, and it had been on the rather dry subject of the redrawing of ecclesiastical districting so bishoprics were better apportioned by population. Current dioceses were perfectly acceptable from a population point of view; it wouldn't be on that.

Likewise Grayland II, while considered pleasantly ineffectual by the bishops in her role as emperox, had not to this point shown any particular affinity for the church as an entity. She had recently been preoccupied with an attempted rebellion by the Nohamapetan family and a theoretical issue regarding the stability of the Flow streams around the Interdependency, neither of which was directly related to the church, its processes or mission.

The idea that the emperox would wish to address the bishops on an ecclesiastical matter was surprising and, some would even say, perhaps cheeky. The general feeling of the bishops assembled was that they were willing to listen tolerantly to whatever musings their young emperox might have, and then go to the formal reception with her afterward, have some nibbles and a photograph with her, and then always have the event as a curious memory and conversation piece. Certainly Lenson thought this was the way it would go.

Thus was Bishop Lenson Ornill — and, to be fair, the rest of the bishops of the church — caught unawares when Grayland II, in the simple vestments of an ordinary priest rather than her cardinal finery, stood at the edge of the chancel and began by saying, "Many years ago, our ancestor and predecessor Rachela had visions. Those miraculous visions brought about our church, this church, this foundation upon which rests our entire civilization. Brothers and sisters, we have good news. We too, have had visions. Wonderful visions. Miraculous visions. Visions which speak to the mission of our church, and its role in the turbulent times of which we stand at the precipice. Rejoice, brothers and sisters. Our church is called to a new spiritual awakening, for the salvation of humanity in this world, and beyond it."

Lenson Ornill took in Grayland II's words, their intent and meaning, what they boded for the church as he understood it, his faith as he had developed it, and the genesis of his engagement with both, trapped in that small cabin, struggling to breathe, all those many long years ago. And then, quite without meaning to, he uttered the words to encapsulate what he was feeling about each, in this one epochal moment.

"Well, *fuck,*" he said.

Book One

Chapter 1

In the beginning was the lie.

The lie was that the Prophet Rachela, the founder of the Holy Empire of Interdependent States and Mercantile Guilds, had mystical visions. These visions prophesied both the creation and the necessity of that far-reaching empire of human settlements, strung out across light-years of space, connected only by the Flow, the metacosmological structure that humans compared to a river. They thought of it as a river mostly because human brains, originally designed for hauling their asses across the African savannah and not much upgraded since then, literally could not comprehend what it actually was, so, fine, "river" it was.

There was no mystical element involved in the so-called prophecies of Rachela at all. The Wu family ginned them up. The Wus, who owned and ran a consortium of businesses, some that built starships and others that hired out mercenaries, looked at the then-current political climate and decided the time was right to make a play for control of the Flow shoals, the places where humanly understandable space-time connected with the Flow and allowed spaceships to enter and exit that metaphorical river between the stars. The Wus understood well that creating tolls and monopolizing their extraction was a much more stable business model than building things, or blowing them up, depending on which of the Wus' businesses one contracted. All they needed to do was to create a reasonable justification to make themselves the toll collectors.

In the meetings of the Wus, the prophecies were proposed, accepted, written, structured, A/B tested and honed before they were attached to Rachela Wu, a young scion of the family who was already well-known as the public charitable face of the Wu family and who also had a razor-sharp mind for marketing and publicity. The prophecies were a family project (well, the project of certain important members of the family — you wouldn't just let *anyone* in on it, too many of the cousins were indiscreet and good only for drinking and being regional executives), but it was Rachela who sold them.

Sold them to whom? To the public at large, who needed to be convinced of the concept of the far-flung and disparate human settlements coming together under a single, unified governmental umbrella, incidentally to be headed by the Wus, who as it happened would collect levies on interstellar travel.

Not just Rachela, to be sure. In each star system, the Wus hired and bribed local politicians and publicly acceptable intelligentsia to promote the idea from a political and social point of view, to the sort of people who would like to imagine they needed a cogent and logical reason to toss away local sovereignty and control to a nascent political union that was already being constructed on imperial lines. But for the ones who either weren't that intellectually vain, or simply preferred to get the idea of an interdependent union from an attractive young woman whose nonthreatening message of unity and peace just made them *feel good,* well, here was the newly dubbed Prophet Rachela.

(The Wus didn't bother selling the mystical idea of the Interdependency to the other families and large corporations that they and their conglomerate moved among. For those they took another tack instead: Support the Wus' plan for rent-seeking disguised as an altruistic exercise for nation-building and in return get a monopoly on a specific, durable good or service — in effect, trade their current businesses, with their annoyingly spikey boom-and-bust cycles, for a stable, predictable and ceaseless income stream, for all time. Plus a discount on the tolls the Wus were about to enact on Flow travel. In point of fact these weren't discounts at all, because the Wus were planning to charge for a thing that used to be without cost to anyone. But the Wus assumed that these families and companies would be so dazzled by the offer of an unassailable monopoly that they wouldn't kick. Which turned out to be mostly correct.)

In the end it took the Wus less time than they expected to pull off their Interdependency scheme — within ten years the other families and companies were in line with their monopolies and promised noble titles, the paid-for politicians and intellectuals made their case, and the Prophet Rachela and her rapidly expanding Interdependent Church mopped up most of the rest of the public. There were holdouts and stragglers and rebellions that would go on for decades, but by and large the Wus had correctly picked their time, their moment, and their goal. And for the troublemakers, they had already decided that the planet called End, the human outpost in the newly imagined Interdependency that took the longest to get to, and to get back from, and had only a single Flow shoal in and out, would be the official dumping ground for anyone who got in their way.

Rachela, already the public and spiritual face of the Interdependency, was selected by (carefully orchestrated) acclamation as the first "emperox." This new gender-neutral title had been chosen because market testing showed that it appealed to nearly all market segments as a fresh, new, and friendly spin on "emperor."

This compact and highly elided history of the formation of the Interdependency may make it appear as if no one questioned the lie — that billions of people uncritically swallowed the fiction of Rachela's prophecies. This was not at all accurate. People *did* question the lie, to the same amount as they would question any bit of pop spirituality marching toward an actual religion, and became alarmed as it gained acceptance, and followers, and respectability. Nor were observers of the time blind to the machinations of the Wu family as it made its play for imperial power. It was the focus of many handwringing editorials, news shows and occasionally attempted legislative action.

What the Wu family had over them was organization, and money, and allies in the form of the other now-noble families. The formation of the Holy Empire of the Interdependent States and Mercantile Guilds was a charging musk ox, and the skeptical observers were a cloud of gnats. Neither did much damage to the other, and in the end there was an empire.

One other reason the lie worked is that once the Interdependency formed, the Prophet-Emperox Rachela declared her visions and prophecies had largely come to an end, for now. She devolved all functional power in the administration of the Interdependent Church to the archbishop of Xi'an and a committee of bishops, who knew a good deal when they saw one. They rapidly built an organization that shoved the explicitly spiritual aspect of the church to the side, to be the spice of the new religion, not its main course.

In other words, neither Rachela nor the church overplayed its spiritual hand in the critical early years of the Interdependency, when the empire was necessarily at its most fragile. Rachela's imperial successors, none of whom added the "prophet" part of the title to their address, largely followed her example, staying out of church business except for the most ceremonial parts, both to the relief, and then as the centuries passed, to the expectation, of the church itself.

The lie of Rachela's visions and prophecy was never acknowledged by the church, of course. Why should it have been? To begin, neither Rachela nor the Wu family ever explicitly said outside of family conferences that the spiritual side of the Interdependent Church was wholly concocted. One could not expect Rachela's successors, either as emperox or in the church, to own up to it, or even to publicly air their own suspicions and undermine their own authority. After that it was simply a matter of waiting until the visions and prophecy became doctrine.

For another thing, Rachela's visions and prophecies largely came true. This was a testament to the fact that the "prophecy" of the Interdependency, while expansive, was also practically achievable, if one had ambition, money, and a certain amount of ruthlessness, all of which the Wu family had, in bulk. Rachela's prophecies did not ask people to change the way they lived, in the small-bore, everyday sense. It just asked them to swap out their system of governance, so that those at the very very top could have even more power, control and money than they had before. As it turned out, this was not too much to ask.

Finally, as it happened, the Wu family wasn't *wrong.* Humanity was widely dispersed, and of all the star systems that the Flow was known to touch, only one of them had a planet capable of sustaining human life in the open: End. All the humans in all the other systems lived in habitats on planets, moons, or floating in space, all monstrously vulnerable in their isolation, none of them entirely able to produce the raw materials needed for their existence or to manufacture all they would need to survive. Humanity needed interdependence to survive.

Whether it needed *the Interdependency* as the political, social and religious structure to implement that interdependence was highly questionable but, a millennium on, a moot point. The Wu family had envisioned a path to long-term, sustainable political and social power for itself and took it, using a lie as a tool to get everybody else to go along. Incidentally, the Wus also created a system under which most humans could have a comfortable life without the existential fear of isolation, entropy, the inevitable horrifying collapse of society and the death of everyone and everything they hold dear hanging over their heads every moment of every day.

The lie worked out for everyone, more or less. It was awesome for the Wus, pretty great for the rest of the noble class, and generally perfectly okay for most other folks. When a lie has negative consequences, people dislike it. But otherwise? They move on, and eventually the lie as a lie is forgotten, or in this case, codified as the foundation of religious practice and buffed and sanded into something prettier and more congenial.

The visions and prophecies of Rachela were a lie, which functioned exactly as intended. Which meant that visions and prophecy remained a doctrinal cornerstone of the Interdependent Church — from a prophet, mind you. There had been one, who had become the first emperox. There was nothing in church doctrine barring another emperox from claiming the power of vision or prophecy. Indeed, church doctrine deeply suggested that, as the head of the Interdependent Church, the visionary power of prophecy was the birthright of the successor emperoxs, all eighty-seven of whom to date could trace their lineage back to the Prophet-Emperox Rachela herself — who aside from being the mother of the Interdependency, was also the mother of seven children, including triplets.

Every emperox was doctrinally capable of having visions and making prophecies. It's just that, excepting Rachela herself, none of them ever did.

None, that is, until now.

In the anteroom of the Chamber of the Executive Committee, the room given over at the imperial palace to the group of the same name, and of which she was the chair, Archbishop Gunda Korbijn abruptly paused, surprising her assistant, and bowed her head.

"Your Eminence?" her assistant, a young priest named Ubes Ici, said.

Korbijn held up her hand to quell the question, and stood there for a moment, collecting her thoughts.

"This used to be easier," she said, under her breath.

Then she smiled ruefully. She had intended to offer up a small prayer, one for patience and calm and serenity in the face of what was likely to be a long day, and month, and possibly rest of her career. But what came out was something else entirely.

Well, and that was about par for the course these days, wasn't it.

"Did you say something, Your Eminence?" Ici asked.

"Only to myself, Ubes," Korbijn said.

The young priest nodded to this, and then pointed to the door of the chamber. "The other members of the executive committee are already here. Minus the emperox, of course. She'll be arriving at the agreed time."

"Thank you," Korbijn said, looking at the door.

"Everything all right?" Ici asked, following his boss's gaze. Ici was deferential but he wasn't stupid, Korbijn knew. He was well aware of recent events. He couldn't have missed them. No one could have. They had rocked the church.

"I'm fine," Korbijn assured him. She moved toward the door and Ici moved with her, but Korbijn held up her hand again. "No one in this meeting but committee members," she said, and then caught the unasked question on Ici's face. "This meeting is likely to have a frank exchange of views, and it's best those are kept in the chamber."

"A frank exchange of views," Ici repeated

skeptically.

"Yes," Korbijn said. "That's the euphemism I'm going with at the moment."

Ici frowned, then bowed and stepped aside.

Korbijn looked up, offered a prayer, for real this time, and then pushed through the doors into the chamber.

The chamber was large and excessively ornate in a way that only a room in an imperial palace could be, filled with the cruft of centuries of artistic gifts, patronage, and acquisitions by emperoxs with more money than taste. Along the far wall of the chamber a mural flowed, representing some of the great historical figures that had been part of the executive committee over the centuries. It was painted by the artist Lambert, who had painted the background in the style of the Italian Renaissance and the figures themselves in early Interdependency realism. From her earliest days on the committee, Korbijn had found the mural both an appalling mishmash, and its heroic representation of figures an almost hilarious overrepresentation of the importance of the executive committee, and what it did on a day-to-day basis.

No one's going to put this *committee in a mural,* Korbijn thought, approaching the long table that featured ten ornate chairs. Eight of those chairs were already filled with the two other representatives of the church, three members of parliament, and three members representing the guilds and the nobility who controlled them. One of the remaining chairs, at one end of the table, was for her, as head of the committee. The other was for the emperox, currently Grayland II, the source of Korbijn's current headache.

As she was reminded the very second she sat down in her seat.

"What the fuck is this about the emperox having *visions*?" said Teran Assan, scion of the House of Assan, and the newest member of the committee. He was a hasty (probably *too* hasty, in Korbijn's estimation) replacement for Nadashe Nohamapetan, who was currently in imperial custody for murder, treason and the attempted assassination of the emperox.

Korbijn missed her relatively polite presence. Nadashe may have been a traitor, but she had decent manners. Assan's current outburst was, alas, standard operating procedure for him. He was one of those people who believed social graces were for the weak.

Korbijn looked around the table to see

the other reactions to this outburst, which ranged from disgust to weary recognition that Assan's behavior probably was setting new, low benchmarks for bad behavior.

"And a good morning to you, too, Lord Teran," Korbijn said. "How good of you to start our meeting off with a round of pleasantries."

"You want pleasantries while our emperox announces that she's having religious delusions about the end of the Interdependency and the destruction of the guild system," Assan said. "May I suggest, Your Eminence, that your sense of priorities is out of whack."

"Insulting the other members of the committee is not a very effective way to work, Lord Teran," said Upeksha Ranatunga, the ranking parliamentarian on the committee. Assan had been rubbing Ranatunga the wrong way from the moment he joined the committee. This took some effort, Korbijn knew. Ranatunga was the very model of the practical politician. She made it her business to get along with everybody, especially the people she loathed.

"Let me offer a rebuttal," Assan said. "In the past month our beloved emperox has announced that she believes the Flow — our way to travel between stars — is collapsing, and trotted out some backwater scientist no one's heard of to bolster her claim. This claim is fueling economic and social unrest, even as other scientists dispute the assertion. And now, in response to *that,* the emperox is claiming mystical *communications.*

"But Her Eminence here" — Assan waved at Korbijn — "wants to exchange *pleasantries.* Fine. Hello, Your Eminence. You are looking very well. Also, wasting time on pleasantries is stupid and unnecessary, and incidentally, in case you haven't heard, the leader of the empire is having fucking *visions,* so maybe we should dispense with the pleasantries and focus on that, what do you say."

"And what is your objection to these visions, Lord Teran?" Korbijn said, as pleasantly as possible, folding her hands together.

"Are you kidding?" Assan leaned forward in his chair. "One, it's obvious that the emperox's claiming visions because she's getting pushback on the idea that the Flow is shutting down. She's trying to do an end run around parliament and the guilds, which are resisting her. Two, so far, the church — *your* end of things, Your Eminence — is giving her cover to do just that. Three, if she is having visions and isn't just using them as a convenient lever, then our young new emperox is in fact delusional, and that just might be a *pressing issue.* All of these need to be addressed, now."

"The church isn't giving the emperox cover," said Bishop Shant Bordleon, who as the second-most junior member of the committee sat across from Assan.

"Really?" Assan shot back. "I haven't heard a peep out of the church about it since Grayland gave her little speech in the cathedral two days ago. That's just a *few* news cycles. You surely could have said something about it by now. A rebuttal, perhaps."

"The emperox is *head of the church,*" Bordleon said, in a tone that suggested he was instructing a particularly stubborn child. "This isn't some minor priest going rogue in a far-flung mining habitat who we can tell to get in line."

"So it's different for emperoxs," Assan cracked, sarcastically.

"In fact, it is," Korbijn said. "The emperox addressed the bishops formally, speaking *ex cathedra,* not in her capacity as the secular head of the empire but in her ecclesiastical person as the successor to the prophet. We can't *dismiss* what she said in that context. Nor can we rebut it. The most we in the church can do is *work* with it.

Interpret it."

"Interpret delusions."

"Interpret *visions.*" Korbijn looked around the table. "The Interdependent Church was founded through the visions of the Prophet Rachela, who also became the first emperox of the Interdependency. The roles have been intertwined since the founding of the empire." She focused on Assan. "Doctrinally speaking, Grayland is doing nothing controversial. The church, whatever its current nature, was founded on visions of a spiritual nature. Our doctrine accepts that the cardinal of Xi'an and Hub, as the head of the church, may have visions of a spiritual nature, just as Rachela did. And that these visions may be revelatory, and may affect doctrine."

"And you expect us to go along with that," Assan said.

"Who is the 'us' you are referring to?" Korbijn asked.

"The guilds, for one." Assan pointed to Ranatunga. "Parliament, for another."

"There *are* still laws for blasphemy," Bordleon noted. "They're even occasionally enforced."

"Well, isn't that convenient," Assan said.

"Lord Teran has a point," Ranatunga said, and Korbijn, for one, respected Ranatunga for being able to say that without stroking out. "Doctrinally correct or not, no emperox in memory has so actively laid claim to the religious mantle of head of the church. Certainly none have claimed visions."

"You believe the timing is suspicious," Korbijn said to Ranatunga.

" 'Suspicious' is not the word I would use," Ranatunga replied, politic as ever. "But I'm not blind to Grayland's political situation, either. Lord Teran is correct. She's disrupted the function of the government with her claims about the Flow. She's panicking people. The answer to this is not to appeal to prophecy, but to science and reason."

Korbijn frowned slightly at this. Ranatunga caught it and held out a placating hand. "This is not a criticism of the church or its doctrines," she said. "But, Gunda, you have to admit it. This is not what emperoxs do. We need at the very least to ask her about it. Directly."

A notification on Korbijn's tablet pinged. She read it, and stood, prompting the others to stand as well. "You're about to have your chance, Up. She's here."

CHAPTER 2

The moment Emperox Grayland II had been waiting for came at the end of a long and frankly mind-numbing meeting.

"Your Majesty, perhaps we should further discuss your . . . visions," Archbishop Gunda Korbijn said. Around the table, the heads of the executive committee, tasked with advising the emperox in her administration of the Interdependency, whether she wanted that advice or not, swiveled to look at her.

On those nine faces, Grayland registered various emotions. Some registered concern, which she appreciated. Some registered contempt, which she did not. Others registered, variously, amusement, irritation, disgust or confusion. Some faces registered some or all of these emotions combined.

Grayland II, Emperox of the Holy Empire of the Interdependent States and Mercantile Guilds, Queen of Hub and Associated Nations, Head of the Interdependent Church, Successor to Earth and Mother to All, Eighty-Eighth Emperox of the House of Wu, studied all these faces, taking in the expressions arrayed across the table, assessing the emotions of the nine arguably most powerful people in the known universe, aside from her.

And then laughed.

Which did not endear her further to them.

"You think us mad," Grayland said, employing the imperial "we," because in point of fact she was busy being the emperox at the moment and could use the imperial address without undue pretension.

"No one has suggested such a thing," Korbijn said, hastily.

"We are very sure *that* is not true," Grayland replied, lightly. "Certainly no one has suggested such a thing, here at this table, to our face. But we are not so naive as to believe that away from our presence, such things are not only whispered but spoken aloud, and perhaps occasionally shouted."

At this, Grayland noticed several sets of eyes shift to Teran Assan, the newest member of the committee. This did not exactly surprise her.

"We are all loyal, Your Majesty," Upeksha Ranatunga said.

Grayland turned to Ranatunga. "We have no reason to doubt the committee's loyalty," she said, kindly. Ranatunga was the one who had had a concerned expression. "To me, and to the Interdependency. Yet we are also aware where 'loyalty' can drive the concerned, if they believe the person to whom they are loyal has taken leave of their senses."

"Your Majesty wishes our obedience, then," said Assan. He'd been one with contempt on his face, although to be fair he'd worn that expression since he'd taken his seat, a few weeks prior.

"We are hoping for your faith," Grayland said, and looked around the table. "You may believe we understand that this faith is difficult for you. No emperox since Rachela has claimed revelatory visions until now. For a millennium the emperoxs have been content to stay out of the revelation business. And even those of us who experienced delusions kept them out of the religious sphere. When Attavio II experienced alcoholic hallucinations near the end of his reign, he saw bejeweled chickens running around the palace." Grayland chuckled at this and then noted that no one else at the table was chuckling with her.

"Some of us worry your visions may be

closer to chickens than actual revelation," Assan said, and Grayland watched as eight pairs of eyebrows, attached to the other committee members, moved up in varying levels of shock and surprise.

Grayland laughed again. "*Thank you,* Lord Teran," she said. "Would that all our advisors were so honest in their opinions."

"I didn't say that to gain your favor," Assan replied.

"You may be assured that we did not think you had," Grayland said. She turned to Korbijn, the head of the executive committee. "And as we had anticipated that this would be a matter of concern for the committee, not to mention the Interdependency as a whole, we have already ordered Qui Drinin, the royal physician, to make himself available to the executive committee, at its pleasure, to discuss our current physical and mental state. You may ask him whatever you like."

"That's good to hear," Korbijn said. "We'll call him very soon."

Grayland nodded, and then returned her attention to Assan. "Our visions aren't phantom chickens, Lord Teran. They are something else entirely. We can't say we wanted them. Times are difficult enough at the moment without adding this spiritual aspect to them. But we are the emperox and a direct line descendant of the Prophet Rachela. The same blood runs through our veins as hers. This *is* the Holy Empire of the Interdependent States, and the empire has seen fit to keep the House of Wu on its throne for a millennium. Is it not reasonable to believe that one of those reasons was to keep open the possibility of revelation?"

"I am skeptical that revelation is a genetically heritable trait, Your Majesty," Assan said.

"Well, if we are honest, so are we," Grayland said. "And yet here we are. We, like Rachela, are the head of the Interdependent Church, a church that was founded on the basis of revelation. We, like Rachela, have had our revelation at the cusp of an immense change in the nature of humanity's existence in space. We, like Rachela, are called to shepherd our people through crisis."

"This is the collapse of the Flow your scientist alleges."

Grayland smiled. "Have you seen the list of ships that arrived to Hub from End in the last month, Lord Teran? We have. The list is very short, because the number is zero. They're not here because they never left End. The Flow stream from here to there has collapsed. If memory serves, one of the ships that has yet to arrive is one of *yours,* by which I mean, one from the house of Assan. Scheduled to arrive from End three weeks ago. I seem to remember my tariffs assessor mentioning it."

Assan looked uncomfortable. "It's still within its acceptable window for arrival."

"And there is a civil war going on at End," Ranatunga noted. "That will have some effect on the arrival of ships."

"The committee may suppose it has the luxury of assuming pedestrian causes for the late arrival of every single ship from one of our states," Grayland said. "We don't. The Count Claremont, at the direction of my father, studied the data from Flow streams for three decades and predicted to within hours the collapse of the Flow stream from End to Hub. Within another month, the Flow stream from Hub to Terhathum is very likely to be next. We have made all this data available to this committee, to parliament and to scientists; and Lord Marce, the Count Claremont's son, has stayed to explain the data to everyone who chooses to listen."

"And yet neither parliament nor the scientists are entirely convinced," murmured Korbijn.

"There is a lot of data to cover, and unfortunately not very much time," Grayland said. "We regret to say they are likely to be better convinced when the Terhathum Flow collapses."

"If," Assan said.

Grayland shook her said. "When."

"And you've seen this in your *visions,*" Assan said, pushing.

Grayland smiled at this. "One does not need visions when one has data. In both cases, however, one does need to be willing to see. We need this committee to see both. We need you to understand the data. We need you to have faith. And if you will not do either, then, yes, Lord Teran, we *will* accept simple obedience. That will do for now." She stood, obliging her executive committee to stand in return. Then she nodded, acknowledging them, and left the room.

"I think I may have made a mistake," Cardenia Wu-Patrick said, to the ghost of her father.

Attavio VI, or more accurately his ghost, or even more accurately the computer simulation of Attavio VI, fashioned from a lifetime of recorded memories, emotions and actions, nodded. "You may have," he said.

"Thanks," Cardenia, who when in her full majesty was called Grayland II, said. "Your vote of confidence here is inspiring."

The two of them were in the Memory Room, a large and largely unadorned room accessible only to the current emperox. Inside of it was a virtual assistant named Jiyi who could, when asked, call up the avatar of any of the previous emperoxs, down to and including the first, Rachela. When Cardenia's time as emperox was done, her memories, emotions and actions would also be downloaded to serve the uses of whomever would be the next emperox.

If there was going to be one, which at the moment struck Cardenia as a question without a very good answer.

"I was only agreeing with you," Attavio VI said. "You seem upset and I thought agreeing with you might make you feel better."

"Not in this particular case, I have to say. We need to work on your program's ability to pick up emotional cues."

"Well, then." Attavio folded his hands together, standing while his daughter sat. "Give me more detail on what you think you've made a mistake about."

"About saying that I'm having visions."

"About the end of the Interdependency."

"Yes."

"Oh. Well, yes. You probably *did* make a mistake about that."

Cardenia threw up her hands.

"I'm wondering what you expected," Attavio VI said.

"Are you really?"

"To the extent that I am able to, yes."

"Tell me why."

"You are attempting to re-create what Rachela did, but you don't have Rachela's starting conditions. You don't have the support of the Wu family or its resources to support you in other areas. You don't have the leverage with the noble houses to make deals. The only support you have is likely to be the Interdependent Church, and that only grudgingly. Finally, you're not building an empire. You're attempting to dismantle one. One that has been successful for a thousand years."

"I know all of that," Cardenia said. "I also considered that we've already had one Flow stream closed up and that more will close soon after. I know that I don't have time to build consensus in the parliament or among the guilds or even among scientists before things start to fall apart. I need to get out ahead of the crisis in a way that lets me save as many people as possible. The way to do that is through the church. And the way to do that is in a way that gives the church no doctrinal way to argue. By claiming prophecy."

"You do understand that 'no doctrinal way to argue' does not mean 'no argument,' " Attavio VI said. "A church is an institution separate from the religion it serves. It's filled with people. And you know how people are."

Cardenia nodded. "I thought I understood that."

"But now you have doubts."

"I do. I didn't think that I could turn the church instantly. I'm not stupid. But I thought there would be more cooperation. More understanding of what it was that I was doing."

"You haven't expressed this to the leaders of the church," Attavio VI said.

Cardenia snorted and looked at her father. "I'm not *that* stupid, either," she said. "As far as the church is concerned I am serenely confident of my visions. The executive committee, too. I met with them today and told all of them I needed their faith. I thought Lord Teran's head, at least, might explode from rage."

"I didn't know him," Attavio VI said. "I knew his father. The House of Assan is a close political ally to the House of Wu."

Cardenia nodded again. "It's why Lord Teran was placed on the committee, I think. The guilds thought they needed to make it up to me for putting Nadashe Nohamapetan on the committee first. But I'm not sure Lord Teran is any better. With Nadashe Nohamapetan, at least, you knew she was plotting for herself and her family. I'm not at all sure what Lord Teran is up to."

"You could find out," Attavio VI suggested.

"I don't think we're there yet."

"You're the emperox. You're always there yet."

Lord Teran Assan swiped his hand over the lock for his suite in the family apartments in Xi'an. His suite was currently minimally appointed; most of his belongings were still in his larger apartments in Hubfall, where prior to his current assignment he'd been acting as the House of Assan's managing director for operations in-system.

Assan's ascent to the imperial executive committee was a coup for the House of Assan, which had been angling to be on the committee for literally centuries. It was always denied a spot because the House of Assan was famously allied with the House of Wu, and the House of Wu was nominally headed by the emperox. In point of fact the emperoxs almost never meddled in the day-to-day operations of the House of Wu. The Wu board of directors, assembled from ranking cousins of the Wu family, would resent it intensely, and anyway the emperox had the rest of the Interdependency to run.

Nevertheless the other guilds, and their respective noble houses, believed the Assan-Wu relationship too close for political comfort. The last thing they wanted on the executive committee was another potential reflexive cheerleader for the policies of whomever was the sitting emperox at the time.

But then Nadashe Nohamapetan had to go and try to assassinate Grayland II — once for sure, possibly twice (the jury was still out on that one; actually the jury had yet to be empaneled for that one, but the metaphor still held), and regardless of that did manage to kill her older brother in the process, foment a rebellion on the planet of End with the help of her other brother, and generally act in all sorts of obviously traitorous ways.

Suddenly, a little light fluffing of the emperox seemed like just what the guilds had ordered. And so, enter, for the first time, the House of Assan onto the executive committee. Assan was obliged, as the ranking family member in-system, to take on the responsibility.

Assan thought it was a real waste of his time. Grayland (and here Assan winced involuntarily, because he had met the emperox when she was still Cardenia Wu-Patrick and not been impressed by her in any way whatsoever; she was about as qualified to be emperox as Assan was qualified to juggle knives) was obliged to meet with the committee and hear their concerns and advice. But she wasn't obliged to consider or follow them in any substantial manner, and it was clear by the end of Assan's first meeting, nearly a month prior now, that Grayland mostly came to the meetings to get them over with.

This was especially problematic because Grayland, immediately prior to his arrival on the committee, had dropped her nonsense about the shift in the Flow streams, trotting out some twit named Lord Marce who purported to have evidence of the same. Marce was, it had to be said, not exactly the most convincing of public speakers, either in front of the committee or testifying in front of parliament. And while the growing lack of shipping from End was beginning to concern a number of houses (including Assan's — the emperox was correct that one of their fivers, the *And for This Gift I Feel Blessed,* was now worryingly overdue), the fact that the emperox's lackey announced that the next Flow stream to collapse would be to the home system of the Nohamapetans was a little *on the nose.*

It hadn't happened yet, in any event. Until (or if) it did, there were all sorts of reasons for ships to be held up at End without the drastic explanation of a Flow stream collapse. Including an imperial freeze on spaceship movement.

Which led to the question of what, exactly, it was that Grayland II was *actually* playing at. And how long she thought she could play at it before it all fell down around her. And whether these goddamned "visions" of hers were now just another tactic to keep her whatever damn fool game she was running going for a few more days or weeks.

All things considered, Assan felt he should have just stayed in his office and stuck to his own business.

Which was not to say that he wasn't going to use his current situation to his own advantage.

Assan walked over to his bar, put ice in a tumbler, poured whiskey over it, and then called Jasin Wu, board member for the House of Wu, on a secure line.

"You wanted a report on this session?" Assan asked.

Jasin grunted and Assan hit the highlights, including the discussion of Grayland's visions. "She asked us to have *faith,*" Assan finished up.

"For fuck's sake," Jasin Wu said, disgusted. "The House of Wu makes starships. She's wandering around saying the Flow is collapsing. We've had orders drop forty percent off their usual clip. It's like she's trying to destroy her own family."

"She never really *was* part of the family, was she," Assan murmured. "It was Rennered who was supposed to take over everything."

"Until he drove a car into a wall, yes," Jasin said. "Stupid. That is, if Nadashe Nohamapetan didn't have him killed by messing with his car."

"She's not really a problem anymore for you."

"She's still alive. So she's still a problem. For now."

" 'For now'?" Assan asked.

Jasin ignored this. "You need to get a one-on-one meeting with Grayland," he said. "Find out what's really going on with her."

"I've been trying to get a meeting with her since I arrived," Assan protested. "I keep being shoved down the schedule. *You* should ask for a meeting with her. And take me with you."

"That's not usually done," Jasin said. "The emperox has an annual courtesy meeting with the House of Wu board once a year, and otherwise everything is handled by underlings."

"The emperox claiming visions isn't usually done either," Assan pointed out.

Jasin grunted again at this. "I'll think about it," he said, and switched off.

Assan took a sip from his whiskey and placed a second secure call, this one to Deran Wu, cousin of Jasin, also on the board of the House of Wu.

"You wanted a report on this session?" Assan asked, and then gave Deran roughly the same report he'd given Jasin.

"You gave Jasin the same report?" Deran asked.

"Pretty much," Assan said.

"And his reaction?"

"He's concerned it will affect shipbuilding."

Deran snorted. "That's because he's an idiot. Anything we lose on ships we gain in weapons sales and security assignments."

"In the short term," Assan pointed out. "If the emperox is correct about the Flow streams collapsing."

Deran made a dismissive motion. "Grayland's loopy, and it's not going to take that long for the rest of the house to recognize that and take steps."

"What's that mean?"

"It means you don't need to worry about it right now. And that it would have been nice if Nadashe Nohamapetan had managed to finish the job when she sent that shuttle to plow into my dear cousin. That was a piece of work."

"I don't think Jasin is pleased she's still alive. Nadashe Nohamapetan, I mean. Not Grayland."

"Trust me, I'm well aware of Jasin's opinions on that matter. He's not shy about that."

"It wouldn't look great for the emperox if something were to happen to Nohamapetan."

"No," Deran said. "And that's not how I would want that particular chess piece to be taken off the board. Either chess piece, in this case. Which is another thing you don't need to worry about right now, Teran."

"Of course."

"You should try to get a meeting with

Grayland one to one."

"She's ducking me."

"Well, let's see what we can do about that, shall we?" Deran smiled and then cut the connection.

Assan smiled too, but to himself. He finished his drink and made his third and final call for the evening.

"Yes?" the voice on the other end said.

"I'm calling for Lady Nohamapetan."

"She is . . . indisposed."

"I'm aware of that. I'm also aware I can leave a message with you and it will get to her."

"What is it?"

"I believe she will want a report on this session."

There was silence on the other end of the line. Then:

"Go on."

CHAPTER 3

As the assassin came at her with a toothbrush shiv, Nadashe Nohamapetan's first thought on the matter was, *Well, that took longer than I had expected.* She had been in the imperial holding facility for more than a month at that point. The fact Grayland II was only sending someone for her now was borderline offensive.

Her second thought, which she vocalized, was, *"Oh, shit."* Whether one is theoretically expecting to get a toothbrush (or whatever) through the ribs, when the sharpened object is honing in on you, carried by someone who looks like her job on the outside was strangling livestock, it's all right to let out a little profanity.

To be honest, it was just a capper on a really less than spectacular month for Nadashe Nohamapetan.

But then, she'd known the risks when she set up her brother Amit — in more than one sense of the term — with Grayland on that starship tour, and then shoved a shuttlecraft into the cargo bay at full speed. She knew them, and that they were manageable. After all, it was *entirely reasonable* to expect that the result of that would have been the emperox smeared over the deck of the bay, or sucked into the vacuum of space, or some combination of the two. The shuttle was big enough, it would be going fast enough, and the bay large enough. Really, it was just bad luck that the proximity alarms had triggered literally seconds too soon, giving Grayland just enough time to be shoved under a rapidly closing vacuum door.

She then also managed to survive the newly constructed ship tearing itself apart due to rotational forces, sealed off in a passage tube that was slowly leaking air. Grayland should have been dead by shuttle, then by the deconstruction of the ship, and then finally by simple clean lack of oxygen.

And that's not even talking about the assassination attempt at her coronation.

Grayland was, literally, a lucky bastard.

Nadashe, not so much these days.

"So here's the rundown," Cal Dorick, Nadashe's personal lawyer, had told her shortly after she was taken into custody. "Murder in the first degree for Amit, murder in the first degree for the shuttle pilot, murder in the second degree for both Grayland and Amit's security people, attempted murder for all the rest of the security contingents, attempted manslaughter for the starship crew — there are several dozen counts here — attempted murder of the emperox, attempted assassination of the emperox, which is technically a separate offense from attempted murder, and of course, treason."

"Is that all?" Nadashe asked.

Dorick looked at her oddly, but went on. "For the moment. I understand the House of Nohamapetan — your house — is currently debating whether or not to ask the state to charge you with destruction of property. The House of Lagos, whose shuttle you stole, will almost certainly ask for those charges, but has not yet. And further charges may be added to the docket, pending further investigation."

"So what are we looking at?" Nadashe asked. "In terms of sentencing?"

Dorick was dumbfounded. "Death, Nadashe," he finally said. "For treason that's traditionally the go-to sentence. You have a chance for death on the first-degree murder cases. For the second-degree charges, life imprisonment. Attempted assassination is typically a life sentence. Lesser sentences for the multiple attempted murders, but the state has already told me they will argue for them to be served consecutively, not concurrently."

Nadashe looked around the drab meeting room the two of them sat in, painted in industrial greens and grays. "So, best-case scenario is something like this, for the rest of my life, and the next several lives to boot."

"That's the best-case scenario, yes," Dorick said. "That's the highly optimistic scenario."

"Any deals on the table?"

"Not really," Dorick said. "When the state believes you tried to assassinate the emperox, it's going to want to set an example."

"Well," Nadashe said, and folded her hands on the table between her and her personal lawyer. "That is simply unacceptable."

Dorick paused, appeared to be about to say something, and then closed his mouth. He adjusted his suit and then reached for his stylus and pad. "So, 'not guilty' is what I'm hearing from you."

"Of course. I'm entirely innocent."

"Of everything."

"Absolutely everything. The idea that I would try to kill Amit, my brother, who I loved, is offensive. And as for Grayland, her brother was once my fiancé. My brother was hoping to be her fiancé. There is no reason, given either of those, that I would want her dead. All of this is ludicrous. I'm not guilty of anything."

Dorick looked over.

"What?" Nadashe said.

"I mean, you did *admit* to treason," Dorick said. "You suborned an entire ship full of Imperial Marines and sent it through the Flow shoal to End in order to support your attempted takeover of that planet. You said it to the emperox herself. And the entire executive committee."

"Excited utterance," Nadashe said.

"That's not how 'excited utterance' works legally, but okay."

"Bravado in the heat of the moment," Nadashe continued, undeterred. "Brought on by being accused of my own brother's death. Honestly I don't remember much of what I said at that point."

"There are *recordings.*"

"I'm sure there are. But I'm fuzzy on the details. A psychological evaluation might be in order to confirm I have a gap in my memory there."

Dorick looked doubtful at this. "Grayland has ordered a top-to-bottom investigation of the service to find out who else you might have suborned."

"*I* haven't suborned anyone. It was Amit."

"Amit."

"Yes."

"Your dead brother who was attempting to marry the emperox."

"He always believed in having a plan B."

"His plan B involved killing himself?"

"People do dramatic things," Nadashe said. "And I think you'll find in your investigation that Amit had left instructions that in the event of his death the *Prophecies of Rachela* was to make its way to End."

"Will I, now," Dorick said, making a note.

"Absolutely."

"A claim that is entirely unverifiable because, if the emperox is correct, the Flow stream from End to here has already collapsed."

"If you believe such a thing, yes."

"Still, your operational knowledge of Amit's plans appears extensive."

"I was investigating him."

Dorick looked up over his pad, eyebrows arched. "For treason."

"Among other things, yes."

"And you didn't think to bring this to the attention of the emperox, the executive committee, or, for that matter, the appropriate law-enforcement authorities, of which there would be . . . several."

"Amit was my *brother,* Cal," Nadashe said. "I had to be sure."

"So, to be clear, all of this . . ." Dorick waved the hand holding the stylus, in an effort to encompass the enormity of the crimes that Amit had attempted.

"On Amit, yes."

"Is there anyone to corroborate any of your claims?"

"My brother Ghreni," Nadashe said. "The two of them were very close."

"Ghreni, also at End, and thus also unable to be called to corroborate your claims here."

"Yes. Unfortunate."

"Quite," Dorick said, in a tone that was maybe two degrees off from being entirely sincere. Nadashe was glad her lawyer was quick on the uptake. "Well, this is certainly an alternate theory of the case, isn't it."

"Yes," Nadashe agreed.

"One that will take some time to investigate. Weeks, certainly. Months, probably. Years?"

"You should take all the time you need," Nadashe said. "I am willing to wait for justice."

"I'm sure you are," Dorick said, and paused. "This won't be cheap. And to put this indelicately, the House of Nohamapetan is up in the air about whether to fund your defense."

Nadashe nodded. "Write this down." She rattled off a long string of numbers. "Take that to the ImperialBanc in Hubfall. The branch across from the Guild House."

"If this account's in your name it may have already been seized."

"It's not in my name. It's in yours."

"Well," Dorick said. "I wish I'd known about my windfall earlier."

"I'd have preferred you never knew about it at all," Nadashe said. "And yet here we are."

Dorick nodded and stood. "The next time we meet will be at the arraignment."

"I want bail," Nadashe said.

"Let me remind you that you are to be charged with the attempted assassination of the emperox," Dorick said. "Getting bail is *optimistic.*"

"Try anyway."

Cal Dorick tried, arguing, not *entirely* unreasonably, that as an accused but entirely innocent attempted assassin, one of the other inmates might try to hurt or kill her out of a desire for notoriety, or a misplaced hope that murdering an attempted assassin of the emperox might better their own chance at a parole or commutation. The arraigning judge was, to put it mildly, not convinced. But he grudgingly admitted the need for extra security for Nadashe. After offering solitary confinement for the duration of her pretrial stay, the judge instead gave Nadashe her own cell in the medium-security wing of the Emperox Hanne II Secured Correctional Facility, thirty klicks outside of Hubfall.

The correctional facility was deemed "secured" because there was no underground passenger rail in or out of the facility. The only way in or out was overland. As Hub was a tidally locked airless planet where the temperature was either 300 degrees or -200 degrees centigrade, depending which side of the planetary terminator line one chose to wander off from, the overland route was not, shall we say, a pleasant drive in the best of circumstances. Only approved vehicles were allowed to approach. Unapproved vehicles approaching the facility were warned at three thousand meters, targeted at two thousand meters and destroyed one klick out. No one was going to go up to the surface of the planet for alone time.

In the month after her arrival Nadashe kept to herself, stayed out of everyone's way and avoided trouble. This was aided by the fact that she was ordered to take meals by herself, which were brought to her cell, and that her shower time was taken in the infirmary area, which had stalls and secured bathing facilities. Once a week she met with Dorick, who kept her up to date on the outside world, informing her of how the House of Lagos was given administration of Nohamapetan businesses in-system, how Grayland II had sparked a social and political crisis by warning about the upcoming collapse of the Flow streams, and more recently how the emperox had begun to claim religious visions, like Rachela in the early days of the Interdependency.

Nadashe, who had more context than nearly everyone else in the universe for these last two actions, said nothing to her lawyer about her thoughts and instead focused on the House of Lagos taking over the House of Nohamapetan's administration. "Who's their point person?" she asked.

"Lady Kiva Lagos," Dorick said.

"Oh. Her."

"You two know each other?"

"She used Ghreni as a boy toy when we were in college. How is she running the house's business?"

"From the outside, she seems to be doing fine."

"And from the inside?"

"No one from the inside is talking that much to me at the moment."

"Well, that's rude."

Dorick shrugged. "You are accused of murdering the head of the company and destroying its newest and most expensive ship. For which, incidentally, the insurance policy has been voided. Since you were an officer of the company at the time of the alleged incident, the insurers are arguing attempted insurance fraud."

"That's ridiculous."

"Given the cost, that would normally make the House of Nohamapetan have a vested interest in you being found not guilty. But since you are trying to pin everything on Amit . . ." Dorick shrugged. "It's not inclined to participate. Especially now that Kiva Lagos is running things."

"For now."

Dorick nodded. "It seems likely your mother will dispatch one of your cousins and a phalanx of lawyers from Terhathum to wrest control back. But they haven't arrived yet, and considering that Grayland suggests that the Flow stream to Terhathum may be on the verge of collapse, that adds another level of . . . *drama* to the situation. I'll be subpoenaing people and documents soon enough, but as you've said, we're not in a rush."

Nadashe filed that away. "And how goes the delaying of the trial date?"

"Surprisingly well. The prosecution wants more time to lay out its own case. It wants to make this as open-and-shut as possible. I am encouraging them to take as much time as they like."

"Good."

"Is there a reason for the delay, other than possibly keeping you alive that much longer?"

"Isn't that enough?" Nadashe asked.

"It is," Dorick said. "But as your lawyer I would prefer to know if there is anything else that's going on relevant to the case."

"Why do you ask?"

Dorick opened up a physical folder and pulled out an actual piece of paper and slid it over to Nadashe. "I got a call the other night. You might find the substance of the call of interest."

Nadashe read the paper silently. "Now, there's nothing there that I found particularly relevant to your legal case, so I don't feel obliged to share it with the prosecution as I might normally," Dorick continued.

"That is, unless you tell me it *is* relevant, in which case I will share it."

Nadashe slid the paper back to Dorick. "I don't think it's relevant, no. Seems like someone might be trying to prank you or to get you to act in a certain way."

"That's a distinct possibility," Dorick said, taking the paper back. "This is obviously a high-profile case, and I do get a lot of crank messages about it."

"Do let me know if you get any similar messages."

"Of course."

On the way back to her cell Nadashe mused on the note Dorick had showed her, from Teran Assan, whom she knew socially. Assan was both a grasping social climber and a prick with a too-high opinion of himself, but he'd also been useful more than once with inside information about his own house and the House of Wu. The fact that he was taking up her seat on the executive committee and was now wanting to share information about the emperox and his contacts within the House of Wu was very interesting.

Nadashe knew this largesse would not come free and that at some point there would need to be payment of one sort or another. But that was for another time. For now, Nadashe's brain was busy putting puzzle pieces together.

So busy, in fact, that she didn't notice the assassin with the toothbrush shiv until she was roughly three steps in front of her and closing fast.

"Oh, *shit,*" Nadashe said, and then the assassin reached out, hooked Nadashe by the neck, pushed her down to the deck and drove the toothbrush shiv into the carotid artery of the woman behind Nadashe, who had been closing in on her with a different shiv entirely, this one sharpened from a spoon.

Spoon Shiv, clearly surprised by the sudden appearance both of the toothbrush shiv–wielding woman, and the toothbrush shiv now lodged in her neck, dropped her own shiv and pawed ineffectually at the toothbrush in her artery. Toothbrush lady slapped her hands aside, and with an open palm drove the toothbrush farther in, eliciting a strangulated gasp. Then she grabbed Spoon Shiv by the front of her prison shirt and hurled her over the side of the railing. Spoon Shiv dropped the four meters to the prison deck, made a wet thud, and died.

Toothbrush looked down, and then picked up Spoon Shiv's weapon. She brandished it at Nadashe. "Don't bring a spoon to a toothbrush fight," she said. She tossed it into the nearest cell.

"What?" Nadashe said, confused.

Toothbrush motioned in the direction of Spoon Shiv. "You know who that was from?"

Nadashe collected herself. "I assume Grayland."

"Close but no. That was from Jasin Wu."

"Okay," Nadashe said. "And who are you from?"

"I'm from Deran Wu. And I have a proposition, from him, to you."

By now the guards and other inmates had crowded around Spoon Shiv's corpse, looking up to see Nadashe there.

"Don't worry about that," Toothbrush said. "That's fixable."

"Good to know."

"Do you want to hear the proposition?"

Nadashe looked back to Toothbrush.

And thought to herself, *Well, this took longer than I expected, too.*

"I'm listening," she said to Toothbrush, and noticed the guards coming up the stairs to them. "Better make it quick."

Chapter 4

Kiva Lagos looked around the empty warehouse that she stood in the middle of, and then turned to Gaye Patz. "You brought me down here to look at fucking nothing," she said.

Gaye Patz, the House of Lagos's top forensic accountant, nodded. "You are looking at nothing," she agreed. "But what you are *supposed* to be looking at is a warehouse filled with several million marks of Nohamapetan grain and other merchandise, ready to be shipped."

Kiva blinked at this. "So was it shipped?"

"It might have been," Patz said. "But if it was, it wasn't done legally, or to the legal buyers. And it's more likely that none of it arrived here at all. Ten million marks' worth of inventory, vanished."

"But on the books," Kiva said.

"Yes. On the books, it's all here. Along with another forty million or so marks of inventory that's supposed to be in other Nohamapetan warehouses across Hub, which is also not there."

"Merchandise we've already accepted the fucking money for."

Patz nodded. "Everything that was supposed to be in this warehouse was ordered and paid for. Everything in those other warehouses was also ordered and paid for. The House of Nohamapetan — and now *you,* because you've been given the responsibility for administering the Nohamapetans' business — is on the hook for that forty million marks' worth of merchandise. But there's good news."

"Yeah? What's that?"

"The inventory was destined to go out of the system. The emperox says the Flow streams are collapsing, so it's possible they'll do so before you're legally required to fulfill the order."

Kiva snorted at this, and looked around again at the empty warehouse. "Why am I only finding out about this now?"

"About this warehouse?"

"Yes."

Patz shrugged. "For as much money is involved in this little graft scheme, it's less than one percent of the local inventory for the House of Nohamapetan and of course even less than that for the total amount of house merchandise. The inventory comes and goes, so these warehouses don't stay empty for long." She waved at the warehouse. "We caught these mostly because House of Lagos taking over for the Nohamapetans meant we had to do an audit. In a few more days this warehouse and several of the others would be full up again."

"How the fuck were they hiding this?"

"That's the magic of having your clients weeks or months away. When the shipments arrive, if there are any shortfalls, the orders are either adjusted to factor in the missing inventory or made good with a later shipment. In both cases the shrinkage is chalked up as business losses and deducted out of taxes. In order to see it as anything else, you'd have to do an audit of the entire business."

"Which the Nohamapetans weren't going to do because they were the ones skimming," Kiva said.

"Well," Patz's voice held a note of caution. "We don't have any concrete evidence of that yet."

"Except for Nadashe Nohamapetan apparently funding an attempted fucking coup of the Interdependency out of petty cash."

"There is that," Patz murmured.

"Are we going to be able to cover these shortfalls?" Kiva asked. "Unlike the fucking Nohamapetans, we can't actually pretend this inventory fell off the ship in the middle of the Flow."

"That's out of my department," Patz said. "I imagine you can shift things around, but regardless you're out the fifty million marks. I'm having my people go through the accounting for the last decade to find out how extensive this skimming operation actually was."

"You think you're going to find more."

Patz looked at her boss levelly. "Lady Kiva, graft on this scale doesn't just happen. We're probably looking at hundreds of millions of marks' worth. Possibly billions."

"Coups don't come cheap," Kiva said.

"I suppose not, ma'am."

"Do we know where the fucking money *is,* at least?"

"Not yet. We don't have the authority to go looking, outside of the House of Nohamapetan's local account. The personal accounts of the family members and any other unrelated accounts are outside our purview. I'm sharing information with the imperial Ministry of Revenue, of course. They'll be able to do a more extensive investigation."

"Any money they find, I want back."

"I have to warn you that the Ministry of Revenue is very unlikely to honor that request."

"Fuck them."

"Yes," agreed Patz. "But there's the matter that the House of Nohamapetan probably owes back taxes and penalties. That will almost certainly be worth more than the amount of the actual missing money."

Kiva grumped about this. Then, "So how much of this is going to be blamed on *me*?"

"I think that depends on who is assigning blame," Patz said. "I don't think Grayland or the Tax Ministry is going to hold it against you, if for no other reason than almost all of *this*" — Patz waved again — "predates your administration. The House of Nohamapetan itself may try to, however. Especially in light of some recent events."

"What recent events?"

"Well, that's the other thing we've found in the audit. Sabotage. Of inventory, of machines, of ships. All in the last month, since the House of Lagos took charge."

"How much?"

Patz said nothing but gave Kiva a look that she interpreted as saying *a whole fuckton.*

"And I reiterate something I just said: And I'm only finding out about this now?"

"You're the new boss. Some people don't want to tell you."

"And the others?"

"Well. They want to wreck you, ma'am."

Three hours later Kiva was back at the Guild House, in her office. It was the former office of the equally former Amit Nohamapetan, who, courtesy of his sister, had recently found himself on the business end of a shuttlecraft, and then smeared across roughly an acre of cargo bay deck as the shuttlecraft rolled over and then in him like a dog in a manure pile.

Kiva didn't think this was a very good way to go. But the more she reflected on it the more she decided there were worse ways. Amit was dead before he knew it, and at least people would be talking about how he died for years. So much more interesting than your basic stroke or heart attack. It was, in fact, the most interesting thing about Amit at all, which Kiva judged was not a great testament to the life he had bothered to live.

The now-dead-and-somewhat-smeary Amit Nohamapetan's office was roomy, as befitted the head of his family's operations in the Hub system, tastefully appointed in the manner that strongly implied it was furnished entirely through the preferences of a hired interior decorator rather than Amit's own inclinations, if he had any, which he probably hadn't, and lardered with all the technological assistants and innovations that any modern executive could want or need.

All except for a "Hey, your fucking sister is planning to shove a shuttle up your ass" alert, Kiva thought to herself. Which to be fair was admittedly a specialized item.

Kiva had that thought as she was looking out the transparent glass wall of the office, down toward the street below. Aside from the usual street noise of Hubfall — the largest city in the Interdependency, as imperial capitals have historically tended to be — there was an extra layer of volume, coming from what looked like a protest below. Kiva was too far up to see the signs or hear clearly whatever was being chanted, but whatever it was about, the crowd seemed pretty excitable.

"Lada Kiva." Kiva turned her head and saw Bunton Salaanadon, her and previously Amit Nohamapetan's executive assistant. Kiva had kept him because it wasn't his fault he had been employed by an ineffectual traitor to the Interdependency, and also he knew things that Kiva didn't, and didn't want to have to wait weeks or months to learn herself. So far he'd been both appropriately grateful he hadn't been sacked, and actually useful in terms of Kiva trying to run the House of Nohamapetan's businesses like something other than a carpetbagging asshole.

Kiva motioned with her head to the glass. "What are they protesting?"

Salaanadon walked to his boss and glanced down at the street. "It's not a protest exactly, I think. The emperox has said that she's been having visions about the future of the Interdependency. I believe the people below are supporting her."

"Huh."

Salaanadon glanced over to Kiva. "Did Her Majesty mention anything about these visions when you met with her, Lady Kiva?"

"No," Kiva said. "When I met her she was mostly still recovering from your old boss's sister blowing up a spaceship around her. She didn't talk all that much. She thanked me for helping uncover Nadashe's plot, and told me I'd be in charge around here. Then I got shoved off."

"Still an honor to meet the emperox."

"It was all right. I think she may be fucking my old boy toy now."

"Ma'am?" Salaanadon said.

Kiva waved him off. "Not important. You came to see me about something?"

"Yes, ma'am. A lawyer is here."

"Toss him out a window."

"Her, actually, I think."

"So toss *her* out, then. Equally defenestratable."

"I would, but this one is from the House of Nohamapetan."

"Someone who works for me now."

"I'm afraid not," Salaanadon said. "This lawyer is here from Terhathum. That's —"

"I know what and where Terhathum is," Kiva said. "She's from the fucking home office."

"Yes, ma'am."

"Does the math even work on that?"

"Terhathum is fifteen days away from Hub by the Flow. So yes, barely."

"What does she want?"

"I believe she wants to discuss your administration of the local Nohamapetan properties."

"Then she'd better bring it up with the emperox, since she's the one who put me here."

"She suggested there were other issues as well."

"More for the emperox."

"I'm afraid she can't be put off. She is

carrying a signet document."

Kiva frowned at this. "Well, fuck." A signet document was a legal document that gave the bearer the same standing as the ranking member of a house. From a legal point of view Kiva couldn't avoid this fucking lawyer, since it would have been the same as avoiding the Countess Nohamapetan, which was not to be done. Technically speaking, and despite the emperox's dispensation, Kiva in her new role as director was the countess's employee.

"She's currently in the waiting area," Salaanadon said.

"Fine," Kiva said. "Send her in. Might as well get this over with."

"Yes, ma'am." Salaanadon bowed his head slightly and exited. Kiva glanced once more down at the placarded crowd in the street, and wondered briefly how many of them were true believers and how many of them Grayland had paid for. Emperoxs had hired crowds for subjects less weighty than mystical visions, after all. And if the Interdependency was about to come to a crashing halt, then she might as well spend her marks before they were all worthless.

Not bad advice for you, either, Kiva thought to herself.

Right, but the problem with *that* was, for

a rich person, Kiva was spectacularly unmotivated by money. She *liked* money, and she liked that she *had* money, and she was aware that a life lived without money would well and truly suck. But having had enough money all her life for literally anything she ever wanted to do — being the daughter of the head of a noble merchant family had its perks — she never thought about money, and her own material needs were fulfilled with a small percentage of the money she had available to her.

Instead, Kiva had two primary pursuits: Fucking, which she was enthusiastic about nearly (but not entirely) to the point of indiscrimination; and running things, which she enjoyed and which as it was turning out she wasn't all that bad at. Kiva was not under the impression that she would ever be running the House of Lagos — as late addition to the Countess Huma Lagos's already numerous family, she was out of contention for inheriting the role of the primary director of the House of Lagos, and, despite the example set by Kiva's erstwhile college chum Nadashe Nohamapetan, was not inclined to murder siblings to improve her chances. But the universe was wide enough to give Kiva things of her own to run, like, in this case, the Nohamapetans' business.

For now, anyway. Until either the Nohamapetans grabbed it back from her, or all the Flow streams collapsed and they were all fucked anyway.

Exciting fucking times, Kiva thought to herself.

The door opened, and Salaanadon came through with a woman roughly Kiva's age. "Lady Kiva Lagos, Madam Senia Fundapellonan," Salaanadon said, motioning to Fundapellonan.

"Lady Kiva," Fundapellonan said, bowing.

"Yeah, yeah," Kiva said, waving her all the way into the room, and motioning her to sit at the chair in front of her capacious desk. Salaanadon frowned to himself at this, but excused himself silently. Kiva sunk into her own chair behind her desk.

"I'd like to begin by delivering the compliments of the Countess Nohamapetan, who thanks you for taking control of her local concerns at this turbulent time."

Kiva rolled her eyes at this. "Look . . . what's your name again?"

"Senia Fundapellonan."

"That's a lot all at once."

"I suppose it is, Lady Kiva."

"Fundapellonan, can we just . . . *not* do

the bullshit parts? I mean, you seem like a smart person."

"Thank you, Lady Kiva."

"So as a smart person, you know as well as I do that of all the things that the Countess Nohamapetan might be feeling toward me right now, *gratitude* is right down at the absolute fucking bottom. I gave the emperox evidence that her kids were traitors, that one murdered the other, and now I'm running her fucking company. What she'd *actually* be wanting to do, I'd guess, is push me out a goddamned window."

Fundapellonan smiled slightly at this.

"Also, presuming you actually did come from Terhathum —"

"I have."

"— then it's likely given transport times to and from there that you were sent almost immediately after the countess got the news about her problem children. In which case the idea that she is thinking *anything* about me at all is pretty laughable. What I imagine the Countess Nohamapetan is actually thinking, aside from 'the *fuck,*' is, one, how to extract her daughter from an almost certain death sentence, and two, prying me or anyone else who isn't a Nohamapetan from her precious fucking company. Are these reasonable assumptions?"

Fundapellonan took a second before responding. "You're not wrong."

"So in the interest of saving both of us some time, I am asking you just to pretty please get to the fucking *point,* already."

"Fair enough," Fundapellonan said. "Then here it is, Lady Kiva: The House of Nohamapetan, which I represent, is asking you to step aside and allow an executive of our own choosing to take over our local interests." She held up the signet document and placed it on Kiva's desk. "That's the official request. Unofficially, as part of your terms of withdrawal, you will receive a substantial bonus payment."

"You mean a bribe."

"I mean a bonus payment. The countess's appreciation for your willingness to step in during a moment of crisis."

"I thought I asked to dispense with bullshit."

"There's bullshit and then there's bullshit, Lady Kiva."

"Well, you're right about that, at least." Kiva pointed to the signet document. "I presume you and the countess both understand that I was put in charge of your house's business by the emperox, yes? I can't just quit."

"We understand that. We also know that

the emperox would be more inclined to allow your exit if you also were willing to voluntarily depart."

"Don't be so sure."

"And why is that?"

"Well, aside from the fact that Nadashe Nohamapetan tried to assassinate the emperox with a spacecraft, which is not great for the reputation of the entire fucking *family,* there's also the matter of the endemic graft my auditors are finding in your books for the last several years."

Fundapellonan tilted her head. "And the House of Lagos's ledgers are entirely free of graft and corruption, Lady Kiva? You know as well as I do that skimming off the top — by employees, by executives, and, yes, even occasionally and regrettably by family members — is not an unusual thing. Regrettable, yes. Unusual, no."

"This is your argument for returning control to a Nohamapetan? Everybody does it?"

"To be fair, everybody does do it."

"To be fair, not everyone tries to fucking murder the emperox."

"So this is a no from you."

"It's a 'you have to be fucking kidding me' from me."

Fundapellonan shrugged. "As you will.

You should know we intend to ask for your removal anyway."

"Good luck with that."

"We don't need luck, Lady Kiva. We have your incompetence."

"The fuck you say."

"You must be aware that there's been a substantial increase in the amount of sabotage of Nohamapetan property and merchandise."

"I've heard."

"Then you're equally aware this challenges the house's ability to fulfill its business relationships. That damages the house's reputation."

"I don't know," Kiva said. "I won't argue there's been a spike in sabotage, but it seems to me the most *prominent* bit of sabotage was when Nadashe turned a brand-new Nohamapetan ship into fucking scrap metal. As long as we're talking about what damages a house's reputation, maybe that should be put on the pile as well."

Fundapellonan frowned at this. "Perhaps the emperox will see things differently."

"I doubt it." Kiva pointed to the signet document. "One of those will get you in to see Grayland, but I don't think the emperox is going to forget your house rose up against her."

"Not the house. One of its members."

"Good luck making that argument."

"*I* won't be making that argument. The Countess Nohamapetan will be."

Kiva blinked at this. "She's coming here?"

"Of course," Fundapellonan said, and smiled. "Lady Kiva, as you astutely note, the reputation of the House of Nohamapetan has taken a few hits recently. This is not something the appearance of a humble lawyer will fix. It's not something a thousand lawyers will fix. The only way to fix this is to bring the countess from Terhathum to speak to the emperox directly. I'm here to take care of some — sorry — relatively minor preliminaries, like speaking to you. The countess will handle the heavy lifting."

"And when is she arriving?"

Fundapellonan glanced at her wrist, which held a timepiece, which annoyed Kiva as being an overly dramatic act. "If the ship she was planning to be on held its schedule, roughly three days from now." She looked back up. "Which gives you that much time to change your mind. But not that much time, Lady Kiva. Not that much time at all."

CHAPTER 5

"So, how *much* time, precisely?"

Marce Claremont managed to keep his face composed — he was learning how to do that much, at least — but on the inside, where it mattered, he was smacking his face with his hand and dragging that hand down across his cheeks. His life for the past month had been answering, time and time and time and time again, the same question, in its infinite but mundane variations, for people who didn't want to be convinced by the answer and who didn't have the math to understand why it was going to be true no matter how much they wanted the answer to be different.

But this was Marce's job now: Special Assistant for Science Policy to Emperox Grayland II, tasked with communicating the issues surrounding the imminent collapse of the Flow to Very Important People. These included but were not limited to imperial ministers, members of parliament, the heads of noble houses and their entourages, bishops and archbishops of the Interdependent Church and any other churches, scientists, journalists, high-ranking celebrities, "thought leaders," noted public intellectuals and the occasional talk show host.

All day, every day, for the last month.

All day, every day, for the foreseeable future.

At this very moment, Marce had brought his now road-tried-and-tested presentation to the Imperial Society of Exogeology, which had convened for its biennial convention on Hub, biennial because it was difficult for members from across the Interdependency to haul their respective butts across Flow streams that took weeks and sometimes months to get them to where they were going, and at Hub because, simply, all Flow streams led to Hub.

(*For now,* some portion on Marce's brain volunteered. Marce shoved that part of his brain back down into its hole.)

One might think that of all groups that Marce would address on the topic of the collapse of the Flow streams, it would be scientists who would be the easiest to convince. After all, what Marce had was data, three decades of data, researched and codified and presented in a format that nearly every scientist would understand. Charts and graphs and columns and footnotes and of course a digital file laden with all the raw information his father, the Count Claremont, had collected over thirty years.

But as it turned out the scientists were uniformly the worst audiences. Marce could understand Flow physicists being balky or dismissive: This was their field, after all, and now some minor lord and even more minor professor from an obscure university at the ass end of space was presenting them information, from his *dad,* informing all of them that everything they thought they understood about the Flow was entirely wrong. That was a real kick to the nether regions, intellectually speaking. Honestly Marce would have been surprised if Flow scientists had done anything *other* than attack, at least until they had time to sit with the data and recognize the terrifying truth of it.

But it wasn't just the Flow physicists. Every group of scientists, in every discipline, had given him static about the data he and his father had collected and interpreted. Marce had been genuinely flummoxed by it until he thought back on his days in academia and what the chair of his department had once told him, about colleagues who were bound and determined to relate every new finding to their own area of expertise and that area only. "When you have a hammer, everything looks like a nail," his chair had said.

This wasn't a new turn of phrase, but the point was new to Marce: There were more than a few scientists who knew one little thing, and then thought that knowledge was universally applicable to every other problem, to the point of excluding or discounting information from people whose specialty *was* that other problem.

Marce didn't particularly have that problem — he was all too aware of everything he didn't know, which these days felt like everything that wasn't about the collapse of the Flow — but he was increasingly aware of the number of scientists brandishing hammers, looking for the nail in his data, and in his presentation.

It was exhausting. More than once Marce longed to throw up his hands, say, *Fine, don't believe me or the data; enjoy being the first turned to jerky when the collapse comes.* But then he remembered that he had promised Grayland — the emperox of the Interdependency, who had improbably and somewhat ridiculously also become his friend — that he would help her find a way to forestall the collapse of their entire civilization.

And that meant *not* bellowing to a theater of recalcitrant exogeologists that the Flow didn't care whether they believed it was collapsing or not, and answering, for the innumereth time, the same damn basic question he received every single time he gave his presentation.

"No time at all," Marce said, to the man who asked the question, a self-important bald fellow who Marce believed was no doubt the preeminent scientist in the entire Interdependency on some very specific type of igneous rock. Marce motioned to the schematic that floated in the air above him, showing the systems of the Interdependency and all the Flow streams that stretched between them all, pointing specifically to the stream connecting Hub, the capital of the Interdependency, and End, which as it happened was Marce's home, and which he wondered if he would ever see again. "As I said, the stream from End to Hub has already started to collapse. It's collapsing from End, in the direction of Hub. One of the last ships to come from End was the one I was on, as it happens. There have been no new arrivals from End in weeks. There will be no more arrivals, as best as the data can predict."

"So End is sealed off," another scientist asked.

"In one direction." Marce pointed to the other stream arcing between Hub and End. "In the other direction the stream remains open for now. We can send ships to End. They just won't be coming back."

Marce then pointed to another stream, connecting Hub to Terhathum. "We're pretty sure this, the Flow stream between Hub and Terhathum, will be the next Flow stream to collapse. We expect this to happen within the next few weeks. The emperox has assigned research craft to monitor the Flow shoal here, and we're sending specialized drones through the shoal to gauge the soundness of the stream."

"How do you do that?" another exogeologist asked.

"Well, it's complicated," Marce said. "The internal topography of the Flow doesn't precisely correspond to the space-time we're familiar with. In fact, if we didn't wrap our own ships inside a little bubble of space-time before they entered the Flow, they'd just cease to exist, at least in a way we understand as existing. I could explain it better but I would need more time, and I have another presentation to give across

Hubfall in two and half hours." This got a small laugh.

"When the stream from Hub to Terhathum collapses, then Terhathum will be cut off, like End is," said the bald probably-expert-in-igneous-rocks-of-some-sort.

"No," Marce said, and was sure he heard a groan. "End is named 'End' in part because there's only one stream in and one stream out, and both lead here, to Hub." Marce pointed to where the Terhathum system was displayed in his floating image. "Terhathum is connected to Hub, but it's also connected to three other systems as well: Shirak, Melaka and Paramaribo. So now instead of going directly to Terhathum from Hub, the quickest route will be going to Melaka first and then to Terhathum. That adds an additional nine days to travel."

"But Terhathum won't be isolated."

"Not yet." Marce went to his display controls and pressed a button to start an animation. "But the collapse of the stream from Hub to Terhathum is just the first. Shortly after that one collapses, we begin to lose more." One by one, the streams dropped out of the display, marking fewer connections between planets. "Within three years some systems are already isolated." The animation ran some more. "Within ten, all the Flow streams are gone."

"And we have no way to get from one system to the next without them?" someone asked, after a moment.

"Not without taking hundreds of years at least," Marce said. "Our ships' engines are designed to move in-system, at a small fraction of the speed of light. Even if we built ships to go faster — say, ten percent of the speed of light — there would still be decades between the closest systems." Marce saw a hand go up. "And of course as scientists I don't have to remind you that going faster than the speed of light is a physical impossibility." The hand went back down, quickly.

"And you're sure about this?" the bald man said. "Because I mentioned to my brother-in-law, who is a Flow physicist, that we were meeting with you today, and he said, bluntly, that you were a crank and that you have somehow managed to scam the emperox."

Marce smiled at this. He was used to this question, too. "Sir, I don't think you understand," he said. "I — and my father, whose work this is — would be *delighted* to be wrong. We would be delighted for every other Flow physicist to sit with the data, which we have provided to anyone who wants it, poke holes in it, and show definitively that we missed some pertinent bit of information that shows we've been reading the data wrong all this time. Isn't that the way science works? You present a hypothesis to your peers, you show them all your measurements and observations and data, and you ask them to make you a liar. The *best-case* scenario, sir, is that my father and I are revealed as cranks and I go home to End in ignominy.

"There's only one problem with this, which I've already covered." Marce motioned again toward End. "It's *already* begun, consistent with our predictions and data. At this point we're still arguing about it only because only one stream has collapsed and we can still make other excuses for why those ships that should have arrived at Hub by now haven't arrived. When the collapse of the Hub–Terhathum Flow stream happens, within weeks, the time for debate about the status of the Flow will be over. And when that happens, what we need to ask ourselves is what we will be prepared to do *as scientists* to help everyone else in the Interdependency to survive."

"You say 'as scientists,' but the emperox has been claiming she is having visions about what's coming," complained an exogeologist.

Marce looked uncomfortable at this. "I can't speak to those. I can speak to Emperox Grayland's commitment to continuing and increasing scientific research on this subject, which was started by her father, Attavio VI."

"But don't you think it's odd that she's engaged in this mystical nonsense? I don't think it helps her case at all."

Marce paused for a moment to consider his words. "My colleagues," he said, finally. "I have just given you an hour-long presentation on a hypothesis whose data fit the observed behavior of the universe, which has been peer-reviewed and which conforms to every accepted standard and stricture for scientific inquiry. Yet I can tell already that something less than half of you are more than half convinced by it. You're scientists. If I can't convince all of *you* with my data, then it's possible I'll do even less well with the general public."

He glanced around at the exogeologists, who were silent. "Now, I'm not going to tell you I understand our emperox's claim of visions and revelation," Marce said. "I certainly can't say I believe them, exactly. But I believe in the emperox. I believe that the emperox is committed to helping all of her subjects prepare for what's coming. And if having a *vision* helps where the actual, observable and verifiable science doesn't, then I'm open to visions. Given what's at stake, maybe you might be, too."

Marce sensed the woman before he saw her, or more accurately, he saw Nadau Wilt, his assistant/bodyguard, tense up as they walked to Marce's waiting car, and step between him and someone who was clearly walking up on both of them. He looked up and saw the approaching woman, a bit older than he was, with an air of dishevelment, carrying a sheaf of papers.

The woman saw Wilt move and stopped a few meters out, hands up guardingly. "Did you tell the truth in there, Dr. Claremont?"

Marce smiled; it had been a while since anyone had called him "doctor." "About the collapse of the Flow? Absolutely."

"No, not about *that,*" the woman said, and the annoyed, dismissive tone came through clearly. "About being delighted to be proven wrong."

Ah, thought Marce. *Here we go.* One persistent feature of giving these presentations on the Flow collapse is one or two attendees who would want to corner him later to share their own "scientific" theories, like how the Flow was actually the ghost plane or how the emperox was actually turning off the Flow stream at the behest of a heretofore never-discovered intelligent alien species, which looked like a cross between a shark and a poodle (that one came with art). Marce's strategy in those situations was to be polite but to let Wilt shove him along to the next thing.

"Yes," he said, politely. "In this case, I would be very happy to be proven wrong."

"Are you sure about that? Because I have to tell you, Dr. Claremont, I wasn't very pleased when you proved *me* wrong."

Marce was confused by this comment for several seconds, until he wasn't. Then his mouth literally dropped open. "You're . . . Hatide Roynold."

"Yes."

"You told the Nohamapetans that the Flow streams are shifting, not going away."

"Yes."

"You were wrong about that."

"Yes, yes," Roynold said, irritably. "Maybe I wouldn't have been wrong if your father had bothered to answer my correspondence to him on the subject, but he never did."

"He was told by the emperox to keep his research to himself," Marce said.

"I understand that's his excuse, yes."

"The Nohamapetans used your data to

attempt a coup."

"Well, they didn't tell me that's what they had planned," Roynold said. "Any more than I imagine the emperox told you she was using your data for that ridiculous 'vision' scheme of hers."

Marce looked back at the conference building they had just come from. "How . . . did you see today's presentation? You're not an exogeologist."

"I grabbed a nametag and snuck in." Roynold motioned to herself, almost dismissively. "I look like this. The other exogeologists aren't exactly fashion plates. I fit in."

"Lord Marce, we should go," Wilt said, knowing when to move things along. Marce turned, allowing himself to be moved.

"You're not right, Dr. Claremont," Roynold said, stepping forward again, and then stopping once more when Wilt gave her a take-the-hint glare, but not walking away.

"What do you mean?" Marce asked.

Roynold pointed to Marce's briefcase, which held his tablet, display projector, and papers. "Your work. It's not right. It's not *wrong,* not entirely. But it's not right. Fully. It's incomplete."

"Incomplete."

Roynold nodded. "That's right."

Marce took a step toward Roynold, much

to Wilt's consternation. "My father's data predicted the collapse of the End Flow stream to an extremely high level of confidence," he said. "I checked the math myself."

"Yes," Roynold said. "It's correct. And you'll be correct with the Hub to Terhathum collapse, too. Look, I said you weren't *wrong.*"

"But how is that incomplete?"

"*That* part isn't incomplete. But your theory is. You and your father have been working on a general theory of Flow collapse." Roynold rattled the papers in her hand. "This is the special theory."

"What do you mean?"

"I mean that your father is accurately predicting when Flow streams are collapsing, and you checked the math on that. But he missed that in the process the Flow would open some streams too. You never checked that because he missed it."

Roynold held the papers out to Marce, who stepped forward and took them.

"I got things wrong because I started out with a few bad assumptions that I didn't check," Roynold said as he read. She shrugged. "Having peer review would have helped, but I was being paid not to tell anyone else. It turns out my *process* was right, I was just plugging in the wrong initial conditions. When I got your data, I saw that your father and I were studying different aspects of the same problem. Related but nearly independent. And I incorporated his findings into my process." She pointed to the papers. "And got this."

Marce looked up from the papers and blinked mutely at Roynold.

"Right?" Roynold said, and waved at the papers. "It's all preliminary, of course. But still."

"Lord Marce," Wilt said, more insistently this time.

Marce acknowledged his bodyguard, and then turned back to Roynold and held up the papers. "Can I keep these?"

"I brought them for you."

"How can I reach you? To talk about this more."

"My contact information is on the cover sheet."

"Is there a good time to call?"

Roynold smiled awkwardly. "There's not a *bad* time to call, Dr. Claremont. I'm between opportunities at the moment."

Marce frowned. "I thought you were a professor."

"Yes, well," Roynold said. "It turns out when your work is used by traitors as the reason to undermine the Interdependency and attempt to assassinate the emperox, it makes going into work at an imperial university . . . *problematic.*"

"It's not your fault they used your data like this. They didn't tell you what they had planned."

"No," Roynold agreed. "On the other hand, I didn't really ask, either, did I." She shrugged. "And anyway I had a lot of free time to work on this. Not entirely sure how I'm going to eat after next week. But I suppose that's what the Interdependency minimum benefit is for."

Marce looked up at this. "Really?" he said.

"That last part was probably too much, wasn't it. Sorry. I have a hard time knowing where the line is sometimes."

Marce smiled and handed the papers back to Roynold. "Come on. I've got another one of these presentations across town, which I'm now late for. We can talk on the way there. And then we can talk after."

"All right." Roynold took the papers. "You really don't mind being proven wrong. I wasn't actually expecting that."

"You said it, Dr. Roynold. I'm not wrong. I'm just not right."

Chapter 6

The Flow stream from Hub to Terhathum collapsed.

The collapse was ahead of schedule but within the penumbra of the prediction cone that Marce Claremont had offered Emperox Grayland II. The last ship through the Flow shoal from Hub to Terhathum was the House of Nohamapetan fiver *I'll Always Remember You Like a Child,* which entered the Flow stream six hours ahead of the collapse. The captain of the *Child* had been cautioned prior to entering the Flow stream that the emperox's science advisor was predicting its collapse and further warned that the collapse was likely to spread from random points within the stream and not, as had happened with the collapse from End to Hub, beginning at one end and moving forward like a wave to the other. Hub's traffic control suggested routing through Melaka and then to Terhathum.

The captain of the *Child,* Daris Moria, expressed to her executive officer Lin Burrotinol her contempt for Grayland II, her science advisor and Hub's traffic control, and ordered her ship into the shoal, on schedule.

The ship would not arrive at Terhathum on schedule, or at all. The *Child* would in fact be lost to the Interdependency forever. It would tumble out of the decaying Flow stream at a point several thousand light-years from any known human outpost. This is because the Flow, while thought of as a river, or road, or another sort of linear bearer of transportation, was not actually remotely like any of those things, or remotely linear. Had the *Child* been tossed out of the Flow stream a second earlier, it would have been only a light-year from the star Sirius A, itself a relative hop and skip from humanity's ancestral solar system. If it had been tossed out a second later, it would have found itself much closer to the Milky Way's galactic core.

Where it would have found itself, in any of these instances, was *away.* Away from Hub, away from Terhathum, away from humanity. Away from rescue. Away from life.

I'll Always Remember You Like a Child was a ship designed to be capable of maintaining the lives and safety of its crew for five years before things would inevitably decline into chaos and madness. But like most commercial fivers, the *Child* was not in fact set up to sustain its crew for five years. In the *Child*'s case, it had been tasked with making short-haul cargo trips from Hub to Terhathum and back again, over and over, trips that took roughly two weeks each leg. There was no *need* to fit the ship for long-term crew survival. Until there was.

Captain Moria appealed to her crew for calm and got it, for two weeks. In another two weeks, Moria would be dead and the crew, which understood all too well what had happened to the *Child,* where it was (and wasn't) and how little food and other resources it had on hand, would begin to fracture. In another month half the crew would be dead, including most of the officers. Six weeks after that and the crew would be down to thirty, in three non-cooperating groups, and ship systems would begin to fail.

It would be another 277 days before the final surviving crew member, a cargo handler named Jayn Brisfelt, would record a lengthy testimonial of the last, extraordinarily depressing days of the *Child* and her crew, before he would then go to the security office, obtain a sidearm, retire to one of the crew lounges, put on one of his favorite comedies, and then shoot himself mid-laugh during his favorite part of the story.

The testimonial, recorded on a tablet, would be unseen and unheard by any other living thing. The tablet itself, whose internal battery would drain within two years, would lose the ability to function fifty years later even if it had been charged. The *Child* itself would be a cold, powerless husk within ten years. It would be never be found by humans or any other intelligent creatures, if there were any. It would drift between the stars for twenty million years before being gravitationally snagged by a passing red dwarf star, which it would orbit for another six million years in a comet-like path before falling into the star and vaporizing into its constituent atoms.

But this was all in the future.

At the moment, the collapse of the Flow stream between Hub and Terhathum was confirmed by a simple procedure: A research drone attempted to fly into the Flow shoal and was unable to. Where the Shoal had been, only moments before, was nothing but conventional space-time, and vacuum. Other ships sounded the area, on the idea that the Flow shoal might have moved, or was moving, a thing that had rarely been seen but which was theoretically possible. It was not moving. It was, simply, gone.

It would take weeks or months for the news of the collapse of the Terhathum stream to reach all the systems of the Interdependency (including Terhathum itself, now nearly one month away from Hub), but within the Hub system, the effect was immediate:

On the Hub Stocks and Commodities Exchange, stocks plunged and commodity futures collapsed and billions of marks' worth of value vaporized almost instantly. A very few speculators, having shorted the market, momentarily found themselves almost ridiculously rich, until trading was halted entirely and gains and losses frozen.

Several mercantile houses filed claims to the House of Aiello, which held the monopoly on insurance, for losses incurred because of the (now almost certainly confirmed) collapse of the Flow stream from End to Hub. The claims were for lost ships, cargo and crew, and ran collectively into the billions of marks. The House of Aiello rejected nearly all of these claims, asserting, not entirely unreasonably, that the collapse of the Flow streams constituted an Act of God.

Shops and markets across the entire Hub

system were swamped by panicked shoppers who came in first for essentials, and then for anything that was left. Overwhelmed store owners and managers tried to assure their customers that the collapse of a single Flow stream did not mean they were immediately doomed to starvation and despair. This did not go as well as they hoped.

Police and security forces across the system shifted to high alert and prepared for rioting. The good news was that the panicking seemed largely contained to the shopping experience. The bad news was that no one believed that would stay true for very long.

The Church of the Interdependency and other religions found their places of worship jammed, as the faithful, the newly faithful and the not-actually-at-all-faithful-but-this-is-some-weird-shit-and-I'm-hedging-my-bets came in and, depending on experience, prayed, meditated or wondered what it was exactly they were supposed to do now that they were there. Priests, ministers, rabbis, imams and other religious leaders were on one hand delighted to be useful in a moment of spiritual and existential crisis and on the other hand well aware that this was the theological equivalent of shoppers making a panic run at the market, with their new parishioners grabbing at anything and hoping it would get them through.

In Hubfall, the newly fervent who weren't at a church found themselves at the gates of Brighton, the local imperial residence. Everyone in the Hub system was aware of Grayland's visions for the future of the Interdependency, and her championing of Lord Marce Claremont, whose scientific findings had predicted the collapse of the End and Terhathum streams. Whether they believed her visions were sincere, a ploy to gull the credulous, or a sign of mental instability, they now had reason to believe she was onto *something.* And so they came to Brighton, some to revere, some to pray, and some because even if they didn't want to go to a church, they wanted to be somewhere in this teleologically deeply unsettling moment.

The emperox, however, was not at Brighton. She was at Xi'an, the massive imperial habitat hovering over the planet of Hub and the city of Hubfall. She was in communion, some suggested, with her ancestor Rachela, the only other prophet-emperox, planning her next move, her next announcement, to save her people and her empire.

Which was not entirely wrong, as far as it went.

Archbishop Korbijn couldn't say she was entirely thrilled to receive her next visitor, but at this point there didn't seem much that she could do to refuse him. And so into her offices at the Xi'an Cathedral Complex walked Lord Teran Assan.

"Welcome, Lord Assan," Korbijn said, with what she hoped was enough politeness.

Assan did a small bow with his head and swiveled his head around, taking in Korbijn's private office, which was immense and exquisitely appointed. "This is impressive," he said.

"Thank you," Korbijn said. "I am the head of my church."

Assan nodded. "Not a church that's big on humility."

"We were founded by a scion of a merchant family who then became the emperox of an interstellar civilization, so, no. Not really."

"Speaking of merchant scions who became emperoxs, I assume that you heard the news that Grayland II is going to address parliament."

"I'd heard," Korbijn said.

"There's speculation that she will use the

occasion to announce martial law. Seeing as how her pet scientist's prediction about the collapse of the Terhathum's Flow stream panned out and now people are in a panic."

"It's not a panic yet."

Assan tilted his head and smirked. "Really."

"Really," Korbijn asserted. "People are shaken and afraid, yes. But they're not burning things."

"Yet."

"Hopefully not ever. Fires in closed habitats are never good things."

Assan motioned with his head out the window, where a crowd had gathered on the lawn of Xi'an Cathedral. "Your business is doing well in this moment of crisis."

"You had a reason to want to see me, Lord Teran?"

"What will the church do if the emperox declares martial law?"

"Is that why you came to see me?"

"It's part of it," Assan said. "As a representative of the guilds on the executive committee, I've been fielding a number of concerned calls and correspondence from noble houses and guild representatives. I know my counterparts in parliament have been doing the same with their own constituents. But your constituency isn't people,

Archbishop. It's the church itself."

"You say that like we don't have parishioners, Lord Teran."

Assan motioned back toward the crowd. "More now."

"I'm saying I disagree with your assessment."

"As you will, but you still haven't answered my question."

"I haven't given it any thought," Korbijn said. "I haven't given it any thought because this is literally the first I've heard of such a thing. I'm not inclined to give snap judgments on hypotheticals. I might as well ask you what you would do if Grayland announced she was abolishing breakfast."

"I'm pro-breakfast."

Korbijn threw up her hands. "You're missing my point."

"I got your point," Assan assured her. "But I dare say you're missing mine. I'm not offering you a random hypothetical, like outlawing a meal. The emperox addressed the church in her capacity as its leader and announced she was having visions — a thing unheard-of in a millennium — and obliged you as a church to follow her lead." He waved toward the crowd at the cathedral. "She played that one very well, I'd say. You have an influx of freaked-out people flooding your churches and cathedrals, and suddenly your institution, the thing you represent, Archbishop, has more power. But it's power you have on loan from the emperox, who set it up with her canard about visions."

"What are you suggesting?"

"I'm not suggesting it, I'm saying it out loud: She pulled a coup on you — on you *specifically,* Archbishop — and used the collapse of two Flow streams to shift the power of the church onto her. And she did it so well that apparently you haven't even noticed it yet. Unless you have and are perfectly fine with it."

Korbijn opened her mouth to address this, but Assan continued. "And now the emperox wants to address parliament, right after the Terhathum Flow collapse, when people are scared, and vulnerable, and looking to be reassured, and politically persuadable. Given all of *that,* does my question about the possibility of the emperox declaring martial law sound like a random hypothetical to you now?"

"No," Korbijn said, after a moment.

"So back to my question."

"But neither does it sound *probable* to me," Korbijn continued, ignoring Assan's interjection. "I've worked with this emperox for her entire reign so far. I knew her before she was emperox. Grayland is many things, Lord Teran, not all of them desirable in an emperox. But power-hungry is not one of them."

"And if you're wrong?"

"What if *you're* wrong?" Now it was Korbijn's turn to motion to the crowd outside. "Your assessment of Grayland's coup of the Interdependent Church glosses over the fact that at no point either before or after her address to the bishops has she tried to exercise any control of the church. She's not the one in this office, setting policies and practices and doctrine. I am. She's not the one assigning priests to churches. Bishop Carnick is. She's not administering our social services. Bishop Ornill is. For now."

"For now?"

"He's thinking of resigning. A sudden crisis of faith, he said. But whoever will take his place, they won't be put there by the emperox. Which is my point to you, Lord Teran. For a coup to occur, power has to shift. None has."

"If you say so, Archbishop," Assan said. "And now I think I have your answer. Thank you." He nodded and left as abruptly as he'd entered, glancing around at the office again as he did.

Korbijn stood there for a moment wondering what in fact had just happened, and then sat down at her desk, disquieted. She buzzed for Ubes Ici, her assistant.

He was at the door in an instant. "Yes, Your Eminence?"

"Set a meeting of my advisors for this evening," Korbijn said. "Seven o'clock. Tell the bishops to clear their schedules if necessary."

"May I tell them what the meeting is for?"

"I need their advice. On the emperox."

Ici paused as if to ask for further guidance, but thought better of it. "Yes, Your Eminence."

"And, Ubes?"

"Yes?"

"Schedule a dinner service and refreshments. It's going to be a long meeting."

"And how did Archbishop Korbijn take to your suggestion she's been played?" asked Jasin Wu.

"She denied it, obviously," Assan said. "But the point wasn't to get her to agree. The point was to plant the seed of doubt. She already had doubts, of course. Someone of her position doesn't just go along with a brand-new emperox spouting about prophecy. That's a threat to her personal power and influence."

Jasin grunted. The two of them were in Jasin's office in the Guild House on Hubfall, all clean lines and executive power, as befitted Jasin's position on the Wu board. The two of them had tumblers of whiskey in their hands, which Assan reflected was as much a cliché of executive power as the big office they now stood in. "When the time comes, I'm going to need her as an ally, Teran."

"I know that, Jasin."

"Good. Because that time looks like it's coming sooner than later."

"Because of the collapse of the Terhathum Flow stream."

"Because that's only going to be the first. Well," Jasin amended, "second. But the other ones are going to happen, and we need to be prepared before too many of them collapse."

"Prepared for your coup."

Jasin grimaced. "Don't say that word out loud, Teran. For fuck's sake."

"Call it what it is, Jasin. You and I both know it's necessary. It's why you maneuvered to put me on the executive committee in the first place. To make the case for it to the other members."

Jasin glanced over. "Word is that you're not all that popular on the committee. The word 'asshole' gets attached to you a lot."

"I'm just being me."

"It's true you've always been an asshole. I say that with respect."

"I know. There's no point in me pretending to be who I'm not. The people on the committee aren't stupid. They would see through that. So I'm an asshole. But I'm an asshole who has a point. And they can't deny the point, as much as they might dislike me."

"That's optimistic."

"It's working."

"Let's hope so." Jasin took a sip from his tumbler. "Nadashe Nohamapetan is still alive."

"I heard."

Jasin glanced over to Teran. "Is she alive because you told Deran I was planning to have her killed?"

"No," Assan said, scornfully. "She's alive because Deran's office is three doors down and the House of Wu is incredibly leaky with information."

"I hinted to you I was planning something."

"And I told no one. You know I talk to Deran, and Deran knows I talk to you. The difference is that Deran thinks I am his double agent, when in fact I'm yours. And as your double agent, let me tell you it's a good thing your attempt failed."

"Nadashe Nohamapetan is dangerous."

"Yes, she is. But she and her house can be your enemy or they can be your ally. The House of Nohamapetan is in disgrace right now, but it's still powerful. It still has powerful friends. And for what you're about to try to do, you're going to need all the friends you can get."

"I wish I could have seen the look on his face when you told him it wasn't you who told me about his plan to murder Nadashe," Deran Wu said, a half hour later, in his office. His office was slightly smaller than Jasin's but perhaps more richly appointed, and his whiskey was better.

"Well, you know," Assan said. "You know I talk to Jasin and Jasin knows I talk to you. The difference is that Jasin thinks I am his double agent, when in fact I'm yours. And as your double agent, let me tell you that now it's time for you to be careful with the Nohamapetans."

"Why? As of right now I have an understanding with Nadashe. She'll put in a positive word for me with her house, through her lawyer. In return I'll use our law enforcement and security contacts to make a mess of the evidence leading to her."

"Which you will necessarily have to try to pin on Amit."

"So?"

"So, Amit is known to have been the favorite child of the countess, so shitting on his memory to spring the child the countess undoubtedly knows killed her favorite might not be the winning play you think it is."

Deran frowned. "I see your point."

"I thought you might."

"Do you have an alternative plan?"

Assan smiled. "It depends on how aggressive you'd like to be in your quest to be emperox."

"So you are playing the two Wu cousins against each other," said Tinda Louentintu, who was the chief of staff for the Countess Nohamapetan. She said this in the imperial suite of the Racheline, Hubfall's most exclusive and secure hotel. She said it there rather than in the offices of the House of Nohamapetan because there was currently a cuckoo in that particular nest, a thing that would need to be addressed presently. The Racheline was an exquisite address, the imperial suite was gorgeously laid out and appointed, and the whiskey, which Assan took care to sip very slowly, given how much alcohol was already in his system at the moment, was almost impossibly fine.

"I'm not exactly playing them against each other," Assan said. "I'm allowing them both to think they are using me to spy on the other while I decide which of them I ultimately want to back in their run for emperox."

"That could turn out poorly for you if they compare notes," Louentintu said.

"For them to do that they would have to stop loathing each other for longer than fifteen seconds. My family is close to the Wus, just like it has been for generations. I'm of an age between Jasin and Deran and grew up socializing with both here in Hubfall. No one outside of the family knows them better than I do. Neither of them is in much danger of having a sudden fit of affection for the other."

"You find it useful to keep them at cross-purposes."

"You say that as if it was me doing it," Teran said. "My family has a saying: 'No one hates a Wu like a Wu.' It's a miracle when anyone on their board of directors agrees on what to have for lunch, much less their actual business. I'm not putting Jasin and Deran at cross-purposes. But I'm not against using their cross-purposes to my advantage, either."

Louentintu nodded. "Which is why you're here, Lord Teran."

"Yes. You have to know that no matter what, Grayland is on her way out. If she's actually having visions, she's not stable. If she's not, then she's playing a game in a moment of crisis that's partly of her own making. For the good of the Interdependency, she has to go."

"If you say so."

"Ah, but it's not me saying so," Assan said. "Or not *just* me, anyway. The other houses are nervous about these changes in the Flow and what Grayland might use them as an excuse for, in terms of their business and monopolies. The parliament is convinced Grayland is about to institute martial law. Even the church is unsure what to do with Grayland now that she's imitating Rachela. Changes are coming. That much is obvious. And I think everyone agrees that when that change comes, we need stability right at the top. In the imperial seat."

"The House of Nohamapetan has already stood out once against the emperox," Louentintu said. "It was not to our advantage."

Assan shook his head. "No. Forgive me,

Minister Louentintu, but the House of Nohamapetan has not stood out against the emperox. One of its members has. And while that member may have acted unwisely, it's also clear they had a legitimate complaint. The imperial house had agreed that the next emperox would marry a Nohamapetan. Then the emperox backed out of the deal. She shouldn't have. It's an error that should be corrected. And can be corrected."

Louentintu raised her eyebrows at this.

"That is, if the House of Nohamapetan is willing to make a deal, with one or the other of the Wu cousins now currently aiming at the throne, and to back it up with their resources, and the resources of their friends."

"When?"

"Soon, I would think. The emperox's scientist has given us a timetable."

"And what do you get out of it?" asked the third person in the room, reclining on the couch, who until this moment had been silent.

"How do you mean, ma'am?"

"How I mean, Lord Teran, is that I am not stupid," said the Countess Nohamapetan. "I know why Jasin and Deran Wu are caught up in this. It's because a Wu must be emperox, and they are foolish enough to want the job, even now, as things are apparently falling apart. And it's clear what you think our interest should be, since you are clearly hinting at a political union between our house and whichever Wu floats to the top of this enterprise. What I want to know is what your interest is. You are already the director of the House of Assan's business affairs. You are already on the executive committee. You are already a lord. You have all the power you will ever have. What else is it that you want?"

Assan smiled. "Not for me," he said, and then pulled out his tablet and opened up a photo. Two small children were there, smiling up at the photographer. Assan showed the photo to the countess.

"Charming," the countess said. "And relevant how?"

"Relevant because one of them will marry the child of the next emperox."

An unknowable play of emotions crossed over the countess's face as she processed his words. "That is ambitious of you, Lord Teran, to plan that far ahead. Considering our civilization is coming to a sudden close."

"Not all of it. Just most of it. There's still End. Which your son Ghreni is attempting to gain control of, and which Nadashe sent a ship full of marines to in order to help him do so. It's the one place in the Interdependency where humans will be able to survive in the long run. Your children planned to secure it, and make the House of Nohamapetan the new imperial house. Well, that didn't go as planned. So it's time to go back to plan A: Marry an Emperox. I'll help you do it."

"And all you want is the throne."

"Yes. Eventually. You can have it first. Which is what you want. Ma'am."

Assan saw the Countess Nohamapetan look over at her chief of staff, who nodded almost imperceptibly. Then her eyes came back to him. "Tell us more, Lord Teran."

"To begin, which Wu would you prefer, ma'am?" Assan asked. "Jasin or Deran?"

Chapter 7

Kiva Lagos was in the middle of receiving some perfectly serviceable oral when her tablet pinged. She glanced over and saw it was Bunton Salaanadon, her executive assistant. Kiva considered not answering it, because she was busy and because she had told Salaanadon not to bother her unless the world was on fire. But then, because there was a possibility the world was on fire, and also because the oral was serviceable rather than full-attention-requiring spectacular, she picked up the tablet and answered it, voice only.

"Is the fucking world on fire?" she asked. From below, her partner looked up, quizzically, and gave Kiva a look that she interpreted as, *Should I hold up?* Kiva gave a motion with her hand, signaling that the oral should continue. Kiva's partner got back to it.

"It depends on whether you consider an

imperial summons a fire-bearing situation, ma'am," Salaanadon said.

"What? Explain."

"The Countess Nohamapetan has asked for, and received, a priority audience from the emperox regarding the disposition of the local activities of the house businesses. Specifically, she is asking you be removed from your position. I assume the emperox thought it only fair that you be allowed to offer your opinion on that, Lady Kiva."

"When is this audience?"

"Two hours from now, ma'am."

"Then I'm going to need a ride."

"I've already arranged for a pickup at your apartments and a priority seat on the Xi'an shuttle. Since you explicitly have an imperial summons, you will have priority seating and clearance. An imperial escort will greet you when you arrive, and I've already filed the paperwork for expedited passage through security."

"No firearms when I go, got it."

"Yes, that would be advisable, ma'am," Salaanadon said. Kiva was never sure if he ever really knew when she was being sarcastic or not and assumed he just chose the straight man lifestyle as a defensive choice.

"Will it just be the three of us?"

"The audience? I understand the countess

will be bringing her lawyer. Ms. Fundapellonan. You met with her the other day, you may recall."

"We're acquainted," Kiva said.

"Should I have one of our lawyers join you for the meeting?"

"I've got this," Kiva said. "Just make sure my 'receipts' file has been updated. I may need it."

"Yes, ma'am."

"When is the car picking me up?"

"It will be at your apartments in fifteen minutes. Unless you would like it to arrive sooner."

"No, that works," Kiva said, disconnected and then refocused herself on the perfectly serviceable oral she was getting.

"You should probably check your messages," Kiva said to her partner, after she came.

"Why is that?" asked Senia Fundapellonan.

"You'll see." Kiva went to her bathroom to go stop smelling like sex.

"You could have told me about this when you got the call," Fundapellonan said when Kiva emerged from the bathroom, no longer having the whiff of being perfectly adequately serviced.

"You were busy."

Fundapellonan waggled her tablet in her hand at Kiva. "This is slightly more important."

"That's a matter of opinion," Kiva said. "And anyway, you're not running any later because of it."

"I have to order a cab to the shuttleport and then catch a shuttle."

"Just come with me."

"And you don't think that looks at all *bad,* you and I taking a car from your apartment, together."

Kiva shrugged. "It's not like the countess doesn't already know we're fucking."

Fundapellonan blinked at this. "What?"

"I assumed she told you I like to fuck around, so you should get with me to see if I would say anything useful while we banged."

"Is that what you really think is going on here?" Fundapellonan asked.

"Isn't it?"

"Well, yes," Fundapellonan admitted. "But you're not supposed to *think* it."

"Just because I like to fuck, doesn't mean I'm stupid," Kiva said.

"If you knew this was a setup, then why did you . . . ?"

"Screw your brains out?"

"Yes."

"Why wouldn't I?"

"Because it's totally insincere?"

Kiva squinted at Fundapellonan. "Do you get out much?"

Fundapellonan was flustered at this. "Apparently not?"

"It's just *sex,* for fuck's sake." Kiva said. "I wasn't planning to fucking propose. You offered, you're cute enough —"

"Thanks," Fundapellonan said, dryly.

"— and I haven't gotten laid that much since Marce Claremont traded up to the emperox. And it's not like I was going to say anything to you about my business."

"You mean, *our* business."

"Well, that's what today's meeting will be about, anyway," Kiva said. "My point is, it was a safe enough opportunity to get laid."

"I don't know how to feel about that," Fundapellonan said.

"It's not like you didn't get anything out of it," Kiva pointed out.

Fundapellonan smiled at that. "True enough." She paused. "This is the first time I've ever done something like this."

"Had sex with someone because your client told you to."

"Yes."

"How was it for you?"

"Mostly okay?"

"Well, good," Kiva said, and patted Fundapellonan's shoulder. "Because you're about to get fucked by me again, this time in front of the emperox."

The Countess Nohamapetan was definitely someone who wanted all the bells and whistles and shiny fucking spangles, so her audience with the emperox was held in the formal receiving room. It was cavernous enough that you could probably land a shuttle in it, although Kiva supposed, given who was both asking for and giving this little farce of an audience, any snippy quips about a shuttlecraft would not be appreciated.

Kiva glanced over at the Countess Nohamapetan and was not impressed. The countess, conspicuously ornate, had overdressed for this particular emperox. Grayland had been overdressed exactly once in her life, at her coronation, and since that event had included a bombing and the murder of Grayland's best friend, it hadn't been exactly a sterling moment in fashion history. The countess's advisors might have told her that Grayland preferred a more understated look. Either they hadn't, or the countess had ignored them, and now she was looking like a grenade went off in a drawer of metallic ribbons.

Kiva's own attire was rather more subtle, a formal suit of merchant black and gold with a pendant that showed off the colors of the House of Lagos: red, yellow, light and dark blue. Kiva thought the formal suit made her look like a waiter or a fucking servant, but it wasn't up to her what to wear to see the emperox, so she just dealt with it.

The emperox herself, as Kiva recalled, preferred a suit rather more like Kiva's than whatever sad monstrosity it was that the countess was wearing, tailored exquisitely (because it would be, wouldn't it) and in the dark imperial green that shouldn't have looked good next to Grayland's skin tone, but managed to look just fine anyway. Being emperox meant everything looked good on you, maybe. A nice perk of an otherwise thankless fucking job.

Kiva, the countess, and Senia Fundapellonan — who was wearing the same nice, conservative suit that Kiva had peeled her out of earlier in the day — all stood in front of the dais that held the throne Grayland would perch upon. Neither the dais nor the throne were particularly ridiculous, which meant they were out of place in the room, but in keeping with Grayland's own sensibility.

From well behind the dais, a door opened and Grayland entered the room. She did it without handlers, which Kiva understood to be increasingly her custom. She accepted bows and handshakes from Kiva and Fundapellonan, and a more elaborate curtsey-bow-whatever-the-fuck-it-was from the countess. Then she stepped up the dais, sat herself into the throne, and smiled.

"We are ready to hear you, our dear Countess Nohamapetan," she said. Kiva noted the use of the royal "we," which was the first time she had personally heard that from Grayland; when she'd met her before, Grayland was all "I" and "me." That said, the last time she'd seen Grayland, the emperox was getting over being attacked with spaceships. It was possible she was not entirely herself.

The countess did whatever that fucked-up bow-curtsey thing was again. "Let me begin, Your Majesty, by assuring you of the unending loyalty of the House of Nohamapetan. I am aware — we as a house are aware — that you have recently had ample reason to doubt the sincerity of this loyalty. I understand that the only way to regain that trust is to earn it again, slowly and with difficulty. It will be the mission of my house to do so. And in earnest of that mission, and as the first small step in recompense, I am pledging all Nohamapetan in-system profits this year to the Naffa Dolg Foundation."

Kiva almost choked on her tongue at this bullshit. To begin, the countess fucking well knew that she couldn't pledge those in-system revenues to anything; they were under Kiva's control, and she had the final word to how they could be used. Since Kiva had been in control of Nohamapetan's local businesses, all revenues had been placed into accounts that Kiva had made accessible to the Ministry of Revenue as a sort of permanent audit. The only way the countess could do anything with the revenues without Kiva's consent was for the emperox to give back control of local operations. Which was something the countess undoubtedly knew as well as Kiva. So either this was the opening gambit to removing Kiva, or it was an attempt to make Kiva the asshole of the day. Which would also be the opening gambit to removing Kiva.

To continue, Naffa Dolg, the emperox's childhood best friend and first chief of staff, was fucking *murdered* on the emperox's coronation day by a bomb that was almost certainly but not yet provably planted by some asshole working for the Nohamapetan siblings, the asshole children of this asshole countess. Whether the countess herself knew about the attempt at the time or not, she certainly knew about it *now.* Just like she knew the bomb was meant to kill Grayland.

So basically the Countess Nohamapetan was currently saying to the emperox, "I'm proving my loyalty by offering money I don't have to the charity named for your friend, who my kids accidentally slaughtered when they tried to fucking assassinate *you.*"

Which struck Kiva as an *interesting* way to try to win favor with the emperox.

Either the countess was laughably oblivious to the insult she was offering to Grayland, or she was daring the emperox to make something of it. Kiva, remembering both Nadashe and Ghreni Nohamapetan from her college days, doubted that the countess was that oblivious. She might currently look like a glittered chicken, but she wasn't stupid.

So this had to be a test of some sort or another, one that the countess thought she was administering to the emperox. To see if Grayland was oblivious, perhaps. Or to see how the emperox would react to what amounted to a bald-faced slap against her and her beloved friend. Or maybe the countess just wanted to see what she could get away with, and what the emperox was willing to take from her. Or maybe she just thought Grayland was a fucking idiot.

Kiva glanced over to Fundapellonan, whose face was pleasantly blank. Kiva wondered briefly whether her recent lover might have suggested this particular course of action to her countess. She doubted it. Fundapellonan didn't seem to have the sufficient level of gutstabbery in her soul to pull a stunt like this. Kiva's eyes went back to Grayland, who took this all in and processed it.

Go on, Kiva thought. *Fucking ask me about this.*

"Your pledge moves us, Countess," Grayland said. "It is a reflection of the quality of your soul, and we are glad to know it."

And then, after that absolute fucking masterpiece of saying, *Oh, I see you, bitch,* and making it sound like a compliment, the emperox turned her attention to Kiva. "We wonder what Lady Kiva, as the countess's in-system director, has to say regarding this remarkable offer."

Watch this, Kiva thought, and began. "No doubt the countess has the best of intentions, Your Majesty, but I regret to say that this year our in-system profits will be close to zero."

Grayland blinked at this. "And why is that, Lady Kiva?"

"Widespread graft, ma'am. I instituted an audit when you asked me to supervise the in-system businesses of the Nohamapetans, and we have uncovered substantial business discrepancies, all of which will affect revenues and profits. We are still uncovering them. It will take months to get a full account, and meanwhile we are in a position of having to deal with make-goods with our customers, as well as fines and penalties which will be assessed by your own Ministry of Revenue."

"This is unhappy news," Grayland said.

"I can have a full report sent to you, if you would like," Kiva said, helpfully. "It has already been sent to the Ministry of Revenue."

"Thank you, Lady Kiva. We would like that very much."

"And if I may," Kiva continued, "I can offer you a solution to this unfortunate problem."

"We are listening."

"No doubt the countess had no intention of offering you nothing when she offered you this year's in-system profits, Your Majesty. Her own accountants were misled and deceived, and as she is newly arrived in-system, I have not had an opportunity to get her or her people up to speed on the financial affairs of the local business. This is almost certainly an innocent mistake. And truth be told, if the graft were not as endemic and widespread as it is, the House of Nohamapetan would be having a banner year, profit-wise."

"What do you suggest, Lady Kiva?" Grayland asked.

"Simple, Your Majesty. I will have my accountants provide you an amount that represents the sum of local profits for the last twelve months, without the graft and penalties. The countess may then present to the Naffa Dolg Foundation a donation of that sum, from the House of Nohamapetan general coffers. Everyone wins."

Grayland nodded and turned back to the Countess Nohamapetan. "If the countess will accept this small emendation to her generous offer, as we are sure she will, then we will be delighted to accept her gracious gesture."

Suck on that, *you duplicitous crab,* Kiva thought. The countess thought she was testing Grayland, and it turned out she was the one who got schooled. The emperox had turned her slap of a gift around and shoved her face right into it.

The Countess Nohamapetan allowed herself roughly a second and a half to blink in surprise. And then, "Of course, Your Majesty. It will be exactly so."

"Wonderful." Grayland turned to Kiva. "When may we expect that number?"

"I can have it to you tomorrow, Your Majesty."

"We will expect it then." Over to the countess again. "And the Naffa Dolg Foundation may expect your contribution quickly after? Within the week?"

"Of course," the countess said.

Grayland nodded. "You are very lucky to have Lady Kiva as your director, Countess Nohamapetan," she said. "Aside from her clever solution to this minor problem, her uncovering of the widespread graft and corruption within your organization must be a great relief to you."

"Yes, quite," the countess answered, not looking at Kiva at all.

"It would have been unfortunate if such practices had leapfrogged from the in-system organization to the Nohamapetan organization at large," Grayland continued. "Then the Ministry of Revenue and the Ministry of Justice would be obliged to step in." She glanced over to Kiva. "But you do not believe that such a thing is the case?"

"Not yet, Your Majesty," Lady Kiva said. "But of course our investigation is not yet over."

"How long do you think it will take, Lady Kiva?"

"Given the complexity of the House of Nohamapetan income streams and books, and the sophistication of the skimming from each, several more months, I think."

"Several more months," Grayland said, with a very slight emphasis on the word "months."

"At least, yes," Kiva amended.

Grayland returned her attention to the Countess Nohamapetan. "We have no doubt you are extending your director here every courtesy and cooperation while she sounds the extent of your local organization's issues, Countess."

"Yes, Your Majesty, but —"

"Yes, Countess?"

"— while Lady Kiva has shown great ingenuity —"

"The countess is too kind with her praise," Kiva interjected, knocking the countess off-balance. "I must admit, however, that there was almost no ingenuity on my part here. To discover these lapses, all it took were fresh eyes."

"Someone from the outside, you would

say, Lady Kiva?" Grayland asked.

"Perhaps that's all that was needed, yes," Kiva replied.

Grayland slapped the arms of her throne, lightly. "In that case, we believe it's best to have those outside eyes continue to look into the issues with the in-system Nohamapetan business, and to help this branch of a great house return to form. And of course, in your continuing role as director, Lady Kiva, you will remain in contact with the countess directly, to keep her informed on what you find, as you will keep *us* informed, to the same extent."

"Of course, Your Majesty," Kiva said.

"The House of Nohamapetan is of great interest to us, Lady Kiva," Grayland said. "You have a great responsibility, both to it, and to us."

"I understand," Kiva intoned. She glanced over at the countess, who it must be said was holding her outrage in admirably.

"Now, Countess, let us discuss your daughter," Grayland said.

"Ma'am?" the Countess Nohamapetan said, thrown entirely off track by this.

"Our understanding was that this was the reason for your visit," Grayland said.

"In fact, ma'am, we came to discuss the matter of Lady Kiva —"

"Well, we've settled that, have we not?" Grayland asked. "And on the matter of your daughter, *we* have an interest to speak to you. If you wish to hear it."

Kiva saw the countess momentarily and almost imperceptibly weigh her desire to revisit the matter of extracting Kiva from her business against the possibility of irritating this emperox who was currently in the process of railroading her sorry ass all around the room. She took the cowardly way out. "I am happy to speak of my daughter, ma'am."

"Your daughter is accused of some of the most grievous crimes, Countess. Murder. Attempted assassination. Treason. These crimes, if she is found guilty of them, come with the penalty of death."

The countess paled a bit at this. "Yes, ma'am."

"It grieves me that she finds herself in this position, Countess Nohamapetan. At one point, we thought she might be our sister, married to our brother Rennered, who was to be emperox. Things would be very different now, had he lived to succeed our father."

"Yes, they would," the countess said. "They would indeed."

"We cannot say what may have led Nadashe to the crimes she is accused of. We cannot stop what must happen. She must be tried. And when tried, if she is found guilty, she must be punished. We must all face the law, and justice. You understand this, Countess Nohamapetan?"

"I do." The countess looked down at the room's exquisite mosaic floor.

Grayland nodded. "Nadashe must face the law, and must face justice, and must be punished," she repeated. "And yet, in earnest of my brother's love for her, and to honor the loyalty you have pledged your house to, I can offer some mercy."

The countess looked up. "Your Majesty?"

"Life instead of death," Grayland said. "If she is found guilty of any of the capital crimes she is accused of, and is sentenced to death, I will commute the sentence to life imprisonment. And she will serve that sentence here on Xi'an, at Silent Water."

Kiva blinked at this. Silent Water wasn't so much a penitentiary as it was a vacation camp you couldn't leave. It was where ministers of parliament went when they were caught taking bribes, or accountants caught embezzling funds. It was the only penal facility on Xi'an, on the basis that one doesn't want to house hardened criminals in the same habitat as the emperox. To house Nadashe there when she straight-up murdered dozens of people, including her brother, was giving her a huge fucking break. Grayland might as well be giving her an ice cream cone while she was at it.

"Is that acceptable to you, Countess Nohamapetan?" Grayland asked.

Kiva watched the Countess Nohamapetan roll through several sets of emotion on her face, some so quickly that Kiva wasn't sure she actually saw them. Then the countess looked directly at Grayland again, and gave that fucked-up curtsey-bow-whatever again.

"Of course, Your Majesty," she said to the emperox. "Thank you."

Grayland nodded and stood. "We have accomplished much today," she said. "We are glad of it. And now you must excuse us, as we have another appointment which we will soon be late for. Countess Nohamapetan, Lady Kiva, Ms. Fundapellonan." Grayland gave a small bow, which the three of them returned and held until the emperox had made it to the door behind the dais from which she had entered.

The door closed.

"What the *fuck* were you even doing here?" the Countess Nohamapetan lashed at Fundapellonan. Fundapellonan opened her mouth to reply, but the countess stormed off toward the entrance, looking like the world's most pissed-off peacock.

Kiva watched her go. "I don't know what she's so upset about," she said to Fundapellonan. "I thought that went very well."

Fundapellonan looked at Kiva with narrowed eyes. "This was a setup," she said.

"Are you fucking kidding me?" Kiva said. "Your boss walks in here with an obvious plan to insult Grayland, and when her ass is handed to her, you whine about a setup?" She nodded in the direction of the departed, furious countess. "This wasn't a setup. It was a massacre, pure and simple. Your boss made the mistake of assuming the emperox was weak and got stuffed. She got stuffed so hard *you* never had a chance to make the argument that I should be out of a job."

"And you didn't speak to the emperox about this at all."

"We're not *friends,*" Kiva said. "We don't have fucking sleepovers where we style each other's hair and giggle about boys. This is the second time I've ever met her."

"Hmmm."

"Don't get me wrong," Kiva said. "The way she crushed your boss just now was fucking *spectacular.* She didn't get a chance to object to me. You didn't get to bring in your sabotage gambit. The emperox made it clear that she was going to watch what happened to me and your local businesses very closely. Then she rubbed the countess's nose in the fact her daughter was a murderer and a traitor, and made her thank her for telling her that her kid would spend the rest of her life in prison."

Fundapellonan looked at Kiva strangely. "Is that what you thought just happened?"

"I was here for it, so yes, actually."

Fundapellonan shook her head. "You don't understand. When Grayland said that she would commute Nadashe's death sentence and house her on Xi'an, she wasn't being *gracious.* She wasn't even rubbing the countess's nose in the fact that Nadashe will be in prison all her life. She was telling the countess that she was making Nadashe a hostage. Right here on Xi'an. Where the emperox can get to her if the countess ever gets out of line again. How could you miss that, Kiva? How could you miss that the emperox made an enemy of the countess today? Countess Nadashe will never forget what Grayland did today. And she will never, ever forgive it."

Chapter 8

Grayland II did have another appointment that she was about to be late for — truth to be told, she always had an appointment that she was about to be late for — but the appointment she was about to be late for was one where, at least, she would not have to be Grayland II. She was meant to be having a meeting with Marce Claremont, which meant she would get to be Cardenia Wu-Patrick for the thirty minutes or so they would have together.

The fact that the meeting was thirty minutes was in itself something of a luxury. To get thirty minutes with the emperox these days you had to be the minister of state or the archbishop of Xi'an, or some major human habitat had to be on fire. But Marce Claremont got thirty minutes because one, he was the linchpin to understanding the changes in the Flow that were currently affecting the Interdependency, and no other Flow scientists had caught up with him; and two, Cardenia had a crush on him and liked spending time looking at him.

"Are you all right, ma'am?" asked her assistant Obelees Atek, who was ferrying her to the next appointment.

"I'm fine," Cardenia said. "Why?"

"You look a little flushed all of a sudden."

This made Cardenia flush a little more. "It's nothing," she said. "I was thinking back on something the Countess Nohamapetan said."

"That bad, ma'am?"

"It could have been worse," Cardenia said, although at the moment she wasn't sure how. Cardenia was aware the countess had been furious at the outcome of the meeting; she'd been sure she was going to roll the emperox and take back control of her local holdings.

This is the nice thing about being underestimated, Cardenia thought. It wasn't the first time recently that she'd outmaneuvered someone because that other person thought she was slow, or naive, or simply too nice to be anything more than an obstacle to be maneuvered, or to be maneuvered around. Cardenia remembered that when she'd started as the emperox, she felt mildly offended that people thought she could be flattered or intellectually bullied into a position or decision.

Then she'd spent time talking to the ghosts of her predecessors in the Memory Room and learned just how much flattery and bullying had worked over the centuries. It didn't leave her with a positive impression either of the former emperoxs or of the people who wheedled concessions out of them. She also learned the value of letting people assume she was less than capable, up until the moment she disabused them of the notion. Like she just had with the Countess Nohamapetan. The countess wouldn't do that again.

That's not necessarily a good thing, one part of Cardenia's mind pointed out. And that was true enough. You were underestimated once, and then when you rubbed someone's face in it, forever after, that trick was out of the toolbox.

I'm the emperox, Cardenia thought. *I do have other tricks.*

And that was also true enough.

Enough of the Countess Nohamapetan, another part of Cardenia's brain said. *We were thinking about Marce.* This part of her brain, Cardenia realized, might be a swoony fifteen-year-old.

But, well. Marce. There was a puzzle, wasn't it.

"I don't know what to do," Cardenia had admitted to the ghost of her father, Attavio VI, in the Memory Room, the night before.

"Have sex with him," Attavio VI said.

"It's not that simple," Cardenia protested.

"It is, actually," Attavio VI replied. "You're the emperox."

"And, what? I just command him into my bed?"

"It's been done before."

"Not by me," Cardenia said. "Leaving everything else aside, I'm not built that way."

"Then invite him," Attavio VI. "Less problematic. Mostly equal success rate, historically speaking."

"How often did *you* do that?" Cardenia asked.

"Before I answer I will remind you that I as a computer simulation of your father have no ego to defend, and thus will answer entirely truthfully," Attavio VI said. "I mention this because at several points in the past I answered questions for you and it made you unhappy. Perhaps you might ask the question of another emperox, to whom you are not emotionally attached."

"You're saying the answer will make me

unhappy?"

"Yes, basically."

"Well, now I have to know," Cardenia said.

"I did *all* the time," Attavio VI said. "It was a pretty great perk of being emperox."

"Oh, God," Cardenia said, and buried her face in her hands. "You're right. I didn't want to know."

"It worked on your mother," Attavio VI said.

"I especially didn't need to know *that.*"

"In her case it led to something more. But you have to know it started because I invited her, and like nearly everyone else, she didn't refuse."

"You understand that doesn't make it *better,* right?" Cardenia said.

"I never coerced anyone," Attavio VI said. "I was turned down from time to time, and I never asked again in those cases. There's never a need for that, especially when you're emperox."

"And you don't think being emperox wasn't a substantial factor in people accepting. That they might feel pressure to have sex with you because you could, say, *wreck their lives.*"

"There's no need for that, either," Attavio VI said. "It's just sex. And it worked the other way as well. There were people who wanted to have sex with me because I was the emperox. They wanted a story to tell their grandchildren. They wanted it more than I did."

"And you fulfilled their wishes, because you were selfless," Cardenia said, sarcastically.

"No, I did it because I wanted sex too," Attavio VI said. "Just not as much."

"Remind me never to ask you for romantic advice ever again."

"I have recorded that request and will remind you of it should this ever come up again."

"Thank you."

"With that said, you have to be aware that you will never stop being the emperox," Attavio VI said. "You will always be more powerful than the people you will be interested in. If you don't want to be alone, or to have your sexual and emotional needs tended to by a professional, you will have to accept that is part of your landscape."

"I haven't had sex since I've been emperox," Cardenia admitted.

"That doesn't seem healthy."

"I don't like it much either. But that's part of the problem too. I don't want Marce to think I'd be using him strictly for tension release."

"I'm not sure I'm qualified to talk to you about this," Attavio VI said. "I'm a computer simulation of your father, not a licensed relationship therapist."

"I doubt this rises to the level of therapy," Cardenia said.

"If you say so," Attavio VI said, and it bothered Cardenia that a computer simulation could perfectly mimic doubt. "Perhaps you should just tell this person you like them. The worst that can happen is he says no."

"I know."

"And then you can have him exiled."

"No," Cardenia said, and then paused. "Did you just make a joke?"

"If it will make you feel better about what I just said, then yes, I did," said Attavio VI.

As Cardenia walked through the imperial palace toward her personal apartments, she realized that her father, or the computer simulation thereof, was not wrong. Ultimately Marce and she were adults and could approach this in an adult manner. She suspected he liked her as well but was shy about making any first move, first because he was kind of a nerd, and second because she was, after all, the emperox, and despite her father's attestations otherwise, Cardenia suspected it took nerves of steel to let an emperox know you were into them. Marce, entirely understandably, was waiting for Cardenia to make that first move.

All right, then, I will, Cardenia said to herself. *It's been weeks since we met. It's time. The worst that can happen is he says no.*

Cardenia walked into her apartments, nodded goodbye to Atek, who made her way back to her own office until she was called for, and then walked into her private dining room, where she knew Marce would be waiting, and was, in fact, waiting.

With another woman.

"Who the hell are *you*?" Cardenia blurted, before she could stop herself.

"We're calling it 'evanescence,' " Marce said. "Flow streams that arise out of the shifting of the Flow topography in our part of space. So even as the streams that we've seen as long-term and stable are collapsing — and they *are* — these other streams will arise and connect star systems for an indeterminate period of time."

"Right," said Hatide Roynold, the woman Marce had brought to their engagement. "Although by 'indeterminate' we don't mean that we can't estimate how long the stream will remain open. We can, probably.

What we mean is that the individual streams might be open for a day. Or a couple of weeks. Or even years."

"But they'll still collapse quickly, relative to the streams we've been used to, the ones that were open for a thousand years," Marce said. "That's why we're calling the phenomenon evanescence."

"Now you see them, now you don't," Roynold said.

Cardenia nodded dumbly at the two of them as they raced through the details of their latest discoveries, and tried to gather her thoughts. She had made a mess of her entrance, and neither Marce nor Roynold had seemed to figure out why exactly that was. Marce had apologized for springing Roynold on Cardenia, but noted that he had cleared the addition with the emperox's secretary and assumed that Cardenia knew he was bringing a guest.

This was entirely possible, since Cardenia had not bothered to check her own personal schedule on her tablet between her appointments, on the basis that she knew where she was going and with whom she was having her next meeting. Roynold's presence meant that she was essentially harmless to Cardenia; security would not have cleared her as an addition if she could have been in any way a threat.

Marce had brought Roynold because of all the Flow physicists currently cranking their way through the Count Claremont's work on the Flow collapse, she was the only one who was already up to speed on the work. She had done her own work on the subject, albeit only relatedly, and also for the Nohamapetans, who then used her work to try to overthrow the Interdependency.

No one seemed to be holding it against Roynold, however. Apparently not the Imperial Guard, which allowed her into the palace, and clearly not Marce, who was talking animatedly with her, with the both of them trading off sentences.

Cardenia watched the way the two of them talked about the subject of the Flow and was aware of a tang of jealousy creeping into her emotions. Marce and Roynold had a communion of ideas that felt to Cardenia like love at first sight — they were obviously into each other, or at least into each other's brains. Roynold was a bit older than Marce, but that wouldn't be that much of an impediment if everything else lined up.

Maybe you should actually pay attention to what they're saying to you, that one annoying voice in her head said. *You can moon after the boy later.* Cardenia made a note to try to find that voice later and strangle it, possibly with alcohol.

So Cardenia held up a hand to stop the both of them from talking. Marce picked up on it right away; Roynold kept prattling on until Marce put a hand on her shoulder to stop her. Cardenia noted it and felt a small pinprick in the general area of her heart.

"I don't need to know the details here," Cardenia said. "I wouldn't *understand* the details even if you tried to tell them to me, and I have to be at another meeting in a few minutes. So let me see if I understand what you're saying so far."

"Okay," Marce said.

"One, the Flow streams are still collapsing."

"Yes," Marce said.

"Two, every once in a while a new Flow stream will appear where there wasn't one before."

"Yes."

"Three, these new Flow streams are only around for a short time; they won't replace the old streams."

"Yes."

"Well," Roynold said.

"Well, what?" Cardenia asked.

"Our preliminary work —" Roynold began.

"And this all *super* preliminary," Marce interjected.

"— shows that eventually a new network of Flow streams with long-term stability is likely to appear in this part of space. Like I'd predicted before, for the Nohamapetans," Roynold finished.

Cardenia looked up at Marce, confused. "Is this accurate?"

"Well," Marce began.

"Because if this is *accurate,* then I have a whole lot of questions for you, Lord Marce. Not all of them friendly. I've risked a whole lot on your predictions being correct."

Marce held up a hand, and then pointed at Roynold. "Ask her what 'eventually' means in this context."

Cardenia directed her attention to Roynold. "And what does 'eventually' mean in this context, Dr. Roynold?"

"Somewhere between five thousand and eight thousand years from now," Roynold said.

Cardenia looked back at Marce, confused.

"Dad and I were right," Marce said. "The Flow streams as we know them are going to collapse, soon, and go away for a very long time. Enough time to bring about the effective end of civilization if we don't act." He pointed again at Roynold. "She was *also* right — the Flow streams are eventually likely to reestablish themselves in this part of space, in a different configuration than they are in now. She was just off on the timescale."

"No one to check my math," Roynold said.

"And we *both* missed something else, until we had access to each other's work," Marce continued. "The evanescence, I mean. It doesn't change the fact the Flow streams are collapsing. It doesn't change that the Interdependency is threatened. But it might buy us all a little more time to deal with it."

"How so?"

"You asked if new Flow streams will open up where there weren't ones before," Marce said. "That's correct, and some will. But there's another effect, too."

"Collapsed ones will open back up again," Roynold said. "Sometimes. Not for very long."

"But long enough to send ships through," Marce said.

"Maybe," Roynold said. "Depends."

"And bring them back again," Marce said.

"Again, maybe and depends," Roynold said.

"Which brings us to the next thing." Marce leaned forward. "And this is a big thing."

"It's really big," Roynold said.

"What?" Cardenia asked, switching her view between the two of them. "What is it?"

"Hatide predicted a previously closed Flow stream would be opening up imminently. After the Terhathum stream closed, I tasked one our drones to go to where this previously closed Flow shoal used to be."

"And?" Cardenia said.

"It went through," Roynold said. "The Flow stream has opened up again. And the one coming back, too. Both of them back in business."

"Not for long," Marce warned.

"No," Roynold agreed. "They're both going to collapse again. The outgoing stream in about a year. The incoming stream much sooner than that. Say three months."

"Why the difference?" Cardenia asked.

"It's like I told you when I first met you," Marce said. "The incoming and outgoing streams aren't actually related. And there's this." He nodded over to Roynold.

"The incoming stream has been open for almost five years," Roynold said.

Cardenia blinked at this. "How is that possible?"

"The Flow doesn't do what it does on our schedule," Roynold said. "The current shift has been happening for decades, maybe even centuries."

"No," Cardenia said, slightly annoyed. "I mean how did *we* miss this open Flow shoal hanging out in Hub space?"

Roynold shrugged. "You weren't looking for it. Nothing was coming out of it. And the outgoing Flow shoal had collapsed so long ago, probably no one has thought about it for centuries."

"Except maybe for you," Marce said, to Cardenia.

Who threw up her hands, exasperated. "Could you please stop being mysterious, and just tell me, already?"

"It's Dalasýsla," Marce said. "The lost star system of the Interdependency. And the reason your namesake was assassinated."

Cardenia was stunned silent by this.

"Ask her," Roynold said, eventually, to Marce.

"Ask me what?" Cardenia said, also looking to Marce.

"We think we should go," Marce said. "To Dalasýsla."

"Why?"

"Because it's the system we lost," Marce said. "What happened there could happen to every other system in the Interdependency. We need to go and find out what we can about how everything broke down, so we can learn how to avoid their mistakes."

"And we need to do it soon," Roynold said. "Before the incoming stream collapses again."

"Hatide's right. We need a ship. And we need it soon."

"And *you* would want to go on the ship," Cardenia said.

"Of course," Marce said, and smiled. "It'll be the most important scientific expedition in hundreds of years. I wouldn't want to miss it." He looked over to Roynold. "Neither of us would."

It was close to midnight before Cardenia finally said *fuck it* to herself and sent for Marce Claremont.

"What sort of scientists are you going to need for this expedition?" she asked, when he appeared, hastily, in her apartments. His own apartment was in the staff wing of the palace, some distance away. Cardenia knew Marce had his own money — his father had sent him to Hub with a substantial portion of his family's wealth in a personal data vault — but Marce Claremont was apparently happy in what was essentially a studio apartment with a lavatory attached. He had walked the several minutes from his apartment to hers, stopping through layers of security on the way. The two of them stood, somewhat awkwardly, in her drawing room a bit of a distance apart.

"I think we'd need all kinds," Marce said, carefully. Cardenia could tell he wasn't aware why he'd been summoned, and now that she'd asked the question, he wasn't sure why this needed to be answered at 11:55 at night. "Flow physicists, obviously, but I'd also think we want biologists, chemists, astrophysicists, ordinary physicists, anthropologists and archeologists —"

"Archeologists?"

"Dalasýsla has been dead for centuries," Marce said. "We need people with an understanding of how to process that sort of history. We'd need forensic scientists and pathologists; we'd need historians, particularly the ones with a knowledge of Dalasýsla and the early Interdependency. We also need engineers and people who were familiar with the computers and systems of the era. That's who I can think of off the top of my head. I can write you a longer report, if you like."

"What if I wanted to keep this small?" Cardenia said. "Small and quiet?"

"Why would you want to do that?" Marce asked.

"Because right now the fewer people who know about it, and about the evanescent Flow streams you and Roynold have discovered, the fewer headaches I have to deal with trying to explain everything without you around," Cardenia said, and then caught Marce's look. "I'm not saying I want to keep this classified forever. I'm saying I want to know what this expedition has found out about Dalasýsla before I make any announcements."

"Other Flow physicists have been working on the data we've given them," Marce pointed out. "Some of them might find out about this anyway."

"They're working on your and your father's data, yes?"

"That's right."

"And not Roynold's."

"No."

"Then it's a risk worth taking."

"If you think so."

"I do. Back to my question. Small and quiet. How many scientists would you need, then?"

"We could double up jobs," Marce said.

"Flow physicists. We can do without the other sorts because we are schooled in general and classical physics, and we can make observations available for others to work with. A forensic pathologist who has some general biological expertise. There are lots of archeologists who have experience in anthropology and vice versa. We'd still need someone familiar with the computer systems of the time. And someone familiar with the habitats of the era as well. Maybe those could combine."

"So five or six, depending."

"I suppose. Plus an actual crew for the ship."

"How much time would you need at Dalasýsla?"

"However much time you want to give us."

"Give me a time frame, Marce."

"Two weeks minimum, I would think."

"How long there and back?"

"We estimate about eight days, going from the data we have and the historical data about the system. We're confident this is a reopened Flow stream and not a new stream mimicking the previous stream. But there's a plus or minus of about three days."

"So maximum eleven days there, two weeks at Dalasýsla, eleven days back. That's more than a month."

"Now you know why we want to get this expedition going sooner than later," Marce said.

"Why would you need two Flow scientists?" Cardenia asked. "If you're doubling up expertise with everyone else."

Marce looked a little hesitant at this. "I don't think that's a question of need," he said.

"Then what is it?"

"This is *our* discovery," Marce said. "Both mine and Hatide's. We both want to be part of it, and I think we both deserve to be part of it. I wouldn't want to ask her to stay here for it. And *I* definitely want to be part of it. Maybe it's a luxury in terms of personnel. But I think we can afford it."

"What if I asked you to stay behind?" Cardenia asked.

Marce gave Cardenia a very slight smile. "Asked?" he said.

"Asked," Cardenia said. "Not ordered."

"Your Majesty, if the emperox asks for something like this, one would be foolish to see it as anything other than an order."

Cardenia had a momentary flashback to her discussion with her father's ghost the night before, on the distinction between an emperox commanding or inviting someone to bed. "Oh, forget it," she said, and walked over to her bar to pour herself a drink.

"I'm confused," Marce said, after a moment.

"Join the club," Cardenia said, and put ice into a tumbler.

"What am I missing here?" Marce said.

Cardenia poured the drink, slugged back a nontrivial amount, and then set her glass down. "I'm really, really bad at this," she said.

"Bad at what?"

"Look, are you with Roynold?" Cardenia asked Marce.

"What?"

"Are you with Roynold? Are you two, you know" — Cardenia made wavy motions with the hand holding the tumbler, sloshing the liquid as a result — "a thing? An item? Romantically involved?"

Cardenia watched as Marce — bless his stupid, oblivious, nerdy heart — finally put it together. "No," he said. "No, we are not an item. We are not romantically involved."

"Are you sure?" Cardenia pressed. "I saw the two of you talking this afternoon. You were very *animated* together."

"It's because we're the only two people in the entire system who know what the other one is talking about," Marce said. "When it comes to the Flow, at least. It's like finding the only other person in the world who speaks your language."

"Well, see, that's what I *mean,*" Cardenia said, and finished the rest of her drink. She went over to refill her tumbler.

"The language is Flow physics," Marce said. "It's specialized. It's very abstruse. And it's not at all romantic."

"Are you sure that's what Roynold thinks?"

"You think she has a thing for me?"

"Maybe."

"I don't think I'm her type," Marce said.

"What do you think her type is?"

"Mathematical symbols, mostly. If you spent any time with her you'd know she doesn't really like humans all that much."

"She likes *you.*"

"She accepts dealing with the fleshy parts of me as part of the price of getting to work with my brain. It's not exactly the same thing."

Cardenia was quiet for a moment. "So, nothing between you two at all."

"If civilization survives we might go down in history as the co-discoverers of the Claremont-Roynold Theory of Flow Stream Distribution, along with my dad," Marce said. "But otherwise, no."

"Well, fuck," Cardenia said. She looked

into her drink, which she had replenished, and then looked back up at Marce. "Did I mention I am really, really bad at this?"

Marce grinned. "You did." He motioned to the tumbler in Cardenia's hand. "May I ask you to put that down, please?"

"Why?"

"Because if we're about to have the conversation I think we're going to have, I'd like to think it wasn't the booze talking."

"You could have said no, you know," Cardenia said, after, as they lay in bed in a classic snuggling pose.

"Why would I do that?" Marce said. "You're the emperox. You could have me shot."

Cardenia swatted him lightly. "That's my point. I didn't want you to think this was some sort of command performance. That I was hitting you up because you couldn't say no."

"Trust me, after tonight's conversation, I would never think you were commanding me into your bed."

"Oh, God," Cardenia said, and buried her face in Marce's chest. "Don't remind me. I will never live it down."

"I thought it was sweet."

"I swear to you I'm not actually the jealous type. That was something else entirely."

"What was it?"

"It was the 'he likes someone else and now I'm sad and want to go eat an entire pie' thing."

"That's a very specific thing."

"Well, pie is amazing." Cardenia lifted up her head and kissed Marce. "But I like this better."

"I'm very happy to know I'm better than pie," Marce said.

"Don't knock it."

"I'm not."

"You still want to go on that Dalasýsla expedition, don't you," Cardenia said, a minute later.

"Yes, of course," Marce said.

"I could go with you."

"I think the Interdependency might notice if the emperox suddenly went missing."

"That's not entirely true," Cardenia said. "Samuel III would disappear for entire months. Nobody much missed him."

"You may be more critical to the well-being to the Interdependency than Samuel III, whoever he was."

"That's possible."

"And given the amount of controversy you've kicked up recently, people would definitely notice if you were gone."

Cardenia looked up at him again. "That's a sly reference to the visions, isn't it."

"I'm going to shut up now," Marce said.

"So? What do you think of them? Really?"

"Does it matter?"

"Yeah. To me it matters."

"What I think is that Emperox Grayland II is doing everything she can to make sure that civilization and all the humans in it survive past the next ten years. And because that's what I think, if she's having visions, and they help humanity survive, then I'm all for them."

Cardenia kissed Marce again. "Thank you."

"I mean, I would have been *happier* if you'd just leaned into the science more," Marce said.

"Maybe next time," Cardenia said.

Marce snorted at that.

"How do you feel about the Imperial Navy?" Cardenia asked.

"I've never really given them much thought," Marce said. "Why?"

"Because I'm going to requisition a ship, crew and scientists from them to get you to Dalasýsla and back. They can do it quickly and quietly, and no one asks any questions when the emperox has a mission for the navy. Well," Cardenia amended, "people will ask. But they won't ask them out of the chain of command."

"When will they be ready?"

"I'm going to tell Admiral Emblad I want them ready in a week. Five days if he can manage it."

"That's fast."

"Yes it is." Cardenia hauled herself on top of Marce. "And that's because you have to go on this expedition, and I want you back as quickly as you can get back. Because whatever *this* is, I want to get back to it as soon as possible."

Book Two

CHAPTER 9

Cal Dorick had managed to spring Nadashe Nohamapetan from prison, for exactly eight hours.

"The judge finally agreed to give us a hearing on your mental state," Dorick told her, at their weekly meeting. "I'm making the argument that your time here is an assault on your already fragile mental state, and that you need to be placed in a secure mental facility instead. The prosecution is fighting this, obviously, so the judge has asked for you to be present so he can evaluate you himself, because who needs an actual medical degree in psychiatry when you have a law degree and an oversized opinion of your own importance."

"And we think that being in a mental institution is going to be better than being here?" Nadashe asked.

"It's not optimal, no. But it beats being somewhere people are trying to stab you with spoons."

"I thought we were sticking to the story that the lady with the spoon and the lady with the toothbrush just happened to be stabbing each other as I was innocently walking by."

Nadashe could see how heroic Dorick was in his effort not to roll his eyes. "Fine. It beats being somewhere people are spontaneously trying to shiv each other whenever you *just happen* to be walking by. What became of the toothbrush lady, anyway?"

"I believe she's still in solitary. Apparently it was not her first toothbrushing."

"You meet such interesting people, Lady Nadashe."

"And yet here I am with you."

Dorick raised a finger as if to say, *A touch, I do admit it.* "To get back to business, we're up in front of the judge in two days, so you know the drill. They'll come and shackle you up, take you up the elevator to the surface level and chain you up in the overland wagon. I made noise about your security, so you'll be happy to know you'll be solo in your chariot, and by 'solo' I mean you'll only have three armed guards with nonlethal but, I am promised, nevertheless extraordinarily painful stun sticks and shock guns. This is apparently a precaution for if you have a burst of adrenaline and burst your chains, or smuggle a lock-pick into the wagon by some method I am not paid enough to imagine. Which reminds me that you'll be searched on both ends of your journey, on both ends of your body. Sorry, that was a nonnegotiable."

Nadashe shrugged. "I was groped worse in college."

"I don't know what to do with that information. I will say that if you do actually wish for the judge to seriously consider that your staying here is detrimental to your fragile mental state, it might help to evince a look of, say, detriment."

"You're saying I don't look sufficiently fragile."

"I'm saying that while I think your flat affect is generally a great look for you, for this particular audience this one particular time you might want to try a different tactic. Or don't, it's fine, you be you."

Nadashe considered her lawyer. "Remind me again why I hired you."

"I honestly don't know, Lady Nadashe. But inasmuch as you've already paid me, in advance, for roughly the next forty years — thank you for that, by the way, my wife loves the new dining room set probably more than she loves me — you might as well keep me."

"We'll see."

"Moving right along, assuming the hearing about your mental state does not take up the entire day, and it won't, as your judge rarely spends more than fifteen minutes on anything if he can avoid it, I've arranged for you, along with your honor guards, to have use of my office conference room. I've arranged several meetings for you, including one with your mother, the Countess Nohamapetan."

Nadashe winced at this.

"Is this not to your liking?" Dorick said. "I can have her moved off the schedule. I live in fear of her righteous fury when I do that, but you are my client, not her."

"No," Nadashe said. "I'd rather meet her on what's nominally my turf than on hers."

"If I don't schedule you, you wouldn't be meeting her at all."

"I think it's nice that you believe that."

"Do you have any particular requests for when you're meeting her?"

"Have her searched for spoons and toothbrushes before she enters the room."

"I have no idea if you are actually joking, so I'm just going to make a note of that." Dorick made a note.

"If you actually try to have her searched you'll probably be thrown out a window by her bodyguard."

"Good to know." Dorick erased the note.

"What about the other thing?"

"What other thing?"

"The *other* thing."

Dorick stared at Nadashe blankly for several seconds before realizing what she was saying. "Oh, *that.* Well, I regret to say that those endorsements you've asked for from your friends, relating to your character, have been hard to come by, and I think a few of your friends are actively avoiding me. So I'm still working on that. *Unrelatedly,* you may be interested to know that several news sources have been coming up with very intriguing information regarding your late and beloved brother Amit."

"Is that so."

"Yes, apparently your brother had been talking to several prominent underworld figures about the possibility of an insurance fraud on some of the house ships. It seems he had been embezzling from the house funds and needed to replace that money before it was noticed. Nothing a good 'destruction of a multibillion-mark spaceship' scam couldn't solve."

Nadashe nodded. "What did I tell you?"

"I can scarcely believe it myself," Dorick said.

Nadashe smiled at this. The little dance Dorick just had to do to make it look like he didn't know about her agreement with Deran Wu, on the grounds it was a criminal scheme and he would be implicated in it up to his eyeballs, was sad and a little pathetic, but necessary. "Who else am I meeting with, aside from my mother?"

"Lord Teran Assan has asked for a meeting."

"For what purpose?"

"He said he wants your wisdom about certain members of the executive committee. He's apparently finding a few of them difficult to reach a rapport with."

"It's because he's an asshole."

"That would have been my guess, too. Nevertheless, given his position on the committee he's someone worth cultivating." Dorick raised his eyebrows at this last part, to indicate to Nadashe that in fact Teran Assan was a useful tool, so maybe throw him a bone.

Nadashe groaned. "Make the meeting as short as humanly possible."

"You got it. Also Lady Kiva Lagos's office called and was curious if you might make time for her."

"Good lord, why?"

Dorick looked at his notes. "She apparently has some questions about financials."

"The house's financials were Amit's job, not mine."

"Lady Kiva's office anticipated this objection and says they suspect you might have some insight that would be useful to her."

What is that woman up to? Nadashe thought. She and Kiva were never close in college, even when they were in the same dormitory and Kiva was banging Ghreni. They both instinctively understood that the way to harmony was to stay out of each other's business. Now Kiva was all up in Nadashe's business and she didn't like it one bit. "You haven't already scheduled that."

"No, I was waiting on your approval."

"Then don't bother. Whatever she's doing with our financials, I don't want to be part of it or anywhere near it. Do you understand what I'm saying?"

"I will work hard to make sure you are untroubled by Lady Kiva's look into your company's finances," Dorick said, blandly, which meant he understood that the order encompassed rather more than just not taking a meeting. Then he looked at his watch. "And that's all our time for the day. I'll see you in two days, Lady Nadashe. Avoid toothbrushes and spoons until then. And work on your sadness."

"It doesn't take much work," Nadashe assured him. And that much was true, at least. Gallows humor or not, flat affect or not, the prison life was getting to Nadashe. The prospect of this, all day, every day, for the rest of her life was not one Nadashe wished to entertain. If it meant faking a little mental breakdown in front of a judge, that was a thing she was willing to try.

One way or another, she was getting out of here.

"What I'm saying is, it doesn't taste like fish," one of the guards was saying to another one as the transport bumped its way across the airless surface of Hub. The two guards had been talking about food for the last half hour; the third was slumped in a seat, snoring. Nadashe envied the third guard.

"Of course it tastes like fish," the other guard said. "Fish always tastes like fish. That's why it's called 'fish.' "

"Right, but what I'm saying is that it doesn't taste fishy like most fish."

"So it's not *as* fishy."

"That's what I'm saying."

"Then it still tastes fishy," said the second guard. "Just in a different way."

"No, you're not getting it," the first guard said, and then turned to Nadashe to include her in the pressing debate about what constituted fishy fish.

Don't do it don't you do it don't you fucking dare, Nadashe thought furiously at the guard, willing the goon into silence.

"So, let me ask *you* about this fish," the guard began, and then there was a hideous bang and the transport launched itself into the air and tumbled violently to the side, and all Nadashe could think about was how grateful she was that her final words would not be some asinine discussion about aquaculture.

A few seconds later she realized she wasn't dying, but that she was now hanging off the ceiling of the truck, because what was now the ceiling used to be the side, and she was strapped in and chained up. Her restraints had held up admirably, so she wasn't dead, and that was good, but the low, violent whistling she was hearing was telling her that the air was leaking out of the transport cabin, which meant she would soon be dead of asphyxiation, and that was not great.

Nadashe looked down and saw the third guard crumpled in a heap, neck at an unsurvivable angle. *Went sleeping,* she thought. *How nice.* The other two were on the floor that used to be a side, dazed.

"I need a mask!" Nadashe yelled at them. "Hey! Do you hear me? I need a mask!"

One of them — the one who was convinced that the fish was not fishy, or what the fuck ever — looked up at her, confused, and then nodded and started looking on the wall for the emergency oxygen masks.

"That's not the wall!" Nadashe said. "They're at your feet!"

This took a few more seconds for Not Fishy to process, and then lo and behold, enlightenment came and the wall-mounted case that was now the floor-mounted case with the emergency oxygen masks was found. Not Fishy put one on, gave another to No Actually It Is Fishy, determined guard number three would not be needing one, and then handed one to Nadashe, who put it on with some difficulty, her hands being shackled.

"You stay there," the guard said, and Nadashe was incredulous, because what else was she going to do, shackled and strapped as she was. "We're going to radio in."

There was another hideous bang, and the rear doors of the transport flew away and all the guards, living and dead, were sucked out into the airless surface of Hub. Nadashe grabbed desperately at her mask to keep it from flying off her face; just before the view fogged up she saw Not Fishy and No Actually Fishy had lost theirs and were simultaneously gasping and freezing to death.

Speaking of which, the cold immediately began to bite into Nadashe's skin. Theoretically the overland road to Hubfall was in the temperate twilight zone of the tidally locked planet, but "temperate" meant different things when there was a 500-degree temperature range. "Temperate" here meant "blisteringly cold."

There was a light in Nadashe's face and then two people in space suits were all up on her, cutting through her shackle chains and restraining straps. Nadashe fell from the ceiling into their arms and was immediately sealed into a clear, bulky full body suit that instantly flooded her with warmth and oxygen. Nadashe stood for a second, basking in warm, and then was hustled out of the shattered transport wagon. As she exited, she saw the bodies of the guards, all dead, and the wreck of the transport. This transport was manually driven. Given the shape of the transport, Nadashe assumed the driver was in the same shape as the guards, if not worse.

Nadashe was drag-walked to what looked like a storage container with an airlock. She was pushed into the airlock and sealed in. When the airlock pressurized, the interior door opened and two more people pulled her out, replacing her in the airlock with a body missing a head, and sealing the door to allow it to cycle. That done, they returned their attention to Nadashe, peeled her out of the full body suit and took the oxygen mask off her face.

The entire operation of cutting her down from the wrecked transport to unshucking her in whatever this was had taken less than sixty seconds.

"Lady Nadashe," someone said to her. She turned and saw it was Lord Teran Assan, kitted out in his own suit. "Lovely to see you."

"What are you doing here?" Nadashe asked.

"Just managing your rescue," Assan said. Nadashe opened her mouth to say more, but Assan held up a hand. "Hold that thought," he said, and headed to the airlock, which by now had recycled. "Your mother sends her regards, by the way."

"Does she?"

"You'll be seeing her soon." Assan gave a little salute at that and then disappeared out the door.

Lord Teran Assan was not going to lie: He was absolutely fucking delighted that his prison break scheme was working out as well as it was.

And it was *his* plan; he was the one who had pitched it to the Countess Nohamapetan. "Look," he had said, presenting the countess with a visualization on a tablet screen. "This section of the road to Hubfall is only lightly surveilled, and that surveillance is easily compromised. I've already had my pet hackers at it. I can make a five-minute window where all the ground surveillance is down."

"That leaves the drone surveillance that comes with the transport itself," Tinda Louentintu said. The countess's chief of staff, as usual, was doing the heavy conversational lifting for the two of them. "They send a constant secure video feed back to the correctional facility."

"Yes they do," Assan agreed. "And that feed is both jammable and fakable. You just need the encryption keys for the individual drones, which I happen to have because the supervisor of the drones likes money more than she likes security."

"And then there is the satellite surveillance," Louentintu said.

Assan smiled. "That was a harder nut to crack. For that, I needed someone who could give us access to the satellite itself. Which means access to the military. The good news is, between Jasin and Deran Wu, the countess in her wisdom has chosen Jasin for her favored Wu cousin. In return Jasin has agreed to help, as part of his thanks for the countess's favor."

"You're going to hide a snatch-and-grab from a military satellite," Louentintu said. "Because when it doesn't show up on the satellite feed, that's not going to look at all suspicious."

"It *is* going to show up on the feed, of course," Assan said. "We're not going to *hide* the transport exploding. But we are going to fake the explosion, and make it look like the transport is running slower than it is, so by the time anyone looks at the satellite feed, we'll be long gone. And we run the same simulation to the drones and the security cameras. No one will know to look for us because no one will see that we were there. They will only see what we want them to see. And what we want them to see will be a tragic freak explosion of the transport."

"They'll notice if Nadashe is missing."

"I've accounted for that."

"How?"

Assan looked directly at the countess, rather than at her chief of staff. "You might prefer not knowing the details of that."

"How long will this take?" Louentintu asked.

"With the right people, less than four minutes on-site. Obviously more time on either side, but those moments are going to be away from prying eyes."

"And you're confident you can manage this."

"With your help and Jasin Wu's, yes."

"What do you need from us?"

"Your assent, and money."

"How much money?" the countess asked.

"Countess, this will need to be done quickly, and it will need to be done well. Doing it cheaply is not part of the equation."

Assan got his assent, he got his access through his own and Jasin Wu's connections, and he got his money, in amounts that allowed impossible things to happen so quickly and smoothly that it was almost magical. Assan was no stranger to vast sums of wealth, of course. He was the director of his family's holdings in the Hub system. More wealth moved through his office on a daily basis than some entire human civilizations had had in their entire existence. But there was a vast difference between the daily and mundane exercise of commerce, and the expenditure of frankly ridiculous piles of cash in the service of malfeasance.

That Assan was doing this while being a director of his house and a member of the executive committee was just icing on the cake as far as he was concerned. The ancient phrase "getting away with murder" had come to mind more than once. He was getting away with murder. And jailbreaking. And at least seven other felonies.

It was delicious, and Assan had never felt more alive in his life.

It was a given to Assan that he would be on-site for the extraction. It was a high-risk, high-reward mission, or so he told the countess. He felt honor-bound to make sure that it was executed within the razor-thin tolerances of time and competence that the entire endeavor required. He'd already spoken to the leader of the mercenary team that would be executing the mission, and she'd agreed that he would need to be present, and to oversee the final few minutes of the extraction, and the execution of the finishing touch that Assan had brought to the party.

Louentintu had been correct, of course. If

Nadashe's body was missing from the transport then no one would believe it was a freak accident. Everyone knew the Nohamapetans had money, and power, and the belief that rules were more like guidelines and optional at best even then. Everyone from the Hubfall police department up to the Imperial Ministry of Investigation would stick their noses in if Nadashe's body went missing.

So Assan discreetly let it be known, through agents untraceable to him, what he was looking for: a woman, Nadashe's height, weight and coloration. Assan made it known he was not looking for a murder. That was splashy and would draw the wrong sort of attention. But if a woman just *happened* to show up dead, well. Assan would be happy to know about it.

It didn't take very long at all. The medical examiner who collected the reward assured Assan's agent that the woman wasn't a murder, but a slip in a tub, which, sure, why not. The woman was single, a drifter with no real friends and no immediate family. There was no one to miss her, including the medical examiner's office files, from which she was conveniently scrubbed.

The woman, whoever she was, ceased to exist outside of the utility for which Assan had planned for her. She was delivered to the extraction mission without a head or fingerprints. Her circulatory system had been flushed and her blood replaced by an oxygen-optional, DNA-destroying accelerant, which was kept inside her body by the use of wax caps at the neck and fingertips.

She was beautiful, and she would go up like a firework. There would be a body of the same size and weight as Nadashe's, but if everything worked to plan, it would be almost all ash. Even if it didn't, what was left would be almost impossible to identify as anyone, much less Nadashe Nohamapetan.

In his space suit, Assan watched as his mercenaries put the woman's body into the remains of the transport, along with the bodies of the guards. The whole truck would then be flash-incinerated again, in exactly the manner that it would burn if the battery pack went up because of internal structural issues. The battery pack didn't need oxygen to burn, which was convenient on an airless world. It was its own fuel, and, to be sure, the battery pack would be *made* to go up. It would just have a little help to make the bodies burn more completely.

There was a tap on his shoulder; his merc commander was signaling him to check his communicator circuit. Assan checked it; he had forgotten to turn it on.

"Sorry about that," he said, over the circuit.

"We're patching a secure call to your suit," she said. "It's the countess."

Assan nodded, and when the call came through he turned away from the commander to give himself and the countess a little privacy. "This is Assan," he said.

"Lord Teran," the countess said. "How goes the extraction?"

"Exactly as planned, and right on time. We'll be up and out of here in the next two minutes."

"That's a remarkable bit of planning."

"Thank you, Countess. I am glad to be of service."

"You have been," the countess assured him. "But I don't think we'll be needing your services any longer, Lord Teran."

Assan was about to ask what she meant by that, but then was distracted by a knife sliding into his right kidney and slicing right. The air in Assan's suit immediately started bleeding away into the vacuum, along with his actual blood. Assan turned, knife still in, to see his mission commander holding another knife. This one went into his stomach and was likewise slid across to the right. Assan's suit started spilling oxygen prodigiously into his helmet to compensate for the loss elsewhere, which meant Assan could still hear the countess speaking to him.

"You were acting as the middleman between me and the Wu cousins," she was saying. "And I was wondering why I needed a middleman at all. So I met with them both. Turns out you've been playing both for a fool, and they didn't like that. We came to an alternate arrangement we were all happy with. We also decided that this little escape plan of yours would look better if it looked like it failed, and you went up with it when it did. We've already framed Nadashe's lawyer as your accomplice. It's very detailed. We've had to tweak your video plans. It shows something different now."

Assan fell stiffly to the ground.

"Well, I imagine you're almost all out of oxygen now, Lord Teran, so this is where we say goodbye. Thank you for being useful. There's just one last thing left for you to do."

There was a thin rustle, and Assan felt himself being lifted, carried, and thrown, into the transport.

The last thing he saw was the headless women he'd been so proud of. In the cold, her fingers had contracted up toward her palm. It occurred to Assan that it looked like she was flipping him off.

He would have laughed at that, but he burned instead.

CHAPTER 10

"What do you mean Nadashe Nohamapetan is dead?" Grayland II asked Hibert Limbar, head of the Imperial Guard. She set down her morning tea, for which she had budgeted exactly five minutes of time in one of her private gardens before she was hustled off to her next meeting.

"There was an escape attempt made this morning," Limbar said. "From the security feeds it looks like it went horrendously wrong. Everyone was killed including the person trying to break out Lady Nadashe. And, ma'am, the person trying to do it appears to have been Lord Teran Assan."

"What?"

"There wasn't much to go on — the transport's batteries ruptured and incinerated nearly everything inside — but the evidence we have is pretty conclusive. Lord Teran had been in contact with Lady Nadashe's personal lawyer fairly extensively recently. I've got people liaising with the Hubfall police, the Corrections Ministry and the Ministry of Investigation on this. We'll pick up Nadashe's lawyer and see if he wants to try to extract himself from this mess."

Grayland nodded at this. "Has someone informed the Countess Nohamapetan?"

"I understand the MoI has taken the task of informing her and getting a statement from her on themselves, and I am willing to let them have that honor." Limbar's tone very subtly made the point that it would not actually be an honor at all, but rather a real trash fire of an event, and Grayland couldn't argue the point.

"I should send a note of condolence to her," Grayland said. Limbar made a small, odd sound at this. Grayland caught it. "No?"

"Lady Nadashe was accused of attempting to assassinate you, ma'am," Limbar said. "Sending a condolence note might appear disingenuous. The Countess Nohamapetan is known to perceive insult where none was given, and to hold grudges. Perhaps a public statement acknowledging the deaths of the lady and Lord Teran, plus a regret that justice was not served in this case."

"You're right, that's better," Grayland

said. “Thank you.”

“There’s another small matter to be aware of, ma’am. Rumors have already begun that you had a hand in this event. That Teran wasn’t acting on his own, for his own reasons, but that you had hired him to act as an assassin on your behalf, because there is growing evidence that the attempt on your life was spearheaded by Amit Nohamapetan, not Nadashe.”

“That’s ridiculous. Particularly the part about Amit planning the assassination attempt.”

“There are news reports that suggest he had dealings with some less-than-reputable characters over money issues,” Limbar said. “Among other things.”

“I was with Amit literally seconds before he died,” Grayland said. “I’m not a mind reader, but I can assure you the look he had just before he was murdered was not one of someone who had a master plan to kill me or destroy his own ship.”

“Of course, ma’am.”

Grayland narrowed her eyes ever so slightly at this response. “You don’t believe there is anything to those reports, do you?”

“What I believe is someone has been making a concerted effort to introduce as much doubt into Lady Nadashe’s culpability for your attempted assassination as they can. Before this, I would have chalked this up to the lady's defense team doing everything they could to open up an alternate theory of the case, to try to gin up reasonable doubt. But this latest bit makes me concerned that there is something else going on."

"It's conspiracy mongering."

"I agree. But not all conspiracies crop up because someone forgot to adjust their tinfoil hat, ma'am. Sometimes they're part of a disinformation campaign. And, you will forgive me for saying so, you've given some cause recently for people to stoke disinformation campaigns."

"You're talking about my visions."

"Yes, among other things. I'm not here to doubt them, ma'am. I am saying they muddy the waters in ways that work against you as much as they work for you. But to be honest I'm less worried about that than the rumors swirling about your upcoming address to the parliament."

"Ah," Grayland said. "The one where I will be declaring martial law across the Interdependency."

"That's correct."

"Our press people have already knocked down that rumor."

Grayland sensed rather than heard Limbar's reproving sigh at this comment. "Your Majesty, it is certainly true that no one expects you to confirm that you are going to announce martial law, until you actually announce it."

"I take your point, Sir Hibert. But the fact remains that martial law is not on my parliament address agenda. I and my messengers have been very clear about this. I don't know what else can be said about it."

"That's the point of rumors. They're not based on anything, so nothing is very effective against them. Truth is no defense, and the people fielding these rumors know it."

"You believe someone is leveraging all this to work against me."

"You are the emperox, ma'am. Someone is always working against you. It's in the job description."

"To what end?"

"Probably several. I have people working on it. The point of telling you was not to make you worried or paranoid, ma'am. Merely to inform you what is out there, to help you craft your own messaging."

"Yes, of course." Grayland picked up her tea and sipped it. She put it back down and looked up at Limbar. "Do you believe Lady Nadashe is actually dead?"

"At this point we have no reason to believe otherwise."

Grayland smiled. "You have a way of not directly answering the question."

"*I* have no reason to believe otherwise, either," Limbar said. "I'm also aware the bodies at the site were incinerated to the point where they are almost impossible to identify by forensic means. Everything is ash and denatured bone. And that is very convenient."

"How paranoid do I need to be about this, Sir Hibert?"

"*You* should not be paranoid of anything, ma'am. The paranoia is my job. Leave it to me. I and my people will discover the truth, whatever it is."

"Thank you," Grayland said. Limbar bowed and excused himself and was immediately replaced by Obelees Atek, who would shuttle her off to her next meeting, and the next, and the next, forever and ever, amen.

Except this time Atek did not shuttle her off. "Archbishop Korbijn is here and wants to speak to you. I believe this is regarding Teran Assan."

"What's the schedule?"

"Your next several meetings are meet-and-greets. I can clear them for you."

Grayland frowned. "Don't clear them; just push them back. I have a half hour for lunch scheduled. Put them there."

"You need to eat, ma'am."

"I can skip an occasional lunch, Obelees. Bring along a protein bar. I can shove it into my face between you taking one group out and another in."

Atek smiled at this. "I'll bring the archbishop right in." She exited.

Grayland finished her tea and frowned to herself.

She was having a bundle of contradictory feelings about the death of Nadashe Nohamapetan. The first, and she had to admit it, was relief. Nadashe had been an irritant literally since the beginning of her reign.

And not *just* Nadashe; the entire Nohamapetan family had been on her, unpleasant and sticky, the whole time. Nadashe with her plotting, Amit with his unappealing stolidness, and now the Countess Nohamapetan with what seemed like inexhaustible anger.

Grayland recounted her meeting with the countess once more. Grayland couldn't deny her intent had been to roll over the countess, and she'd done just that. But she'd also extended the proverbial olive branch to the countess by offering clemency to Nadashe and placing her in the closest thing the imperial penal system had to a four-star hotel. Grayland had hoped this smallest offering of goodwill would be appreciated; instead the countess could hardly keep her rage in check. Grayland was aware she had missed a step in there somewhere, but for the life of her she couldn't understand where she had.

Nadashe's death, whatever else it did, cleared all of that away. No more worrying about Nadashe out there plotting; no more of the countess's fury on her daughter's behalf.

Don't count on that, that annoying part of Grayland's brain was telling her, and she had to admit that the annoying part of her brain was probably right about that. Limbar had told her that rumors were already spreading about her having Nadashe killed. They were ridiculous, and Limbar was correct that it wouldn't matter, especially to someone like the Countess Nohamapetan. If the countess could get enraged when Grayland was showing her daughter mercy, she'd probably be a volcano of fury at the thought she had her killed.

The second feeling Grayland had at the death of Nadashe Nohamapetan was sadness, and that was a fact that confused her and made her a little angry. Nadashe, it was clear, had never thought much of Grayland. Grayland had met her once when she was still Cardenia Wu-Patrick and her brother Rennered was the crown prince. Nadashe, who had been in the early days of dating Rennered, had sized her up, figured out the absolute minimum amount of courtesy she needed to provide the bastard sister of her royal boyfriend, and provided exactly that. Cardenia had not been emotionally sophisticated enough at the time to understand why she felt vaguely hurt and unhappy around Nadashe that day. Even now it was disquieting to her.

And perhaps that was the reason for her sadness. Had Nadashe been even a tiny bit kinder, or more wise, or simply fractionally better as a human being, she and Cardenia (and also Grayland II, now in all her glory, waiting with her empty teacup for yet another meeting) could have been friends, and perhaps even more than friends. Confidantes.

Even now, Nadashe represented positive things to Grayland. She was smart and confident and beautiful and all the other sorts of things that Grayland had always had a hard time seeing in herself, and still did. To have won the friendship and the confidence of such a creature would have meant the world to her. To have missed that because Nadashe simply couldn't see her, and didn't feel like she was worth seeing, felt like a genuine tragedy.

You just miss having friends, Grayland's brain said to her, and that was true enough. She thought back to her dear and departed Naffa, who had been all the things Nadashe could also have been, had Nadashe wanted that. Grayland's heart ached for Naffa, not in a sexual or romantic way, just in the way you miss your dearest friend, the one person who just *gets* you.

Marce gets you, said the part of her brain that was a fifteen-year-old girl. And, well. Maybe he did at that. Grayland thought back to their first night together and was warmed with an almost languid happiness at the memory. The two of them had been ridiculously awkward with each other and then suddenly they weren't, as the *Oh God what is happening is this actually going to work* commentary track was replaced by the *Holy crap this* is *actually working and in fact is pretty amazing* commentary track, which in turn was replaced by no commentary track for once, thank *God,* just happiness and contentment. For the first time since the loss of Naffa, and in a completely different way that was not unexpected and yet still entirely unanticipated in its scope, Grayland felt her whole self again.

Marce did that for her. Naffa had done that for her. Grayland sensed that Nadashe could have done that for her too, given all her strengths, which would have complemented Grayland's own.

But Nadashe was . . . Nadashe. She was not the sum of her qualities. She was something else apart from that. Something that didn't want what Grayland had to offer, except for her position, and what it could do for the House of Nohamapetan.

Obelees Atek reentered the garden, with Archbishop Korbijn in tow, Korbijn wearing a simple and conservative suit rather than her full archbishop's finery. Grayland smiled at this. Korbijn was sending her a message that she was paying attention to Grayland's own muted sartorial choices.

Grayland smiled and rose to greet her visitor and put Nadashe and the entire House of Nohamapetan out of her mind. Nadashe was gone now, and everything she had ever wanted for herself and her family was in the past tense, and everything she was or could have ever possibly been to Grayland had now slipped into the past as well. Grayland allowed herself to feel both the relief and the sadness she felt at Nadashe's passing, and then put it aside to deal with Korbijn, and her real and present concerns.

Goodbye, Nadashe, Grayland thought. *I wish you peace now. And I hope you will stay dead.*

Chapter 11

After a day of hiding and skulking around with mercenaries, which was a thing too tedious to recount or indeed ever to think of again, Nadashe found herself on the *You Can Blame It All on Me,* her mother's personal fiver.

Nadashe thought it was an almost unconscionable extravagance that her mother used a fiver to haul herself from star system to star system, but on the other hand her mother didn't really live anywhere else. The fiver was her home, even when it was parked in orbit over Terhathum. She never went down to Terhathum, or Basantapur, its largest city.

Well, that was the deal, wasn't it, Nadashe thought to herself. *Dad got Terhathum. Mom got the rest of the universe.*

Nadashe was tucked quite comfortably into her own private apartment on the *Blame.* It was the one her mother always kept for her, because it was a whole huge goddamn spaceship, and she could keep an apartment for a couple hundred of her closest friends if she wanted. And in fact she did travel with an entourage of friends and lackeys and what have you. She was a countess, and she was the head of the House of Nohamapetan, and she was a narcissist who needed and wanted attention. All of these things conspired to have her travel with a village in tow. But the villagers were kept on the other side of the ship's ring from Mother and her quarters. The only living quarters on her side of the ring were the ones for her and her three children.

Two now, Nadashe said to herself, and sighed. She wasn't ready to have that conversation with her mother.

But she didn't have to, yet; Mother wasn't on the *Blame.* She was down at Hubfall, where she was being told the horrible news that her daughter, the traitor, the murderer, the imperial assassin, had gone up like a firework in a botched escape attempt that killed her, three guards, a driver and the Lord Teran Assan.

The presence of Assan was a spicy bit of news that the media glommed onto and ran with. Everyone loved the idea of Assan, obsessed with the traitorous Nadashe Nohamapetan, planning her escape with her witless lawyer as their go-between. The lawyer who, incidentally, had jumped to his death while his family was at the zoo looking at miniature giraffes and long-haired otters.

Nadashe pursed her lips at that thought. Alas, poor Dorick. He had had no idea what he was getting into, and probably continued to have no idea, up to and including the moment whichever of the countess's bodyguards it was pushed him out of that window. At least his family would be well cared for, as long as Dorick had told his wife where his stash of money was, and also the authorities didn't find it.

No one as yet had seemed to suggest that Nadashe might still be alive. The escape scene featured a body for everyone plus one extra, and what was left in all cases was hardly identifiable. Assan's presence, for example, had been identified by a titanium signet ring he was known to have been proud of. Nearly everything else had melted, burned and turned to ash. The only ones who knew Nadashe was still alive were the mercs who had retrieved her, and who Nadashe was sure would all find themselves at the wrong end of some death-dealing weapon sometime in the reasonably near future, and the crew of the *Blame,* none of whom would have any intention of speaking about her presence to anyone else, because their lives and jobs depended on it.

Well, and Nadashe's *mother,* who was no doubt wailing up a storm right now down on Hubfall. Nadashe imagined her mother gnashing her teeth and rending her garments, all for the benefit of the various local and imperial investigators who would be looking for something, anything, to suggest that this escape attempt was something other than a horrible failure.

Let them look, Nadashe thought. Meanwhile, she was safe, she was secure, and as much any place could be called it, she was home. The beds were unspeakably soft and the bedclothes were warm and caressing, the food was exquisite, the showers were hot for as long as you wanted them to be hot, and the clothes weren't all the same fucking shade of orange. Nadashe celebrated by eating a ridiculously large sandwich, taking a forty-minute shower, and then falling asleep under a pile of blankets for most of a day.

She woke up to her mother sitting in a chair beside her bed. The countess had been watching Nadashe while she slept. Nadashe wondered how long it was that her mother had been watching her, and also, idly, at what point the watching would transmute from warmly maternal to something else entirely, something not quite seemly.

Nadashe propped herself up and smiled at her mother. "Hi, Mom," she said.

The Countess Nohamapetan slapped her daughter hard across the face.

"That's for killing your brother," she said.

Then she slapped Nadashe again.

"What's that one for?" Nadashe asked.

"For getting caught."

Nadashe rubbed her cheek. "I thought you'd be more upset about Amit."

"I'm absolutely furious about it," the countess said. "He was my favorite."

"I know. So did Ghreni."

"I didn't make a secret about it."

"You might have. Other parents do."

"I loved your brother. And he would have made a fine consort for the current emperox. And then there would have been a Nohamapetan on the throne."

"I have to tell you, Mom, that wasn't going to happen."

"It could have been managed."

Nadashe smiled ruefully. "Have you met the new emperox? She's not *manageable.*"

"I learned that."

"So did I," Nadashe said. "Early on. And when it was clear she wasn't going to marry Amit, it was time to try again. There are a lot of Wu cousins. We could have made it work."

"You didn't have to kill *Amit* to get to her."

"There were other complications."

"Your damn fool plan to take over End. And yes, I know about that," the countess said when she caught Nadashe's expression. "You and Amit and Ghreni. You weren't as clever as you thought you were about covering your tracks when you skimmed accounts to pay for your little adventures. That Kiva Lagos person is going through our financials for the last decade. You've put the entire house at risk."

"That's mostly on Amit," Nadashe said. "He was the one cooking the books."

"But *you* were the one telling him to do it," the countess countered. "You're the *smart* one, Nadashe. You were always the smart one."

"I am what you made me, Mom."

"Not smart enough to keep Rennered Wu, though."

Nadashe groaned, fell back on the bed and put a pillow over her head. "I'm not listening to this again."

The countess removed the pillow. "You

had one job. Become the imperial consort. I wanted it. The *emperox* wanted it. We spent years managing that. And you let it slip past you."

"For the last goddamned time, Mother, I didn't *let* it slip past me. Rennered decided he liked fucking a variety of people and didn't want to narrow down his enthusiasms."

"You could have dealt with that."

"I *did.* He and I had that conversation. I told him he could stick his dick anywhere he wanted, as long as I was the one he had children with. I thought that was what he wanted. A political marriage with benefits. But it turns out he wanted me to be jealous. Or *something.* He wanted monogamy and true love, *and* he wanted sex with just about anything that moved. And he was offended that I offered him the sex, which he was going to have anyway, instead of the monogamy, which he had no intention of practicing. He was a pig."

"You could have still brought him around."

"If you really believed that, Mom, then you shouldn't have had him killed."

The countess shrugged. "He hurt you. I was angry. And anyway you're right. The window for you with him was closing, and we couldn't risk him marrying someone else."

Nadashe gaped at her mother. "You were just saying I could have brought him around!"

"I was agreeing with you," the countess said. "I thought you'd be happy about it."

Nadashe closed her eyes. "God, you are so *exhausting,* Mother. Please pick another topic."

"Marriage."

"That's the same topic."

"Same topic, different players."

"What are you talking about?"

"Jasin Wu."

"What about him?"

"You should consider marrying him."

"He's already married."

"This is a small detail. Also he has no children, which is useful."

"Useful for what?"

"We're going to make him emperox."

Nadashe sat up for this. "He's not in the line of succession."

"He's a Wu. When Grayland's gone, whatever 'line of succession' there was will be tossed to the wayside. What's left after that is negotiation."

"There will be other Wus who want to be emperox."

"There's only one serious competitor, Deran Wu. And we've already taken care of that."

"How?"

"Deran supports Jasin's bid to be emperox and gets his supporters to fall in line. In return, when Jasin is emperox, he gives Deran sole control of the House of Wu. No more of this 'board of directors' nonsense that keeps the house paralyzed."

"And the other cousins are just going to fall in line for this."

"By the time it's done they won't be in a position to argue. You'll be meeting both Jasin and Deran soon enough. You can judge how serious they are about the plan."

"And Jasin will have me as consort."

"Yes, he's already agreed to that."

"He tried to have me murdered in prison."

"He didn't know you as a person yet."

"Also, there's the minor detail that I'm supposed to be dead."

"We'll fix that. We're already fixing it. *You* were already fixing it. I know how you were working on shifting the blame for everything to Amit. Deran Wu laid it out for me. I told him to keep doing it."

Nadashe was genuinely shocked. "You just said Amit was your favorite."

"He is. Always will be. But he's also dead,

and we need you alive and relatively unimplicated. Jasin is offering you a throne."

"In return for what?"

"Obviously, for us helping to unseat Grayland."

" 'Unseat' is such an ambiguous verb, Mother."

"We don't have to *kill* her," the countess said. "Isolating and exiling her would work just as well."

"And how do you plan to do that?"

"She is already doing it herself with this visions nonsense. She's alienating the church and she's about to alienate the parliament. Some of the noble houses are already turning against her. It's just a matter of time. That and we remove some of her key allies. Starting with Kiva Lagos, who is just causing trouble for us anyway."

"How do you plan to remove her?"

"Let me worry about that, Nadashe."

"Grayland's not actually that close to Lagos," Nadashe said. "Getting rid of her benefits us more than it wounds her."

"I have something else to wound her."

"What?"

The countess was silent for a moment. "Did you know that Grayland was going to make you a hostage?"

"How was she going to do that?"

"She told me was going to commute your death sentences and have you serve your time on Xi'an. Somewhere you would always be within reach. It was her way of letting me know that if I ever got out of line, your life was forfeit."

This got a wry smile from Nadashe. "She doesn't know you very well. Or our family."

"That's not the point," the countess said. "The point was that she thought she could get to me through someone she thought I loved. *Control* me with someone she thought I loved."

Nadashe noted the construction of her mother's sentences but didn't say anything about it. "So what are you going to do?"

"I'm going to make Grayland feel what she wanted me to feel. I'm going to make it known that I can touch the people she cares about the most."

"And who does she care about?" Nadashe asked. "Enough to make an example out of?"

CHAPTER 12

Marce Claremont watched as the *Oliveer Bransid* turned on its floodlights and illuminated the outer hull of the structure it floated next to.

"You wanted to see Dalasýsla," Captain Kinta Laure said to him. She pointed toward the bridge viewscreen. "There it is."

"There it is," Marce agreed. The *Bransid* was illuminating only a tiny area of Dalasýsla's hull. The primary habitat structure stretched on for klicks, a long cylinder that used to be filled with humans and all of their lives. Beyond Dalasýsla, blocked by the structure, the giant planet of Dalasýsla Prime lurked, roughly the size of Neptune back in humanity's home system.

"It's amazing it's actually still here," Captain Laure said.

"It was in a stable orbit when the Flow stream collapsed," Marce said.

"That was eight hundred years ago. That's

a long time for any nonnatural object's orbit to stay stable. The other moons might have perturbed it gravitationally. A passing comet could have done the same. An impact from a meteor or outgassing from damage might have nudged it. Probably did nudge it, since Klupper here" — Laure acknowledged one of her bridge crew — "tells me that in fact Dalasýsla isn't in a stable orbit anymore. It's beginning to spiral into the planet."

Marce frowned. "Is that going to affect us?"

"Not unless we're here in about a hundred years," Laure said. "Let's try not to be."

Marce nodded at this and turned back to the viewscreen. Superficially Dalasýsla didn't look substantially any different from any number of large spacebound human habitats; humans had settled on six or seven basic large habitat designs that could scale up and allow for some semblance of standard gravity by rotation. Dalasýsla was a modified O'Neill cylinder, a model that had not undergone major revision for centuries. It was efficient, relatively simple, and just worked.

That is, as long as you had the people and resources to make it work. When you ran short of either, you developed problems.

"It's dead?" Marce asked Laure.

"It's dead," Laure said. "Long dead. We took its temperature on the way in. No substantial difference from anything else out here. Cold on the inside as it is on the outside. Your team will be wearing suits to go over."

Marce nodded again. His small team of scientists would have been wearing suits regardless. Eight hundred years is a long time. No one wanted to contaminate anything, or be contaminated. "So we shouldn't worry about bringing along our marine detachment," he joked.

"You'll bring along your detachment," Laure said. "Just because that place is dead doesn't mean it can't kill you."

"That's a fact."

"This will be your first actual away mission, yes?" Laure regarded Marce as she said it.

"That's right."

"And you've never done any other sort of fieldwork."

"Not really, no. I'm a Flow physicist. It's higher-order math. You don't have to go out into the field for that."

Laure nodded. "It's your show, Lord Marce. Our orders say so. But you should know that you've got a team of Imperial Navy scientists. All of them have been in the field. You have your marines. Field is what they do. Are you open to advice?"

"Yes, of course."

"Then here it is. It's your show. But if you're wise you'll listen to your team when they talk. And you'll listen to Sergeant Sherrill and her people when she tells you to go somewhere or not to go somewhere. You'll listen and you'll play it safe. We're all a long way from home, Lord Marce. We all want to get back to ours."

"Thank you, Captain Laure," Marce said. "You'll be glad to know that was pretty much my plan anyway."

"Good," Laure said. "You don't strike me as particularly stupid, but you never know."

Marce grinned at this.

Laure motioned her head toward the viewscreen. "Our visual inspection of the structure will be done in a couple of hours, and then your team is up. Since Dalasýsla is dead you're probably going to have to go through access ports on the surface."

Marce nodded. "We were planning on that. We have the schematics of the structure from the imperial archives. We know where we want to go in. If that port is accessible, then it'll be a short hike to the control room for the computer network."

"You still think you're going to be able to

fire up their system?"

"Not really, no," Marce said. "Eight hundred years is a long time. But it's worth the attempt. It would save us a lot of time, anyway. And possibly answer a lot of questions."

"I heard the recordings from the last days of this place," Laure said. "I'll be surprised if everything's not just rubble."

"Right." Marce had read the transcripts and heard recordings of the last set of transmissions to come from Dalasýsla, a few years after the Flow stream had collapsed. The short version was death, disease, despots and destruction. The longer version had kept him up wondering what the hell was wrong with people.

The answer to that was probably simple enough: When people knew that they were doomed no matter what they did, their long-term decision-making skills often went right out the airlock. Marce couldn't blame them, but given the fact that the whole of the Interdependency was now facing the same fate as Dalasýsla, he was hoping for other options.

Laure put her hand on Marce's back. "Go get your people ready. And, Lord Marce."

"Yes?"

"I hope you find something good in there.

Something we can use to save us all."

Dalasýsla was dead, which meant that all the mechanisms to open the service airlocks to the habitat's surface were dead as well. Opening them up was going to take time and effort by someone, probably PFC Gamis, who was the mechanical specialist in the marine detachment. The *Bransid* had the tools for the job — they had known they would probably need them, so they brought them — but then Laure's people discovered an open service airlock, not too far from where they wanted to be anyway. Suddenly Marce and his team had one less thing to worry about.

"Don't get too excited," Sergeant Sherrill said as she and Marce suited up with the rest of the mission team. "It just means a closed bulkhead further in. No matter what, we're slogging our way to that network operations room."

The suits on the mission were the latest design and tech, light and flexible, puncture- and tear- and vacuum-resistant, self-resealing (up to a point, and if you reached that point you were probably already screwed), and featured magnetized feet and an oxygen rebreather efficient enough to make the oxygen canister they went out with last for an average of fifteen hours. You could relieve yourself in them, also up to a point. Marce was hoping they would not be away long enough for that to be an issue. The helmets had full recording suites; everything they saw and heard would be recorded.

For this mission the team was small — Marce and Gennety Hanton, a navy computer scientist and historian who specialized in ancient computing systems like the ones on Dalasýsla, Sergeant Sherrill and PFCs Gamis and Lyton. No one was expecting to reach the network operations room on this trip. This trip was mostly about making a path to it, through as many sealed bulkheads as it took.

Except that sometime in the last eight hundred years someone had done most of the work for them.

"Take a look at this," Gamis said. The recon team, all in their suits, crowded around the display the private sat at. From the display Gamis was navigating a drone into the service areas past the airlocks. The drone's-eye view could see the bulkheads beyond and farther into the habitat had been pried into, pulled up or out, and sometimes entirely destroyed.

"Someone really wanted to get in there,"

Hanton said.

"Or get out," Lyton said.

"How far in can you get?" Sherrill asked Gamis.

Gamis paused, pulled up a three-dimensional map of the section of Dalasýsla the drone was in, and floated it alongside the drone's view. "Birdie's here." Gamis motioned to a corridor on the map. "And where we want to go is here, about a klick and a half away." Gamis went back to the drone and pushed it forward, zooming it through the corridor. "Honestly, Sarge, after the first few bulkheads it's looking like a straight shot. It doesn't look like this part of Dalasýsla had been sealed off for pressure loss."

"Which means the habitat lost power before this particular area bled out its air," Hanton said.

"Maybe," Gamis said, still navigating the drone. The drone's view was a combination of several wavelengths of light — above, below and within the normal human range — all merged down into a monochrome report. "Or there was a malfunction. Or a hundred different other things. Whoops." Gamis maneuvered the drone around some floating debris. "Should have put on the auto collision detect."

"No gravity," Marce said.

"No, there wouldn't be, would there?" Gamis said. "The habitat's not spinning anymore."

"More like tidally locked at this point."

"Well, fine, all right, if you want to get *technical* about it, sir."

"No bodies," Sherrill said.

"What, Sergeant?" Gamis turned to look at his superior.

Sherrill pointed at the monitor. "You've driven a klick into the structure and I don't see any bodies yet."

"We're still in the service areas, Sarge," Gamis said. "People are down there only if they have work to do on the structure itself. I would guess most of whatever bodies there are would be in the habitat proper."

"It's still weird."

"I'm fine not seeing any eight-hundred-year-old frozen mummies before I have to." Gamis maneuvered the drone some more and then stopped at a door. "This is it," he said. "Your network ops room for Dalasýsla. One of them, anyway. And all we have to do is walk to it slowly in our magnetized boots."

"So we brought all that bulkhead-prying hardware for nothing," Sherrill said.

"I wouldn't say for nothing," Gamis replied. "This is just one small section of the habitat. Other areas are probably sealed off. We'll have to see. But at least for this, we got lucky."

"Well, enjoy it," Hanton said. "Once we get in there I'll have to see if I can power up any part of that network center. We may have blown all our luck already."

Marce decided he didn't like the suits. His nose started to itch pretty much the second he put on his helmet, and he'd already subconsciously tried to scratch his nose three times, smashing his fingers against the helmet each time. After the third time, he gave out a frustrated grunt, which Hanton noticed over the communication circuit.

"You get used to it eventually, sir," he said.

"I *hope* so," Marce said, exasperated.

The walk to the network operations room was slow, as Gamis promised. The magnetic feet in the suits kept the team on the deck, but they were all tethered to each other regardless, just in case one of them lost their footing and started to float off. Marce found the deliberate gait of magnetized walking enervating, compounded by the walking being done in a blackness punctuated only by their helmet lamps. By the time they got to the door of the operations room, he felt like he had run a marathon.

"See, I did need this after all," Gamis said, retrieving the door-spreading hardware from the case of equipment they had brought with them. The lack of gravity made it easy for Gamis and Lyton to carry the case between them, but hard for them to maneuver it. Its inertia wanted to take it places they didn't want it to go.

Gamis and Lyton set the door-spreader. It did its magic, cranking open the sealed hatch. Marce was surprised he could hear the protesting of the door as it opened, then realized he was hearing it through his feet. The sound had carried through the floor and into his suit.

As he walked into the ops room Marce noticed marks on the door, and pointed them out to PFC Gamis, who nodded. "We're not the first ones to do this," he said.

"Can you tell how old those other marks are?" Marce asked.

"Not really," Gamis said. "Could have been made five hundred years ago, could have been made last week. But I'm guessing probably not last week."

Inside the operations center everyone untethered. Lyton tossed something toward the ceiling of the room, and suddenly the entire operations center was bathed in light, shadows radiating out from the single source.

"Let there be light," she said, and looked over to Hanton. "You've got about six hours of that."

"More than enough," Hanton said. He walked over to the equipment case and retrieved a small computer module and a portable keyboard, and a tiny cube power source. He carried all of them over to a workstation.

"You got a power cord for that?" Gamis joked.

"Don't need one," Hanton said, turning on the power cube. A monitor light flashed on it, three times in red, then in steady blue. "I checked the archives. These workstations had induction plates. All you have to do is feed power to them and they'll turn on."

"If it's just a terminal then that won't do you any good," Lyton said.

Hanton shook his head. "It's mostly used as a terminal, but there's a cache of onboard local memory. It's pretty substantial because habitats believe in redundancy. If the primary computer system here ever went down, the primary operational systems could still have basic functionality with the information in these terminals. At least long enough to get the primary back up and running."

"Assuming you can get in," Gamis said.

Hanton patted the computer module he'd brought with him. "If it turns on at all, I brought some fun toys with me, folks. Eight-hundred-year-old security is about to meet modern cracking tools. It should be an instructive event."

"And if it doesn't work?" Marce asked.

"Then there are a dozen other workstations in here."

Marce nodded at this and regarded the room. It was large and circular and in the lighting, which threw razor-sharp shadows, was a little creepy. Along one arc was a window and a doorway into another room, which held silent rows of black metal boxes. The actual processing heart of the habitat, or one of them — workstations aside, a habitat this large could have several rooms like this sprinkled around. Redundant systems save lives.

For a while, at least. The computers in those black boxes were probably long past their expiration date, as would be any others elsewhere on the habitat. Turning them on would require more than the power cube Hanton had brought with him.

Marce wondered what it would have been

like on Dalasýsla when the power systems stopped working. The habitat had been powered by a combination of reactors and solar. Those generators and arrays were prone to the same mechanical failures as any system, as was the power transport grid. So many ways for things to go wrong. Marce imagined it was the systems that failed before the knowledge base for maintaining them died off, but it was hard to be sure. When the world is breaking down, scientists might be the scapegoats.

"Oh, hello there," Hanton said. "Someone's awake." Marce turned and saw that the workstation had sprung to life, booting into a diagnostic screen.

"That's kind of amazing," Gamis said.

"This system is mostly solid-state," Hanton said as he went through menus. "Made out of mostly stable materials. Industrial grade, not consumer grade. When you're building a habitat, you build to last, not for flash."

"Okay," Gamis said. "But eight hundred years."

"Oh, we're lucky as hell," Hanton agreed. "But some of that luck is built on design. Okay, here." He activated a tab, and a storage structure came up. "All the local data files. I'm transferring them over to my own computer now and can open them in a virtual environment."

"What's there?" Sergeant Sherrill asked.

"Lots of things," Hanton said. "What do you want?"

Sherrill looked over to Marce. "It's your show, Lord Marce."

Marce thought about it. "I'd like to know when Dalasýsla went dark," he said. "That would give us some idea of what to expect for other habitats in the same situation."

Hanton nodded. "I have an access log file here."

"Just for the workstation?"

"There's one of those, yes. There also another one here that looks to be for this ops center as a whole. This must have been the administrator's workstation."

"And it would have everything?"

"As long as there was power to it, sure," Hanton said.

"Pull it up."

Hanton pulled up the file. "Huh," he said, a minute later.

"What is it?" Marce asked.

"I'm not sure you're going to believe me if I tell you," Hanton said.

"Try me."

"Let me reorganize this to make it easier to understand." Hanton did some typing for a minute, then waved Marce over to his screen. "I just dumped this data into a spreadsheet. It tallies logins by year. So, here's the year before the Flow stream collapsed. Several thousand logins, because people are logging in and out every day, right. The year of the collapse, the same thing, and the year after that. Scroll down over the next twenty years, and the logins get fewer and fewer, because whatever shit is going down here, it's pretty serious. Twenty-three years after, everything stops. If you were wondering when things got real bad, this is when."

"Twenty-three years is not very long," Sherrill said.

"No it's not," Hanton said. He scrolled again. "So, that's it, right? No, it's not, because look what happens fifty years out." He pointed to a spate of logins.

"Somebody's still alive," Marce said.

"More than one, it looks like. Now, look." Hanton kept scrolling. "Logins every few years until three hundred years ago. And then *this.*" For the next twenty years there were a massive number of logins. "Someone got Dalasýsla back online. Or at least part of it back online."

"Temporarily," Marce said.

"Twenty years is a pretty long temporary,

as far as temporary goes," Hanton said. "And then after those twenty years, the same thing happens. The logins decrease and then drop off, this time after seven years."

Marce peered into the screen again. "But not entirely."

"No," Hanton agreed. "Every few years again, for almost three hundred years." He scrolled again. "Here. Here. Here. And on and on."

"Until when?" Gamis asked.

"Until thirty years ago," Hanton said. "That's the last login. The last time anyone accessed this very room."

"All right, so how is that possible?" Lyton asked. "This place is dead as a fucking rock."

"I have no idea how it's possible," Hanton said. "I'm just telling you what the file is telling me. But it explains why the computer system hasn't entirely degraded. Every time it boots up it runs a diagnostic and fixes the little problems that crop up over time." He pointed over to the workstation. "It's doing it now."

"So Dalasýsla is alive," Marce said.

"Dalasýsla, no," Hanton said. "Lyton is right. This place is dead. Whoever was coming here was probably using this habitat for resources, and using the computer system to help extract them. But someone is still alive in this part of space. Or was, until thirty years ago."

A voice popped into Marce's ear. It was Roynold, back on the *Bransid.* "Marce, you there?"

Marce stepped away from Hanton and his workstation, put his hand to his ear to hear Roynold better, and was annoyed again by the presence of the helmet. "I'm here. Things are very interesting on Dalasýsla, Hat."

"Did you find evidence that someone's still alive in the system?"

"Yeah, we did," Marce said. "How did you know?"

"Because Captain Laure has been having her crew do a search for the other smaller habitats in the area."

"And she found some?"

"She found lots. Three dozen."

"And?"

"They're all dead as Dalasýsla. Cold like Dalasýsla. Same ambient temperature as the rest of space."

"Okay," Marce said, confused.

"But then they found something else. Not a habitat, exactly. More like a tenner."

"A spaceship."

"Yes," Roynold. "And here's the thing about that tenner, Marce. It's *warm.*"

CHAPTER 13

"A peace offering," Senia Fundapellonan said as she entered Kiva Lagos's office for her meeting. She reached over the desk to hand Kiva an object. Kiva took it; it was a bracelet of oxidized silver filigree, with golden brown topaz gems set in it.

"Don't tell me," Kiva said. "You went to a fair and knocked down the bottles. You had to choose between this and the stuffed elephant."

"I didn't choose. I just kept the elephant."

"Okay, but why give me this?" Kiva asked, setting the bracelet down on the desk. "I'm not mad at you for not seeing me since our little meeting with the emperox. We're not *dating.*"

"It's not actually from me," Fundapellonan said. "That's a gift from the Countess Nohamapetan. Terhathum is famous for our topazes. Not that most people would know that, because the Nohamapetan monopoly is for maize and rice, and the House of Hoak doesn't tell people where the topaz they sell comes from."

"And I get a gift from the countess why, exactly? Rumor is, she hates my fucking guts."

"The countess believes you and she may have gotten off on the wrong foot. And coming on the heels of the death of her daughter, I think she believes that it might be time to reassess relationships." Fundapellonan pointed to the bracelet. "That bracelet is a token. I should tell you its financial value is negligible — it's probably worth a thousand marks at most — but it belonged to Nadashe as she was growing up. The countess hopes that fact convinces you of her sincerity in wanting to make a new start between the two of you."

"Uh-huh," Kiva said. She picked up the bracelet again, which to be fair was lovely, and looked at it. "You suggested this to her, didn't you."

"Why do you say that?"

"Because I don't know if you've ever met the Countess Nohamapetan, but she's about as sentimental as a fucking alligator. There is no way in hell she got all mopey about her daughter, picked this thing up, and sent you here to help her realize a healing journey of the fucking soul."

"I think you may be underselling the countess."

"I doubt it."

"You're a doubter of the perfectibility of the human soul."

"I think to perfect a soul you have to have one to begin with."

"That's mean, Kiva Lagos," Fundapellonan said.

Kiva shrugged.

"Shall I tell the countess that you've rejected her gift?"

"Sure, because I need to give her another reason to hate me, thanks."

Fundapellonan smiled. "Then I will just tell her that you expressed your delight and humble thanks."

"Yes, that sounds exactly like me."

"Just as much as the countess giving bracelets sounds like her."

"So you *did* suggest it to her."

"I might have said the bracelet would suit you."

"I'm not sure why. I don't wear much jewelry."

"Maybe it was because I thought I'd like to see it on you."

Kiva put it on. "Well?"

"It's not bad," Fundapellonan said, after a minute.

"Fine, then." Kiva took off the bracelet and set it back on the table. "Now that we've had our maudlin moment of gawking and sharing, do the thing so I can say no and we can get on with our lives."

"The countess invites you to reassess your stewardship of the House of Nohamapetan's businesses here in the Hub system."

"All right."

"Really?"

"Sure," Kiva said, and counted to one in her head. "Now I'm done. And my answer to the countess is 'fuck you.' I already told her no once. She already took her case to the fucking emperox and was turned down. And not only did she say no, she explicitly said that I was to stay on and to have the full cooperation of the House of Nohamapetan in my investigation of the in-system. Which, by the way, I still don't have, and it's beginning to piss me off."

"I will communicate that issue to the countess."

"Do that. Also communicate to her the part where I said 'fuck you.' Make sure you phrase it precisely that way. And while you're at it let her know that if you or anyone else shows up in this office again to suggest to me that I shouldn't do the fucking job that the actual goddamn ruler of the entire known inhabited universe has told me to do, I'm going to start getting angry about it."

Fundapellonan blinked at this. "This is you not angry?"

"You haven't actually seen me angry yet."

"I'm going to make a note of that."

"And neither has the countess. And if she gets me angry, no amount of fucking friendship bracelets is going to help her."

"And there is nothing else that will cause you to reconsider your position?"

Kiva tilted her head. "Again with the bribe offers."

Fundapellonan spread her hands. "I need to be able to go back and say I walked through the checklist."

"What else is on the checklist?"

"That was it."

"Are you sure? We haven't gotten to the veiled threats yet."

"No veiled threats."

"The countess must be off her game."

"Well, she is dealing with the death of her child. For the second time this year."

"There is that." Kiva looked at the bracelet again, and then over to Fundapellonan. "What are you doing later?"

"I'm busy."

"What about after that?"

"I'm always busy."

"I know for a fact you're not *that* busy."

"What are you saying?"

"I'm saying you should come over."

"Maybe I'm avoiding you."

"You're doing a fucking poor job of it, then, standing in my office."

"I was on assignment."

"Bearing gifts."

"From someone else."

"Which you chose."

"Yes I did."

"Come over later, and I'll wear it for you. And not much else."

"Deal."

"So why do you work for evil fucks?" Kiva asked Fundapellonan later, as they were lying in Kiva's bed after some better-than-average sex.

Fundapellonan looked over at Kiva, annoyed. "The House of Nohamapetan is not evil."

"Sounds like someone needs a refresher course on certain recent events."

"Fine," Fundapellonan said. "Some members of the House of Nohamapetan may be evil."

"Fratricide. Murder. Attempted assassination. Embezzlement. Questionable taste in men. That's just one of those motherfuckers."

"Are evil. Well, *were* evil."

"Still evil, just dead."

"But I didn't even work for her."

"You work for her mom. Where did you think she got it?"

"But I don't even technically work for her. I work for the house."

"Which is run by the countess, your boss, and her family. You're splitting hairs here pretty fucking fine."

"I'm a lawyer; that's my actual job. Look, Kiva, I'm not arguing that the individual members of the Nohamapetan family are perfect angels, or even decent human beings. But I work for the house. And on a day-to-day basis the House of Nohamapetan is a middling decent noble house."

"If you say so."

Fundapellonan propped herself up on an elbow. "And what about the House of Lagos, hmmm? You probably won't be entirely surprised to discover that before I met you I did a little, shall we say, opposition research on your house. Would you like a rundown on the labor issues and various other workplace and safety laws the House of Lagos endemically runs afoul of? How many times in the last two years alone the House of Lagos has been hauled up in front of the guilds for bad practices? How many marks the House of Lagos has as a line item in its annual budget for 'conflict resolution'? You actually have a line item for payouts, and you don't change your practices unless you overshoot that line item three years in a row. Which you're about to do, by the way."

"I could do the same opposition research on the House of Nohamapetan and come away with a similar list."

"Which is my point exactly," Fundapellonan said. "The house is a business; it needs representation; it's not perfect but not pure evil either."

"But your boss is."

"That stings, coming from a woman who charged refugees millions of marks to get on her ship to flee from a devastating civil war."

Kiva looked over. "Wow. You really did your research."

"Why did you do it?"

"I needed the money."

Fundapellonan grinned and rolled on top of Kiva. "See, *that* is actually fucking evil, Kiva Lagos."

"And yet you're still here with me."

Fundapellonan sat up with Kiva still underneath her. "Maybe I just like bad people." She grabbed at Kiva's wrist and slid the silver-and-topaz bracelet off it, and on to her own. She held it up to look at it.

"It looks good on you," Kiva said.

"It's nice with my skin tone," Fundapellonan agreed, and then flew sideways off the bed.

"Hey," Kiva said to Fundapellonan, several hours later.

Fundapellonan tried to croak something, and Kiva moved her hand. "Don't bother. You've got a tube in your throat. Your entire respiratory system is kind of fucked at the moment. Along with the rest of you. You were shot. Right off my fucking bed."

Fundapellonan's eyes widened and she looked around frantically.

"Relax, relax, hey, relax," Kiva said. "You're fine. You're safe. Well, you're not *fine.* You almost died several times. But you're not going to die now. And you're very safe. I called in a favor." Kiva made a sweeping motion with her hand. "Welcome to the emperox's private medical suite at Brighton Palace."

Fundapellonan eyes, already wide, became like plates.

"Don't worry, I'm paying."

This got Fundapellonan's eyes to shrink a little.

"Let me catch you up on events," Kiva said. "You were shot in the chest. The bullet came through the sliding glass door. I'm on the seventeenth fucking floor, so it's unlikely it was a random occurrence. My best guess is that someone meant to shoot me and shot you instead. I think this because, no offense, more people probably want me dead than want you dead, including your own actual fucking boss. Does that sound like a reasonable guess to you?"

Fundapellonan nodded, very very slightly.

"Did you tell anyone at House of Nohamapetan you were coming to see me tonight?"

Fundapellonan was still for this, still looking at Kiva.

"I'm not angry at you, Senia. I don't think you set me up. But I need to know if you told anyone at the House of Nohamapetan that you were going to see me."

Nod.

"Did you tell them I said I would wear the bracelet for you?"

Nod.

Kiva smiled. "That's how I know you didn't set me up. If you had set me up, there is no way in fucking hell that you would have put on the bracelet. And I would be dead. You saved my life tonight, Senia. You took a bullet for me."

Fundapellonan's eyes squinted.

"Yes, I know. If it was all the same you would have preferred not to. But I still appreciate it. Also, thank you for not dying on me. I'm not saying that because I *like* you or anything. It's just having someone murdered in your house is not great for property values."

The squint was back.

"Too soon. Okay. Fair. Well, how about this, then. One, you should clearly quit your job because your boss, who is *fucking evil,* probably just had you shot. And yes, I know she was aiming at me, but the very fact she was willing to take a shot at me while you were there should let you know she was perfectly fine with you as collateral damage, or blowing my brains out while you watched. Two, if you *do* quit your job at the House of Nohamapetan, you have a job at the House of Lagos. Yes, we have shaky labor practices. Maybe you can help us fix that. Three, no matter what you do, remember you fucking deserve better than this. And four, do you remember how I said you haven't seen me angry?"

Fundapellonan nodded.

"Well, that's about to fucking change."

Kiva tickled the nose of Tinda Louentintu, the Countess Nohamapetan's chief of staff. Louentintu snorted in her sleep, swatted at her nose, and then rolled onto her side.

Kiva watched this fucking piece of shit snore lightly for a few more minutes. Then she went to the bathroom of Louentintu's hotel room, set down the universal room key she had just paid an outrageous sum for to one of the hotel's less ethically minded assistant managers, unwrapped one of the hygienically sealed glasses on the sink, filled it with water, walked back to the bed and poured it into Louentintu's ears and face. Louentintu came up, awake and sputtering.

"Oh, good, you're awake," Kiva said. "Hi, I'm Kiva Lagos." Then she punched Louentintu square in the face.

There was a crunch, and blood burst out of Louentintu's nose. She gasped and put her hands to her face and came away with bloody fingers. She looked up at Kiva, asked, "Why?" and then screamed as Kiva punched her right flat square in her fucking nose again.

"I'm sorry, did you have a question?" Kiva asked. She shook out her hand, grimacing.

She was pretty fucking sure she just broke a finger on the nose of this thundering twat, but she wasn't going to give her the satisfaction of knowing that, so she drew her hand back again, ready to punch. "Go ahead, ask another fucking question, you feculent pile of shit."

Louentintu shut up. Then Kiva fucking punched her again. Louentintu went down onto her pillows, blood everywhere, her breathing making a horrible fucking noise through her broken nose.

"Now that we've gotten the preliminaries out of the way, let me explain why I'm here," Kiva said. "Tonight a friend of mine — and an employee of your boss, you walking fucking wastestream — was shot right in front of me. One second she was on top of me, showing off a nice piece of jewelry, and the next she was two fucking meters away on the floor with a hole in her chest. It was a fucking miracle she survived."

"I don't know what you're talking about," Louentintu said, in between snorts.

"Don't you fucking dare," Kiva said. "I will fucking drag you off this bloody fucking bed and launch you right off the goddamned balcony and I won't give a shit what happens to me after. So if you want to see if you can fucking *fly,* lady, tell me one more time you don't have the first fucking idea of what I'm talking about."

Louentintu was silent.

"Now, we both know who that bullet was meant for," Kiva continued. "But it happened to go through Senia Fundapellonan instead. Well, fine. That face bashing I just gave you was meant for the Countess Nohamapetan. I guess my aim is as bad as hers. The difference is that Senia didn't fucking deserve what happened to her. You, on the other hand, are an entirely different matter. I know that when the Countess Nohamapetan takes a shit, you wipe her ass for her.

"So here's what you're going to do. You're going to take that newly fucked-up face of yours and you're going to go up the six floors to where your boss is sleeping, and you're going to wake her up. You're going to tell her that she fucking *missed.* And you're going to tell her that tomorrow bright and early I'm walking into the fucking Guild House and going up to *my* office and I'm going to sit in my nice fucking chair behind my nice fucking desk with my nice fucking tea, and then I'm going to rip *her* fucking business apart.

"Every minute of every day of the rest of my natural life will be dedicated to doing to her house what I just did to your shitty, complicit nose. I *already* have enough on the countess's greedy, asshole family to make the guilds seriously consider disenfranchising the house and throwing every last one of you into prison. And that was just me farting around. Imagine what I will do now that I am *fucking motivated.*"

"Or," Louentintu said.

"What?"

"I said 'or.' " Louentintu's nose had stopped bleeding and she had wiped her face on her sheet, making a bloody mess of both. "When someone comes in and makes threats there is always an 'or.' 'Give me what I want, or I will burn your house down.' You've made the threat, Lady Kiva. I'm waiting to hear the 'or.' "

"How's your nose?" Kiva asked.

"It's been better."

Kiva nodded at this and punched Louentintu in the nose again. Louentintu slumped back against her headboard.

"That was the 'or,' " Kiva said. "Make sure the countess gets it. And tell her to get her ass out of Hubfall. She's got a great big fucking spaceship. From now on, she can sleep there."

Chapter 14

The spaceship was large, like a tenner, and featured a ring, like a tenner. Unlike a tenner, the ring wasn't rotating, providing itself with the force to pin people and objects down to the inside of its walls. Lights were on here and there across the ship. If Marce had to guess, he'd say the ship's power and systems were intermittent, at best. The ship was indeed "warm," but that warm was only relative to the space around it. Except for one arc of its ring, the ship registered a temperature of a couple of degrees above zero, Celsius.

What was interesting about the ship was not the ship itself, but the swarm of objects around it: dozens of small cylindrical objects, each no longer than thirty meters wide, connected to one or more other similar objects by cables, rotating around a central point, which was itself connected to the larger ship. Marce looked at one of the cables in his crew's ready room on the *Bransid,* and saw something moving on it: a small container, attached to a mechanized pulley. As he watched, the pulley brought the container to one of the cylinders, which swallowed it up.

"Are we actually seeing this?" asked Jill Seve, watching the container disappear. She was a navy linguist, and had a degree in anthropology as well, which Admiral Emblad had decided was close enough for this mission.

"Oh, we're seeing it," said Plenn Gitsen, the naval biologist. "Are we believing it, is the actual question."

"I mean, how the fuck are people actually *alive* out here?" Seve asked. "How long has it been since the collapse of the Flow stream?"

"Eight hundred years," Roynold said. She was standing by Marce, watching the monitor.

"How do people live like that" — Seve pointed at the monitor — "for eight hundred goddamned years?"

"They probably didn't live like *that* for eight hundred years," said Gennety Hanton. "We have evidence there were people on Dalasýsla thirty years ago. If we had time to examine the other habitats in the local space, we'd probably find some of them were inhabited or at least visited recently. Well, relatively recently."

"So you're saying that people have been living like that for thirty years at least," Seve said.

"Looks like," Hanton said.

"Okay, how the hell do you live like *that* for thirty years?"

"Got me."

"They live like that because they don't have any other *choice,*" Roynold said, testily. "Obviously. Our job is to find out why. And how."

"So are we going over there?" Hanton asked Marce.

Marce turned to Gitsen, the biologist. "Are we?"

"Whoever they are, they've been isolated here in Dalasýsla for most of a millennium," he said. "The number of people they've lived among all their life can't number more than a few hundred at best. That's not a lot."

"You're worried that if we breathe on them, they'll die of our diseases," Roynold said.

"Or the other way around," Gitsen said. "We have no idea how the bacteria and viruses in their very limited environment have mutated and evolved. We aren't going to just walk up to them and give them a hug. That might be mutually assured destruction."

"So that's a vote for no," Marce said.

Gitsen shook his head. "I didn't say that. I think we have to go over there. Whoever these people are, they represent a miracle of science. Somehow they managed to survive eight hundred years after the collapse of their civilization. We need to talk to them. But we have to be careful."

"Back into the suits," Hanton said.

"*You* don't have to go," Seve said, to Hanton. "There are no computer systems that need to be hacked."

"That you know of," Hanton replied.

Roynold looked over to Marce. "Who does need to go?" she asked.

"Seve and Gitsen, definitely," Marce said. "I think we might want to ask Merta Ells." She was the ship's doctor on the *Bransid.* "And I know that Captain Laure is going to want at least a few marines. And you can go too, Hat."

"What makes you think I want to go?" Roynold asked.

"I went on the last mission," Marce said.

"*That's* the one I should have been on,"

Roynold said. "You know I don't like people much."

"Sorry," Marce said.

"It's fine," Roynold said, then turned her attention back to the ship. "But *how* are you going to do it? You just going to go to the front door and knock?"

"Hey," Hanton said, pointing to the screen. "Do you see that?"

"See what?" Marce asked.

"One of the lights on the ring started blinking."

Marce looked at the ship and could barely make out the light in question. "Can you zoom in on that at all?"

"On it," Hanton said.

"It's not random or regular," Seve said after a minute. "You got long blinks and short blinks going on. It's code."

Hanton looked at it for a moment, then pulled out his tablet and opened up a search function. "I know what this is," he said. "The Imperial Navy has a code system for ships in distress that it can use if their communications are otherwise down."

"Using ship lights?" Roynold said, incredulously. "Given the average distance between ships, that's *optimistic.*"

"I didn't say it made *sense,*" Hanton said, annoyed. "I just said we had it. And anyway it's not meant just for spaceships. You can use it for land and sea vessels."

"And this messaging system has been the same for eight hundred years," Marce said.

"Of course not," Hanton said. He flipped the tablet around to show Marce. "But as part of the mission informational database I have the key for the code from eight hundred years ago."

"Well played," Marce said.

"It was just part of a larger download on ships generally, but I'll go ahead and take the credit," Hanton said. "Now give me a minute so I can pay attention to this."

"There are three individual messages," he said, a couple of minutes later. "The first is 'communications inoperable.' "

"We knew that," Roynold said.

Hanton held up his hand. "The second is 'systems critical.' "

"What's the third?" Marce asked.

" 'Help.' "

The Dalasýslans were simultaneously short and elongated, a result, Marce imagined, of poor nutrition and low gravity. Marce could see Dr. Ells next to him clearly wishing she could get one into her medical bay for examination. He couldn't blame her; in her position, he would probably want to do the same thing.

For the moment, however, what Marce really wanted to do was understand them.

Captain Laure had balked at Marce's request to be sent over without security, and didn't want to risk a full crew of scientists. In the end Marce, Ells, Seve and PFC Lyton put on their suits, took a shuttle and waited by an airlock while one of the Dalasýslans manually cranked it open for them. The Dalasýslan was wearing an ill-fitting suit that looked ancient and patched, because it was both of these things.

When the four of them were in, the Dalasýslan cranked the airlock shut again and waited as air flooded back in. Then it cranked the inner door open, shed its suit and left it by the airlock. The Dalasýslan was mostly naked, of indeterminate sex, and appeared to wait for the crew from the *Bransid* to shuck their suits as well. When they did not, the Dalasýslan did what looked like a *suit yourself* shrug, kicked off in the microgravity and waved the four of them along to follow. They did, clomping along with their magnetized feet on the deck.

The interior of the ship was falling apart, or it looked great for an at least eight-hundred-year-old ship, take your pick. Marce noted how every part of it was cobbled together and jury-rigged. It was a Frankenstein monster of a ship, clearly refurbished with bits and pieces of other ships and habitats. The citizens of the ship were scavengers, as well they would have to be to survive as long as they had.

The crew from the *Bransid* were taken to what appeared to be a mess hall, or would have been a mess hall if the ship had been anything approaching a normal ship. Inside were several dozen other Dalasýslans, each looking not dissimilar from the one that had led them in.

They were human, but of a sort of human that Marce had never seen before. They were creatures of space and of spaceships in a way that no other member of the Interdependency was. Billions of Interdependency citizens lived in space, of course. But they lived in habitats with full gravity and full atmosphere and all the essentials and most of the luxuries. They lived *in* space. They weren't *of* space, like these Dalasýslans now were.

This is what our future is, Marce thought, and hoped the involuntary shudder that went across his body was not visible outside of his suit.

The Dalasýslan who had escorted them into the room maneuvered over to a group of its compatriots, and another unfurled, oriented itself to Marce's team, and began to speak. Marce couldn't understand a single thing it was saying.

"Jill?" Marce said, to his linguist, after the Dalasýslan had stopped speaking.

"It's Interdependency Standard," Seve said. "Or *was.* There's some sort of vowel shift going on."

"Can you understand it?"

"Sort of." Seve stepped forward to the standing Dalasýslan, and pointed to herself. "Human." She pointed to Marce. "Human." She did the same with Ells and Seve.

The Dalasýslan caught on easily enough and said a word that might have been "human" if someone had recorded the word, run it backward through a recording device, said that resulting word, reversed that, said that and then repeated the process a couple dozen times. Seve did the word game several more times with different objects in the room, getting the Dalasýslan version of it. Then she said something to the Dalasýslan in something that sounded, to Marce's ears, like nothing resembling language.

The Dalasýslan nodded and waited.

"Wait, what did you just say?" Marce asked.

"I *think* I said, 'Speak slow, your words

are hard for us,' " Seve said. "I guess we'll find out."

The Dalasýslan started again, much more slowly, and this time Marce could almost make out things that sounded like they might have been words he might have known.

"This is Chuch and he — I think 'he' is right — is their captain, and this is what remains of Dalasýsla," Seve said, then nodded at Chuch to continue. "He says that this ship has been the home of what remains of Dalasýsla for the last hundred years." More talking. "There used to be more, but other ships and habitats failed over time. He says that they have survived by moving the ship from habitat to habitat and from ship to ship and scavenging what they need." Another burst. "But now they are no longer able to do that."

"Why not?"

More listening. "I think their propulsion systems are screwed," Seve said. "They have enough power to propel the ship, but they don't have the ability to maneuver it." Another pause. "They have power to run some ship systems, but they can't get to any of the habitats they scavenge to repair the ship anymore. It's falling apart around them, and eventually, it'll fail entirely."

"How long?"

Seve asked, and Chuch looked at another Dalasýslan, who answered. "It's been eighteen months since the propulsion system failed," Seve said. "This person is the chief engineer, and he estimates another year to two before too many critical systems fail."

"They have a chief engineer?" Lyton said.

"They've kept this ship running this long," Marce said. "Of course they have a chief engineer. Don't assume these people are stupid, Lyton."

"Sorry," she said.

Chuch asked Seve something, and Seve responded. "He just asked me what was said."

"Did you tell him?"

"Yes." Chuch said something and Seve listened. "He agrees they are not stupid, just desperate. He asks for our help."

"What kind of help?" Marce asked.

"Help with the propulsion systems, for a start. Other technical assistance. Food — sorry, not food, food stock. Things they can grow. Medical supplies. Information. New technology."

Chuch looked at Marce and said a word. Marce looked over to Seve. "Did he just say 'everything'?"

"I think so, yeah."

"Well, I can't blame him for that," Marce said. He was quiet for a moment.

"What is it?" Seve asked.

"They don't seem surprised to see us," Marce said.

"What do you mean?"

Marce motioned around the room, to the Dalasýslans assembled there. "They've lived on this ship for a hundred years at least. Before that they were eking out an existence on one of the habitats. The Flow stream to here collapsed eight hundred years ago. How would you react if after hundreds of years of isolation you were suddenly discovered?"

"I really don't know," Seve said.

"I'd probably shit myself," Lyton said. Seve looked at her oddly.

"You think they should be treating us like gods or something?" asked Dr. Ells.

"No," Marce said. "But I don't think this is the way I'd be reacting, either." He turned to Seve. "Ask him."

"Ask him what?"

"Ask him why he doesn't seem surprised to see us."

Seve asked, and blinked at the answer.

"What did he say?" Marce asked.

"He said he wasn't surprised to see us because the last ship to come always said that more would come back."

"What?" Marce said.

Chuch spoke again. "He says the last ship arrived three hundred years ago, and its crew stayed here. He says that every one of his crew, including him, has some of their blood. And he says that their captain always said more would come, eventually. So they weren't surprised when we came. We were expected. They were waiting for us. And we chose a good time to arrive, so thanks for that."

CHAPTER 15

Archbishop Gunda Korbijn was thinking about art again.

Specifically, she was thinking of the statue *Rachela at the Assembly,* by Admirable Pritof ("Admirable" was not Pritof's actual first name, but sometime after his death a particularly canny art dealer with an overabundance of his sculpture did a very good job of PR). The sculpture was itself based off a painting of the same name by Hippolyta Moulton, which hung in the Imperial Art Institute, not too far from Xi'an Cathedral.

In the painting Rachela is expounding to an assembly of political and corporate luminaries who will be so moved by her words that they will immediately put aside all their petty differences and form the Interdependency. Moulton imagined the moment with Rachela pretty, her face serene and her expressions iconically blank; apparently the politicians and the businessmen were so amazed at her words that they didn't mind they were coming from a mannequin.

Pritof's sculpture had another take on the moment. The sculptor had kept Rachela's pose exactly the same as in Moulton's painting, but the expression on her face was wildly different. Instead of serenity and blankness was canniness, and awareness, and, some would argue — exhaustively, in art and academic journals for centuries — sardonicism. Moulton's Rachela was a religious icon; Pritof's Rachela was a woman with an agenda.

Of the two Moulton's was the more famous representation, which was why it was in the IAI whilst Pritof's sculpture existed in relative exile at the Interdependent Church's cathedral in Šumadija, Pritof's home habitat. But Korbijn didn't care for it. Archbishop and effective head of the church though she was, blank-faced iconography gave Korbijn the willies. It depersonalized Rachela and made her less human, and more inevitable. And while it suited the Interdependent Church to give itself an air of inevitability — it suited nearly all churches to do that — Korbijn, who by profession and inclination was a student of its history, knew that there was nothing inevitable about it at all.

The famous assembly both works of art memorialized, for example: The politicians and captains of industry had not stared, stunned into amazement, at Rachela. They had laughed and jeered at her foolishness. Certainly they had not walked out of the room and lined up to create the Interdependency. It took years and countless backroom deals for that, with details a great deal more profane than exalted. Moulton's painting was after-the-fact propaganda, commissioned by one of Korbijn's long-dead predecessors as archbishop of Xi'an. The real story of the assembly was not stricken from the historical record, of course, but people liked Moulton's version better. To the extent that anyone thought of *Rachela at the Assembly* at all, the vast majority of them pictured it like Moulton had.

And this is why Korbijn liked the sculpture better. She suspected Rachela's actual expression during the assembly was far closer to what Pritof had depicted than what Moulton had. Not for the first time, Korbijn wished that Rachela had actually been something more divine than human, because at least then she could summon her and ask her what the hell she was actually thinking when she chose to speak to those politicians and businesspeople — what her "prophecies" really were and to what extent they should have ever guided the church that Korbijn had now given close to forty years of her life to.

Barring that she wished that she could be the emperox for a day. It was an open secret that the emperoxs were all embedded with a technology denied to every other subject of the Interdependency, one that recorded their every thought and then on death reconstituted them to advise their successor. There was a room in the imperial palace dedicated to it. Korbijn didn't know if this recording scheme went all the way back to Rachela, but if it did, Korbijn would have some pointed questions for her digital ghost.

If Rachela's memory is in there, then surely Grayland has asked her the same questions I would, Korbijn thought.

And that was why Korbijn was thinking of Pritof's sculpture in the first place. Because like Rachela, Grayland II was going to address an assembly.

Nominally she was going to be addressing the Parliament of the Interdependency, a body that she as emperox was officially a member of as the simple and sole representative of the Xi'an habitat, although by tradition the emperox neither attended nor voted.

But the audience would not be merely the parliament. The gallery of the parliament had become the hottest ticket in Xi'an, with members of the great houses of the Interdependency fighting each other for seats. Korbijn would not have to fight for a seat — she had been invited to offer a formal benediction prior to the emperox speaking, and she had accepted — but other bishops and officers of the church were in the same seating scrum as the great houses. At the end of the day all the major powers of the Interdependency — political, commercial and ecclesiastical — would be there.

Whenever it would be, Korbijn amended in her head. It was common knowledge that the emperox would make an address, but she hadn't quite set a date; all that came from her press minister was "imminently." Grayland was waiting for something, although what that something could be was a matter of intense speculation.

Unlike Rachela, when Grayland II addressed her assembly, she would already be emperox, and nominally at least the most powerful person in the known universe. Korbijn was not entirely sure this was the advantage it might seem to be. Rachela might have been seen as a charismatic crank when she addressed her skeptics. Grayland was seen as a danger. Korbijn was well aware of the rumors that Grayland intended to use the address as an announcement of martial law, under the rationale that the closing of the Flow streams would require a higher level of order. Then under writ of martial law, Grayland would go about dispatching her enemies, just as she had done with Nadashe Nohamapetan.

Korbijn had rolled her eyes when she was told of this particular rumor, but stopped rolling them when she accepted a rush meeting from Tinda Louentintu. The chief of staff to the Countess Nohamapetan arrived in a startling manner, looking like her face had been used to stop weights. When Korbijn asked her if she was all right, Louentintu gave some excuse about tripping over her balcony door sill, which Korbijn immediately intuited to be entirely bullshit, but which Louentintu was making clear she didn't want to address any further, in part by suggesting that Korbijn consider a schism in the Interdependent Church.

"On what grounds would I do that?" Korbijn asked, instead of immediately charging Louentintu with blasphemy, which was her right as an ecclesiastical officer of the church but which was very rarely done and would needlessly complicate matters in any event.

"For the continuation of the church, of course," Louentintu said. "The countess knows you recently convened your bishops to talk about the emperox and her visions and what they have meant to your control of the Interdependent Church. She knows not a few of them advocated for a schism, to preserve the integrity of the church."

Korbijn remembered the hours-long debate/shouting match Louentintu was referring to and was annoyed that one of her bishops had chosen to leak about it. She would deal with whomever that was later. "I suppose a few did," Korbijn said. "But I'd caution you that the meeting was understood to be a free intellectual exercise. No policy was intended to come out of it, or will come out of it."

"Of course not. But there could."

"Please come to your point, Lady Louentintu."

"I am saying that if you were to advocate a schism, you would find that you have allies."

"With all due respect to the Countess Nohamapetan, the church does not need to be seen to have allies like her."

"As unfortunate as your statement is, I understand why you say it. So you'll be glad to know that you will not have to be seen with us. Other, more substantial allies will stand with you."

"And by 'stand with us,' you mean what, exactly?"

"I would imagine it would mean financial and material support for the new church to keep the real estate holdings of the previous church, for a start."

"So not really a schism, merely a coup."

"It wouldn't even have to be that. But a great many people — in the parliament, in the great houses and, yes, in the church — are beginning to see the necessity of inviting this emperox off the throne."

" 'Inviting,' " Korbijn said. "What a polite word for it."

"It doesn't have to be violent," Louentintu said. "The Countess Nohamapetan understands better than almost anyone else at this point the futility of violence against this emperox. She has felt the cost of it more than anyone else, including the emperox herself. Two dead children and the third at End, where she will never see him again. But violence can be avoided, if enough pressure is brought to bear. At the right time. And the right place."

A dawning realization came over Korbijn. "The emperox's address to parliament. You're planning something."

"*We're* not planning it," Louentintu said. "But it is being planned."

"You're running a huge risk telling me this," Korbijn said. "I am on the executive committee. And I'm close to this emperox."

"You are close to her, yes. And it is a risk. But then you could have had me arrested for blasphemy several minutes ago. You are also a power in your own right, Archbishop. Your church owes little to this emperox. And when there is a new emperox, he, or she, might decide to formally separate the office of emperox from the church and to raise the current archbishop of Xi'an to be the new cardinal of Xi'an and Hub."

"You have it planned that far out."

"Again, not the House of Nohamapetan. But we know there are plans."

"And yet it's *you* who have come to try to tempt me, Lady Louentintu."

"I'm not here to tempt you, Archbishop. I am only making you aware of possibilities. And to appeal to your better angels. We are in turbulent times, and with the collapse of the Flow streams things will only get more uncertain. We are — we all are — assuredly heading into dark times. The emperox means well, but she isn't the one to lead us through what comes next for the Interdependency. Someone else will have to do it. And it's better for everyone to have that decided sooner than later."

Korbijn smiled. "It's funny. You sound very much like someone of my acquaintance who came to see me recently on the same subject."

"Talk to them again. Maybe they'll tell you the same thing."

"I can't. He just died."

It took Louentintu a minute to get it, but she got it. "That's unfortunate."

"It certainly was for him," Korbijn said.

"Be thinking about what I've talked to you about here, Archbishop," Louentintu said. "Many things are coming. The church will have a role in those things. But what that role is and what its future will be are going to be up to you. The emperox will make her address soon. And on the day she does, time's up."

Well, Korbijn thought, after Louentintu had gone, *that went almost exactly like Grayland said it would.*

"They're going to be coming to you soon, you know," Grayland had said to her, when Korbijn had visited her to discuss what had befallen Teran Assan. They had briefly discussed Assan's fate, and what it would mean to the functioning of the executive committee, and then Korbijn had broached the conversation she and Assan had had about her upcoming address, and how it had prompted her into meeting with her bishops. Grayland had nodded to all of that and made that cryptic pronouncement.

"They?" Korbijn had asked.

"I don't mean to sound conspiratorial. On the other hand, Lord Teran is newly dead trying to rescue Nadashe Nohamapetan. I expect the Countess Nohamapetan to deny that she or her house had anything to do with it, of course. But Lord Teran, whatever his other qualities, was not someone to do things freelance."

"You think this was part of something bigger."

"I think I have spooked a great number of powers with my talk of visions," Grayland said. "Which is not a surprise. Visions are unsettling and they disrupt order, and no one in power wants order messed with. They don't understand that disruption is coming whether they want it or not. My visions disrupt order now to prevent chaos later. But that's not useful for them. So they're planning something to preserve the order they know."

"And what is that?"

Grayland smiled at Korbijn. "Oh, I think you know well enough."

"A coup."

Grayland nodded again. "Or something close enough to it. Not just a clumsy assassination attempt like Nadashe made. Something large and elegant and irrefutable. So of course they're going to need you for that. You, and the church. So, yes, they're coming to sound you out for a deal."

"And you want me to tell you who they are when they do," Korbijn suggested.

To her amazement, Grayland shrugged at this. "You give me the name of the person who comes to you, and what then? I have them investigated or I have them arrested. You can be assured that Hibert Limbar is *already* investigating everyone and everything, including you and me, because that's his job. If I have them arrested, then I only arrest one person. The rest of them will cut them off and burn any connection, like they did to Lord Teran. Meanwhile the rest of them continue doing what they do in the background. So, no, Archbishop. I don't need you to tell me who comes to see you. Either I'll know or it won't matter."

"Then what do you want me to do?"

Grayland smiled. "I want you to ask

yourself what sort of church you want the Interdependent Church to be," she said.

"I don't understand."

"Actually, I think you do," Grayland said. "Or you will, when you think about it."

"All right," Korbijn said, dubiously.

Grayland laughed. "I'm not trying to be mysterious! I'm just saying that none of your predecessors in the last thousand years has been put on the spot like you have, because I had to go and sprout visions. But now that I have, you have to decide whether the church can still accommodate someone like me."

"A prophet."

"Oh, I don't know if I would go that far," Grayland said. "But yes."

Korbijn smiled at this.

"If it can, then you'll know what to do when you're asked for your allegiance. And if it can't, then I guess you'll know what to do then, too. Either way, I apologize."

"For what?"

"For being a real pain in your ass," Grayland said. "Things would be much easier for you if I had just stuck to the script. I'm sorry."

"Apology accepted," Korbijn said. And then blurted out, "They would have come for you anyway, you know."

Grayland had smiled again, and in remembering that, Korbijn knew why she had thought of Pritof's sculpture at all: because in that moment, Rachela and Grayland had the same smile.

Chapter 16

"What sort of ship am I looking for?" Captain Laure said.

"A ship like this one," Marce said. "Only larger."

"That narrows it down," Laure said.

"The Dalasýslans said that the ship didn't have a ring on it," Marce said. "So it's not like a fiver or a tenner. It probably had push-field technology to mimic gravity like the *Bransid* does. But it was larger than us. The legend has the crew complement at two hundred, two hundred fifty."

"So to reiterate," Laure said. "We're looking for a mythical ship that appeared three hundred years ago, without a ring, big enough to have a crew of two hundred."

"It's not mythical," Marce said.

"It *sounds* mythical."

"Dr. Gitsen did genetic typing of some of the Dalasýslans," Marce said. "Do you know what she found?"

"Inbreeding?"

"No," Marce said. "Well, yes. But not as much as you would think, considering."

"That's a relief," Laure said.

"What Gitsen found was a genetic component that doesn't conform to the historical genetic makeup of the Dalasýslans, and doesn't much align with the DNA of people from the Interdependency."

"What does that mean?"

"It means that after over a thousand years, the humans of the Interdependency are distinct enough from the humans from Earth that we can tell the difference. We're pretty good at typing people's immediate ancestry. And a hefty part of these people's ancestry isn't from here. Or anywhere else in the Interdependency."

"Not to be cruel, but have you seen these people?" Laure said. "They spent the last century at least in a ship that doesn't offer them much protection from cosmic rays. Their DNA is probably more scrambled than most."

"Gitsen controlled for that," Marce said. "There's still something else in there."

"That sounds ominous."

"It's not ominous, but it *is* important. Someone *else* came here, Captain. Long after the Flow stream from the Interdependency collapsed. Long before *we* came. The Dalasýslans say the ship is still here somewhere."

"They've probably scavenged it down to parts by now."

Marce shook his head. "It's apparently not convenient for scavenging. But even if it were, they said they wouldn't because nothing on the ship would be compatible with their ships or habitats. And *that* tells you something, too."

Laure shook her head. "I still think you're having me chase a ghost."

"You're cataloging every man-made object in the area anyway," Marce said. "All I'm asking is that if you find one that even vaguely resembles the one the Dalasýslans talk about, you tell me about it. It's been over a thousand years since we've seen evidence of human civilization outside the Interdependency. I think that's worth checking into."

Laure nodded. "We'll look into it. Don't expect miracles. And don't bother me about it."

"Fair enough," Marce said.

"On another note entirely, I know you brought one of the Dalasýslans over for a tour."

"Chuch, their captain, yes," Marce said.

"Thank you for the permission."

"I thought we worried about infecting them with our germs."

"He was in his own suit, and it was sterilized before he came on board."

"He has an eight-hundred-year-old space suit."

"Actually he claims it's from that newer arrival."

"Is it?"

"No," Marce said. "It's standard-issue Interdependency from just pre-collapse."

"And how did he enjoy his trip?"

"It tired him out because he wasn't used to full gravity. We had him in a chair for a lot of the visit. He said it was interesting to see a ship that had all of its insides actually in its insides. He would still be questioning your engineering staff if we hadn't reminded him he was about to run out of his oxygen."

"And he was able to understand what they were saying."

"Yes, Captain. Most of it. Probably more than me. They really are exceptionally intelligent. They would have to be to have survived this long out here."

"Everyone keeps telling me that," Laure said. "They still look like little goblins to me."

"She's not wrong," Roynold told Marce

later, as they ate. "They creep me the hell out, that's for sure."

"You don't like people anyway," Marce reminded her. "You said so yourself."

"Right, but this is more so."

"That's prejudiced."

"I'm aware of that," Roynold said. "So I'm doing them the favor of staying away."

"What about the other thing we were talking about?" Marce asked her.

"About the idea of another Flow stream opening up here from somewhere else?" Roynold shrugged. "It's entirely possible. The Interdependency has more Flow streams in it by an order of magnitude than anywhere else in local space because of a quirk in the multidimensional topography, but there's nothing that says they're only confined to our local space, or that Flow streams can't emerge in Interdependency space from elsewhere. That's how humans originally *got* here."

"I'm asking if you're seeing any evidence of it."

"Not yet, but that could change," Roynold said. "I've got the probe we brought looking at the local topography and I'm feeding it into our latest models, but aside from our current streams I'm not seeing anything yet. I'll know more the more data

I get. This is what I'm doing while you are out gallivanting."

"I don't gallivant," said Marce.

"Call it what you want. You're not doing much Flow physics research, is what I'm saying. It's all me so far. I'm going to want that noted when it comes time to publish, by the way."

"That seems fair."

"This is how I can tell you're not in academia anymore. If you were still a professor you'd be screaming to be the primary author."

"How much more data will we need before we potentially see evidence of other streams into here?"

"It's hard to say, and a lot will depend on how old the streams in and out are. This aspect isn't entirely surprising. Our model doesn't do very well predicting individual streams more than about two decades out on either side of the timeline. Even that massive stream shift we're predicting comes with a margin of a couple thousand years on either side."

"That still bothers me," Marce said.

"We won't be around for it, so I don't lose any sleep over it."

"That's an interesting life philosophy."

"Not really," Roynold said. "Look, if you

find that ship, see if you can discover exactly where it came from and exactly when it arrived in local space. If we have all that data, we can work backward and maybe construct a model."

"If we know where it comes from, then we don't need to construct a model," Marce pointed out. "We already know where it comes from."

"If we have a model, then we can predict if that particular Flow stream is coming back anytime soon."

"Does it matter?" Marce said. "The Flow stream out of here is collapsing in two months. It won't do us any good."

"Not us, dimwit," Roynold said. "The goblin people."

"The Dalasýslans?"

"Yes, them. Maybe they would like a way out of a life of endless desperate scavenging. Unless you think you can get their ship up and running before the Flow stream back to the Interdependency collapses."

"We checked their propulsion system," said Commander Vyno Junn, the chief engineer of the *Bransid,* when Marce came to him for an update. "It's shot and it can't be fixed. Not with what I have on hand or what they have on hand, in the time we have before we have to leave."

"Can we raid some of the nearby habitats?" Marce asked.

"For what?" Junn asked. "Check the schematics. Habitats don't have propulsion or navigation systems that work even remotely like the ones on starships. They're there to maintain rotational speed and orbital position, not to accelerate to Flow shoals or travel to planets. And before you ask, we already checked the hulls of close-by ships. These guys have already hollowed them out."

"So they're screwed," Marce said.

"They were already screwed when we got here," Junn said. "We're buying them a little more time, at least. We're helping them rebuild some of their life support and power systems, very slapdash, but better than what they have now. And I'm pretty sure we can get that ring of theirs moving again before we go, which will help them with their agriculture. And I know we're basically carving up all the fresh fruit we have on the ship to give them the seeds. Plus bags of potatoes and turnips and all that other root vegetable stuff."

"We're breaking Interdependency law to do that," Marce said. He thought back to his friend and former lover Kiva Lagos, who probably would have skinned someone who handed out citrus seeds without a payment to her house.

"The way I see it is if anyone has a problem they can come here and try to collect," Junn said. "But they better hurry."

"What about bringing them back with us?" Marce said, to Captain Laure, after his visit with Junn.

"The Dalasýslans?" Laure said.

"Of course."

"Where will we put them, Lord Marce?"

"We can squeeze in," Marce said.

"We really can't," Laure said. "This ship crews with fifty, and includes a dozen marines and your science crew on top of that. You'll have noticed that your berth is roughly the size of a broom closet. Mine, I regret to say, is not much larger. Every square centimeter that's not allocated for occupancy is already claimed for something else. How many Dalasýslans are there?"

"Almost two hundred."

"Again I ask: Where will we put them? We literally have no space for them on this ship."

"We have a cargo hold."

"Yes," Laure said. "That will work quite well as long as we don't ever expect them to sit. Which brings up another salient point, Lord Marce. The Dalasýslans have never been exposed to full gravity. They're used to, what, a third of a g?"

"That's what their living quarters pull, yes."

"So we'd be exposing them to three times the weight on their bodies that they're used to."

"We can draw down our own push fields."

"That works fine until they get to the Interdependency. I don't know of a habitat that functions at a third of a g on a constant basis. Living on Hub for them would be like you or me living on a gas giant. And finally, even if I *did* stuff them into the cargo hold and drive home on a third of a g push field, how do you propose we keep them sequestered, to keep them from catching a disease from us they have no defenses for, or vice versa? The cargo hold ventilation system is tied in to the rest of the ship. The only time we close it off is when we're purging the air out of the hold for sterilization. We'd leave with two hundred refugees but arrive with not so many, I suspect, Lord Marce."

"They'll die if they stay here," Marce said.

"No," Laure said. "They'll die if they stay here with that broken ship of theirs. Maybe we can help with that."

"I don't understand."

Laure smiled. "Sensing that I might be having this conversation with you at some point, Lord Marce, and anticipating your objections, you may be interested to know that I have already sent a courier drone to Admiral Emblad, with a confidential message outlining the problems the Dalasýslans are facing. The Imperial Navy has several ships that have been recently decommissioned, including at least one fiver. There's nothing wrong with them except that they are old. But none as old as what Captain Chuch and his crew are sailing in. It's possible the navy may be interested in saving the expenditure of tearing that fiver down for scrap. Especially if you, sir, drop a similar hint to your good friend the emperox."

"That's an excellent idea," Marce said, then did some math in his head. "The timing will be tight for anyone hoping to get back."

"Captains don't like to talk about this, but it's possible for a ship to be navigated to and from a Flow shoal entirely by computer, even more so if there is no crew to manage."

"Got it."

"Don't tell anyone I told you that. I'll have you tossed out an airlock. Sir."

"Your secret is safe with me."

"I'm glad to hear it. And since you are being so accommodating to me at the moment, Lord Marce, let me say it's good you went looking for me, because it saves me the trouble of having to look for you. I have news for you."

"What is it?"

"That ship of yours. We think we found it. Way the hell away from here."

"Another ship, another airlock," PFC Gamis said, and cranked open the airlock to Marce's mystery ship with his spreader. Marce, Gennety Hanton and Sergeant Sherrill floated in, and Gamis uncranked the airlock's outer door closed behind them. He opened the inner door to the ship and was surprised, as was everyone else, to hear and feel the air rushing in.

"It's still got an atmosphere," Sherrill said.

"Want to take off your helmet, Sarge?" Gamis asked.

"I wouldn't suggest it," Hanton said. "Not unless you like breathing air that's two hundred and seventy degrees below zero."

"Come on," Marce said, and led the team away from the airlock, in the exhausting magnetized gait.

"This is odd," Sherrill said as they walked the length of the ship. "All the bulkheads are open. Nothing is secured."

"And no one here," Gamis said. "Not a single frozen corpse."

"Captain Chuch said the crew of this ship joined the survivors of Dalasýsla," Marce said. "This ship didn't meet a violent end. It probably just got parked."

"A hell of a long way from Dalasýsla," Hanton said. The ship had been parked in the trailing orbital Lagrange point of Dalvik, Dalasýsla Prime's largest moon. The *Bransid*'s crew spotted the ship only several hours after Dalvik emerged from the far side of its planet. Dalasýsla itself orbited much farther out than Dalvik, to avoid the large moon's gravity and also Dalasýsla Prime's violent magnetic field. The shuttle, flying flat-out, took six hours to get there. The team would have only a few hours before this ship winged itself back behind Dalasýsla Prime.

"Maybe that was the point," Marce said.

"I think they hid the bridge as well they hid the ship," Gamis complained. "This would be easier if we had a deck plan."

"Found it," Sherrill said, ahead of them. Gamis grumbled at this.

The bridge was small, almost intimate, and dark, with only one glowing light, positioned at what looked like the navigator's workstation.

"There's a light on," Hanton said, pointing. "This ship still has power. After all this time."

"Let's find the heater," Gamis said.

Marce walked over to the workstation and peered in close at the small light, which was embedded in the workstation itself.

The light flashed in Marce's eye. He sputtered and took a step back.

The lights on the bridge flickered on.

"What the hell?" Sherrill said, looking around.

"What did you do?" Hanton said to Marce.

"I looked at a light," Marce said.

"Well, don't do that anymore."

"I think it's a little late for that."

From away in the ship, thrumming began. The sound of a ship waking itself up. Marce felt a pressing on his shoulders. A push field, or something very much like it, had turned on and had begun to simulate something like a full g.

"Okay, I'm very officially not liking this now," Gamis said, and turned to exit the deck.

There was someone standing in the doorway.

Gamis yelled in alarm and raised his weapon. Sherrill did the same.

The person in the doorway held up a hand, as if to say, *Don't do that, please.*

"Wait," Marce said. Gamis and Sherrill both held their ground and didn't back up, but stayed where they were. Marce walked up to the person in the doorway, who watched him approach, his hand still up.

Marce stood in front of the person and poked at his hand. His finger went through the hand like he wasn't there.

Because in reality, he wasn't there.

"Gamis, if you'd shot him, you just would have put holes in the wall," Marce said.

"That's a projection?" Gamis said.

"Either that or a ghost."

"That's great," Sherrill said. "Of who?"

Marce looked back at the image of the person in the doorway. "That's a really good question."

"Your accent and grammar are strange to me, but I think I can follow it now," the apparition said. Its accent was as strange to Marce as his was to the apparition, but perfectly understandable. "You speak like the Dalasýslans, but not *quite* the same as they do."

"I'm speaking Standard," Marce said.

"Standard. Yes," the apparition said, and tilted its head slightly. "Are you from the Interdependency? Aside from the Dalasýslans, I've never met anyone from there. I would be delighted to change that."

"I am from the Interdependency," Marce said. "We all are."

"That's wonderful."

"I'm Lord Marce Claremont, of End."

"An actual lord," the apparition said. "How unexpected. And the duo still aiming their weapons at me, although it will do them no good at all?"

"Sergeant Sherrill and Private First Class Gamis," Marce said, and motioned to them to lower their weapons. Both of them complied, reluctantly. "And over there is Gennety Hanton, computer expert."

"I thought I was, anyway," Hanton said. "Looking at you, I'm maybe changing my mind."

"You think I'm a computer projection and *not* a ghost, Mr. Hanton?"

"Dr. Hanton."

"Dr. Hanton. My apologies."

"And aren't you?"

"It's accurate to say I'm a little of both," said the apparition.

"Who and what are you, then?" Marce asked.

"My name is Tomas. Tomas Reynauld Chenevert. Or was, when I died, which now I find was more than three hundred years ago. Good lord. I was the owner of the *Auvergne,* the ship you are now standing on. And now you could say I *am* the *Auvergne.* How I became a ship after I had been a human is a long story which is perhaps best saved for another time. But I still prefer to be called Tomas, if it's all the same to you. Or Monsieur Chenevert, if you prefer."

"Hello, Monsieur Chenevert," Marce said.

"Hello, Lord Marce. Or is it Lord Claremont?"

"Lord Marce. The Count Claremont is my father."

"A count. Indeed."

"This is *very* weird," Hanton said.

"It is indeed," Chenevert said, to Marce. "I put myself to sleep with the full expectation that I would not ever fully wake up. Except for the most minimal of maintenance, the ship has been dormant for three centuries. But now I find myself awake, and with guests. Can you please tell me why you are here?"

"I was curious about this ship," Marce said.

"What about it made you curious?"

"To begin, where it was from."

"That's answered simply enough. It's from Ponthieu."

"Where is that? Is that on Earth?"

Chenevert smiled at this. "Oh, no, Lord Marce. Nothing's really from *Earth* anymore, is it?"

Before Marce could respond to that there was a ping in his ear: a message from Captain Laure, recorded because the *Bransid* was several light-seconds away.

"We have a problem," it said. "Another ship has come through the Flow shoal. It's located us and is heading our way. Our attempts to hail it have been unsuccessful. We're assuming it is hostile."

"Are you hearing this?" Gamis said. The message had been sent to the entire team. Sherrill waved him to silence.

"Do not return to the *Bransid,*" Laure continued. "If the ship is hostile, all your shuttle will be is an easy target. We are powering up and heading away from the Dalasýslan ship to draw the other ship away. Dr. Seve and Lyton are still with the Dalasýslans. If necessary and possible the *Bransid* will make a break for the Flow shoal back to Hub. If that happens head to the Dalasýslan ship and take refuge there. We will arrange for rescue. Do not respond. Radio silence until further notice. Good luck." The message ended.

"Can the *Bransid* defend itself?" Marce asked Sherrill.

"Back in the day the *Bransid* was a naval interceptor," Sherrill said. "But these days it pulls courier duty. It's not armed for battle. It has defensive weaponry. That's it."

"So if that other ship is hostile, the *Bransid* is a soft target," Hanton said.

"Captain Laure will put up a fight," Sherrill said.

"That's not what I asked, though."

"Your ship is under attack?" Chenevert asked Marce, watching the conversation.

"Not yet," Marce said. "But maybe soon."

"Not from the Dalasýslans."

"No." It occurred to Marce that Chenevert, asleep for three hundred years, might not be caught up on current events.

"Then from whom?"

"We don't know yet."

"I regret to say that I'm not in a position to offer much help," Chenevert said. "I'm using stored battery power for gravity and life support — the ship will be warm enough for you soon — but reactivating the engines will take several hours."

"Anything we can do to help?"

"Thank you, no. This ship's engineering section is entirely automated and was even before I became the ship. You'd just be in the way."

"This ship is going to go behind Dalasýsla

Prime soon," Hanton said. "We'll be cut off from the *Bransid* no matter what."

"If anything happens to the *Bransid,* we're screwed," Gamis said.

"You're welcome to stay here," Chenevert said to him.

"That's great," Gamis replied, sarcastically. "Got any sandwiches?"

"Quiet, Private," Sherrill said. Gamis shut up. Sherrill looked over to Marce. "He's not wrong, though."

Marce nodded. "What supplies do we have on the shuttle?"

"Enough protein bars for about five days for each of us. Probably about three days of water each."

"I have water," Chenevert said.

"No food, though," Marce said.

"Sorry, no. Even if I did, after three hundred years you wouldn't want it."

"So all the water we need but still only five days of food," Sherrill said.

"The Dalasýslans would feed us," Marce said.

"They can barely feed themselves, sir. Not to mention we can't get out of our suits without risking infecting them."

"What's happened to the Dalasýslans?" Chenevert asked.

Marce considered what to tell Chenevert

about the Dalasýslans and how to say it. "It's complicated," he finally settled on. "But the last three hundred years have not been great for them."

"Oh," Chenevert said. "Oh, dear."

"Are you sure the engines will come back online?" Marce asked.

"They should," Chenevert said. "I've been asleep, but the *Auvergne* has done regular checkups on its systems and processes. I can tell you every system on the ship is functional."

"What about weapons?" Sherrill asked.

"This is not a warship," Chenevert said. "No missiles or physical weaponry, and after three centuries those would be of questionable utility anyway. But as it happens, before I left Ponthieu I had cause to install an array of beam weapons."

"What was the cause?" Gamis asked.

"Let's just say that I anticipated that when I needed to leave Ponthieu, it would be suddenly, and that I might be chased. And that those chasing me might prefer that if I couldn't be caught, that I should be rendered into very small pieces."

"What are you, a criminal?"

"That would depend on who you ask, Private Gamis," Chenevert said. "Although anyone you might ask that of is now dead."

"The beam weapons," Sherrill asked. "Do they work?"

"They should once the engines are spun up. They are not routed through the engines, of course. But they draw power from them."

"You're thinking we should go after the other ship," Marce said to Sherrill.

"I would if it were my ship," Sherrill said. "But it's not my ship."

Everyone turned to Chenevert.

"Well, this is all very sudden," Chenevert said. "I sleep for three hundred years, wake up to four strangers on my ship and not fifteen minutes later am asked to ride into battle for them. That's a very different situation than just offering temporary hospitality."

"Is that a no?" Sherrill asked.

"It's an 'I'm giving it thought.' " Chenevert turned to Marce. "We have another six hours at least before the engines are spun up, Lord Marce. I suggest we spend it with you getting me up to speed on current events."

"That's a lot," Marce said.

Chenevert nodded. "Just the last three hundred years will do."

Chapter 17

Nadashe had not seen her mother in this much of a state for years. Part of that was Kiva Lagos having turned Tinda Louentintu into a punching bag, although that was less about the well-being of poor Louentintu than it was about Lagos sending the message for the countess to get the fuck off her planet. The countess did get the fuck off the planet and returned to the *Blame* in a fury.

But that was only a small part. The larger part was that Jasin and Deran Wu were coming for a clandestine visit to the *Blame,* to meet Nadashe and to detail to the countess all their plotting in this exciting nascent conspiracy they had going. Nadashe's brain put sarcastic emphasis on the word "exciting" here, because to date, it had been anything but that to her. In point of fact her only role in the current conspiracy to overthrow Grayland II was to be married off.

This rankled Nadashe. She had no problem with being married off when she was a full participant in a scheme; that's how it had worked with Rennered Wu, the crown prince. Nadashe had gone into that one with eyes open and with full consent and active participation. She had wooed Rennered by letting him think he was the one who had been doing the wooing, charmed him and amused him and fucked him and complemented his skills all well enough that Rennered would think the match was something more than a practical political union.

It would have meant that Nadashe had to wear a mask for the rest of her life (well, the rest of Rennered's life, at least) — one that showed what could be thought of as love for the man. Nadashe had been willing to do that, in return for everything she and the House of Nohamapetan would have gotten out of it. And anyway she hadn't *hated* Rennered. He was shallow and had a facile intelligence at best — this was why Amit had liked him so well, since they were cut from the same thin cloth — and he was led by his dick enough that Nadashe had known that it was a thing she would be required to manage, since she wouldn't be able to curtail it entirely. But he was not a horrible person, or cruel. He was appropriately respectful and affectionate and knew the correct times and place for each, and he was tractable. Nadashe could have easily worked with that.

And then one day suddenly he wasn't affectionate and tractable, and he was going to call off the announcement of their engagement. Aside from the massive loss of face Nadashe would endure, which was significant but something she could live with, the House of Nohamapetan would suffer a significant decline in its status. All the other houses had been doing business with the Nohamapetans with the implicit understanding that in a generation, one of its own would be on the throne. With the name Wu, to be sure, but there was no one who thought that once Nadashe was the emperox's wife, the Nohamapetans would not be the ones running the show. Everyone acted accordingly.

But if Nadashe was thrown over, all that went by the wayside. And then the other houses would begin their own frantic competition for the crown. The emperox's marriages were almost always political unions in one way or another.

If there was a little love thrown in there, that was fine; Attavio VI, as an example, was known to have been excessively fond of his consort Glenna Costu, whom he married because the House of Costu had bailed out his mother, the infamous Zetian III, from some ruinous personal investments that would have bankrupted the imperial private accounts. But in an empire that was aggressively dynastical, the only way for a house to move up was to marry into the House of Wu. Every marriage was political. And in the political arena, if Nadashe was tossed to the side, so was the House of Nohamapetan.

In the end the problem solved itself when Rennered rammed his car into a wall during that race, before he could formally announce that he would not be moving forward with his engagement to Nadashe. He was dead and there would be a different emperox, and given what was known of the mousy, indifferent creature that was Cardenia Wu-Patrick, it would be highly unlikely that Nadashe would be the imperial consort. But the House of Nohamapetan was still first in line to marry into the throne.

Nadashe had always been impressed with how well her mother had managed that assassination. It had been flawlessly executed, done so well that even those with suspicions, which would have been the entire Imperial Guard and the Ministry of Investigation, could find nothing suspicious in the wreck.

The countess had not told Nadashe she was going to do it, or how it was going to be done, or when it would happen. The countess had not even been in the system at the time.

Nadashe had been as shocked and horrified as anyone when Rennered died. For five minutes. After that she had wondered how it had been done. She had been smart enough until just the last few days never to outright say to her mother that she knew her mother had done it. The only reason Nadashe had said it at all was that she was meant to be dead herself. It couldn't hurt.

And her mother was all, *Of course I did it. It had to be done.*

The point was, from the moment that Nadashe pointed herself at Rennered Wu to the moment he crumpled into that speedway wall, she had been a full participant in events. She was aiming to be a wife. But *she* was the one doing the aiming.

This time, she was just being offered up.

"Stand straighter," the countess said to her daughter as they stood, waiting for their visitors.

"I am entirely straight," Nadashe said.

"You look like you're slouching."

"Does it actually matter, Mother? I've already been bought and sold, have I not?"

"Yes, you have," the countess said. "But you haven't been taken home yet. You could still be returned. It's happened before. So straighten up."

Nadashe sighed and overextended her back ever so slightly. The countess, satisfied, returned her attention to the door.

Jasin and Deran Wu were about five years apart in age, but looking at the two of them Nadashe would have thought there was a decade or more between them. Jasin, more than a decade older than Nadashe, was heavyset and untoned, with a face the consistency of dough and a haircut that could only be described as brusque. His face showed intelligence but not curiosity. This was a conservative man, Nadashe could see, and not in the useful way of being cautious but practical and deliberate. He simply wanted things done the way he wanted them done, which was the way they had always been done. Nadashe expected in bed he would be a sodden lump.

Deran's hair was great, in a way that was cared for but not overattended. His suit fit well and he fit well into it. His face was intelligent and also engaged; Nadashe watched as his eyes took in the room and the details of it, not neglecting herself and her mother. He had energy in his step. He was also a conservative man, it was clear, but his conservatism had a method and ethos to it beyond "this is just how it's done." Deran, Nadashe was sure, would be happy to be flexible on methods if the results were the same, and what he wanted, which would be the status quo, with him on top. Nadashe expected that in bed Deran would get her off and then get his, making sure always to get his.

And of course I will be stuck with the lump, Nadashe thought.

The countess welcomed both of the men to the room, Deran warmly but perfunctorily, and Jasin with more effusion. It was clear to anyone who looked which of the two the countess had decided was the more important. Deran, for his part, seemed to be amused by this.

"Jasin, this is of course my daughter, Nadashe," the countess said, and Nadashe took her cue to walk up, hand extended. Jasin took it in a very businesslike grip.

"Lady Nadashe," he said. "I am delighted."

"Wonderful to see you, Lord Jasin," Nadashe said.

"I, uh, wanted to apologize to you, Lady Nadashe," Jasin said.

"What for, sir?"

"While you were in prison, one of my associates —"

"Oh, yes. Right. The spoon murderer."

"In retrospect, not the best decision I could have made."

"Lord Jasin, you were acting in what you believed were the best interests of your house," Nadashe said. "As you are doing now. I can honor that sentiment, even as I can say I'm grateful that your associate was not as competent as you might have hoped for at the time."

"Even so, you have my apologies."

"My dear Jasin," Nadashe said, dropping the "lord" to give the appearance of fond familiarity. "If we are to be emperox and consort, then the first things we have to let go of are the trivial matters of the past. There is nothing to apologize for. There is only what we can accomplish moving forward."

"Well, good, then," Jasin said, smiled, and turned his attention back to the Countess Nohamapetan. Nadashe, who had tuned what she said to be warm with just a hint of intimate, was nonplussed by this. All that effort for nothing. She turned to see Deran, a small smirk on his face. He at least had gotten what she had been up to, and how it had failed to be received.

Indeed, as the four of them sat down and began to discuss matters of a conspiratorial nature, it became abundantly clear that Jasin was entirely about business, that being the business of the Countess Nohamapetan's plan, which she laid out in detail. Jasin listened and offered cogent but unremarkable comments and details, and within ten minutes it became clear that for this plan and the organization of it, Nadashe and Deran were surplus to requirements. Every now and again she or Deran would chime in with a comment or idea. That comment or idea was momentarily acknowledged to exist by the countess and Jasin, and then the both of them proceeded with their own planning. After a half hour of this, Nadashe needed a drink.

Deran accompanied her to the bar. "You're feeling as useful as I am right now, I imagine."

" 'Useful' is an interesting way to put it." She poured herself a whiskey.

"Well, I don't know," Deran said, and looked over to the countess and Jasin, both intensely focused on each other. "I think it's nice that the revolution will happen and all we have to do to reap the benefits is show up."

"For as long as it lasts, anyway," Nadashe

said. She pulled out a second tumbler, poured whiskey into it, and handed it to Deran.

"Thank you," he said, and then raised it to her. "Here's to 'for as long as it lasts.' "

"Amen." Nadashe looked at him, took a sip of her drink, and made a snap decision. She turned to her mother. "Deran wants to see the ship," she said. "I'm going to give him a tour."

"Yes, fine," the countess said, and went back to her discussion with Jasin.

Deran turned to Nadashe. "I want to see the ship, do I?"

"Yes you do," Nadashe said. "Some parts of it more than others."

"Thank you, by the way," Nadashe said, after she had gotten off and Deran had made sure to get his, too.

"You're welcome," Deran said. "And thank you too."

"Not for this," Nadashe said.

"Wow. That bad."

"It was definitely not bad," Nadashe assured him. "I meant for making sure I didn't get stabbed with a spoon in prison."

"Oh, *that,*" Deran said. "It was nothing. Your savior is a former member of the house's security detail. Had a divorce, got into some hard stuff to forget, messed up her life pretty badly because of it. Being in prison dried her out and got her back in shape. Honestly the best thing for her. She was happy to take the assignment from me. Made her feel a little like being on the job again."

"She toothbrushed the shit out of that other woman, that's for sure. I'm pretty sure it added a few years to her visit."

"Nah, no extra time. It'll turn out to be self-defense."

"While she was carrying a sharpened dental instrument."

"It's prison. Everyone does it."

"I didn't."

"And you almost got spooned for it."

"Point taken. So why did you offer to help me back there?"

"Because I knew Jasin was planning to have you killed, and I didn't think it was good business for our house to make things worse with your house."

"Is that it?"

"And because I thought doing you a favor would be better business for our house."

"Anything else?"

"And because I was thinking we might need a new emperox soon and the emperox would need a consort. One whose house would be unendingly grateful for a second chance. Plus, you'd already been vetted."

"You've certainly vetted me now."

"I think it was the other way around, actually, but yes."

"Forgive me. I was in prison. It's been a while."

"Believe me, there is nothing to forgive."

"But you're not going to be emperox anymore. You've settled for something less."

"One, the chances I was going to be emperox were slim. Jasin is hidebound and slow, but he has a lot of inertia, and he's just slightly up the food chain from me. We'd fight it out and it would be close, but he's got the reach. Two, 'settling' for total control of the House of Wu is a high settle. It's a pretty decent consolation prize."

"It's too bad," Nadashe said. "I could have gotten used to this."

Deran grinned. "You don't have to give it up, you know."

"Sorry, but that's not the way these things work. I can have my toys, and Jasin, if he wants them, can have his. What we can't have are people who are an actual threat."

"You think I would be a threat."

"I *know* you would be. That's why you're getting the House of Wu. You're going to be so busy running the house and fending off the enraged cousins that you've thrown out of power that you won't even be able to look up from your desk for the next thirty years."

"When you put it that way, it doesn't sound so great."

"That's because it's not. At least not compared to what you could have, which is everything."

Deran was silent for a moment and then sat up in the bed. "I'm not sure why you care," he said. "Jasin is perfect for you. He's ambitious but he has no imagination. You can point him in whatever direction you want and he'll go there and knock down everything in his way. Isn't that what the House of Nohamapetan wants in an emperox?"

"It's what the house wants," Nadashe said. "It's what my *mother* wants. Look how she's locked on to Jasin. She knows a good, maneuverable thing when she sees it."

"And you don't want that?"

Nadashe lifted herself up, placed herself in Deran's lap and locked her legs around him. She put her arms around his neck and started playing with the back of his cared-for but not over-attended hair. "Maybe what I want is someone I don't have to wind up and point in a particular direction. Maybe what I want is someone who appreciates what I have to offer rather than just agreeing to use me for their own plans and benefit. Maybe what I want is someone who will give me children who don't run the risk of being depressingly dull. Maybe what I want is someone who knows how to fuck and will keep me happy doing it."

Deran grinned at this again and Nadashe could feel him stirring under her, which meant he had a tolerably short refractory period, which is a thing she could appreciate, just not right this second, when she was still mid-pitch.

"Maybe, Deran Wu, what I want is someone who will actually be an emperox, and not just a tool for me and my family. Grayland is wrong about a lot, but she's not wrong that everything is changing. We need someone who is up to it. Grayland isn't up to it. And look at Jasin. I'm willing to bet he doesn't actually want to engage with the fact that things are going to be different and chaotic and dangerous for the next decade. I can push him and prod him, but he's limited to how fast and far he'll go. He'll knock down everything in his way, but he won't ever get to where we need him to go. So maybe what I want is someone who will get there, with me helping, not pushing."

" 'Not pushing' doesn't sound very Nohamapetan," Deran said.

"I'm willing to work on it," Nadashe said.

Deran smiled at her, and there was a flash of something actually human there: the smallest bit of uncertainty. "You don't actually know me," he said. "I don't actually know you. You're asking a lot from a complete stranger."

"I'm scheduled to be married to your cousin, who I know even less. And anyway, Deran, let's be clear what's on the table, here. This is a political union. Pure and simple. We know each other well enough to understand that, at least."

"So you 'showed me the ship' to get me to make a deal," Deran said.

"No, I did that because I needed to get laid," Nadashe said. "But I'm not going to lie to you, Deran. You did the tour well enough that offering you a political deal became more interesting."

"I'll take that as a compliment."

"You should," Nadashe said. "But now I need you to tell me if you're taking me up on my offer. If not, thank you for breaking my drought. If yes, then we need to get to work."

"Undermining your mother and my cousin."

"No," Nadashe said. "I want them to keep doing everything they're doing."

Chapter 18

Just before the *Auvergne* slipped behind Dalasýsla Prime, Marce received an encrypted text message from Hatide Roynold.

> Ship coming for us definitely not friendly, *it said.* We launched a drone to the Flow shoal; it was blasted down. The crew is at stations and the rest of us are on lockdown. Looks like we're running and fighting this one out. Pretty sure Captain Laure doesn't think this one is looking good. Someone has to have sent them, whoever they are.
>
> Laure is letting me send this one message to you. Says that if things get bad, she'll dump all the data we have for the mission in a powered-down drone and put a delayed transponder on it for you to find. It includes some new work from me you'll find interesting. Says that the request for a ship for the Dalasýslans

was already sent. If it was, you'll just have to tough it out for a couple of weeks before it arrives. Breathe only when necessary.

I'm not going to lie. Kind of wish I stayed home. Or actually went on this last away mission with you. This is what a lifetime of introversion gets me.

But thanks anyway. You didn't have to listen to me when I came to you. You did. You believed me and made me a friend. I liked that about you.

— H

By the time the *Auvergne* came out of the planet's shadow, the *Bransid* was an expanding cloud of debris.

"Here's that ship," Hanton said. He pointed on the *Auvergne*'s command screen to a dot, moving toward the Flow Shoal back to Hub.

"We're sure that's it," Sherrill asked.

"We're sure. It's the only thing in this part of the system that's moving that fast that's not in an orbit around Dalasýsla Prime." He pointed to another dot on the screen. "Here's the Flow shoal back to Hub. "At its current speed it's going to take twenty hours to get there. It's not accelerating at the moment, which is interesting."

"Why is that interesting?" Marce asked.

"It means they're not using their engines right now," Sherrill said. "Constant engine use would mean constant acceleration. Instead they're just using inertia to coast."

"Their engines could be damaged," Marce said.

"Could be."

"Or they just aren't in a *rush,*" Gamis said.

"Maybe," Sherrill said. "But we accelerated into the shoal on the way here. I know that was the captain's plan on the way back. These Flow shoals are on a clock" — she looked over at Marce — "and your predictions on how long they could be open could be wrong. No offense."

"None taken," Marce said.

"Captain Laure didn't want to stay here a minute longer than she had to. We would have accelerated all the way back, as fast as we could." Sherrill pointed to the dot, representing the ship. "If these people aren't stupid, they would be doing the same thing. So there's a reason they're not."

"It's a lot to suppose on," Gamis said.

"But it's not a bad supposition," Marce said. "If the engines are damaged, then the *Bransid* got some hits in. They're limping home."

"But they *are* still planning to go home," Hanton said. "Which means their field generator is still functional."

"As long as their engines don't give out," Sherrill said. "In which case they won't have power for the field generator."

"Monsieur Chenevert," Marce said, turning to the apparition.

Who smiled. "I was wondering when you would remember I was here, Lord Marce."

"Can we overtake this ship?"

"Their path takes them past Dalasýsla Prime. If we stay where we are, we'll be behind the planet when that happens. But of course there's no reason we have to stay where we are now. The *Auvergne*'s engines and power systems are fully functional at this point." Chenevert nodded toward the command screen, which blanked out, surprising Hanton, and then reappeared with a new image, charting an intercept course.

"If they don't accelerate, we can intercept them in ten hours," Chenevert said. "If they do accelerate, that changes things, but if their specs are similar to what you've given me for the *Bransid,* then we intercept them in eighteen hours at the latest. Well before they reach the Flow shoal."

"And then we blast the shit out of them,"

Gamis said. "Do what they did to the *Bransid.*"

Chenevert looked over to Marce. "Is that your intention, Lord Marce?"

"No," Marce said.

"What?" Gamis was pissed at this. "These fuckers just killed our crew, sir. Returning the favor seems just about *fair.*"

Marce shook his head. "Dead isn't useful."

"I don't understand."

Marce looked over to Chenevert. "But you do, I hope."

"I think I do, Lord Marce," Chenevert said.

"Can it be managed?"

"It depends on what shape their ship is in and what I can figure out about it from my scans and visualizations. I have to warn you that means we'll have to get close."

"Define 'close.' "

"You won't like it if I do."

"I think they know we're here," Hanton said as the ship launched a pair of missiles at the *Auvergne* a thousand klicks out.

Sherrill looked at the visualization of the missiles from the *Auvergne*'s sensors as they streaked toward them. "Those look like beehives," she said. "They've got multiple warheads in them. They'll break open just before they hit."

"That's rude," Chenevert said, and waited for the missiles to get within a hundred klicks before lancing them with his beam weapons. They vaporized soundlessly in the void.

"Your beams are coherent a hundred klicks out," Hanton said.

"That's what I want this other ship to believe, yes," he said. "I don't expect that our friends in that ship launched those missiles with the belief that they were going to hit us with them. They wanted to know how and when we would respond. And now they think they know."

"You've done this before."

"I told you that I've had practice being chased."

"How far out are they actually effective?" Marce asked.

"Not this far," Chenevert said. He popped up a visualization of the ship they were pursuing on the command screen. From slightly less than a thousand kilometers away, the ship was a mostly indistinct wedge. The *Auvergne* was coming at it from an above angle, relative to Dalasýsla system's ecliptic plane. *Death from above,* thought Marce.

"Any thoughts on this ship?" Chenevert asked.

"It looks like a Farthing-class ship," Sherrill said, after a minute.

"I'm afraid that means nothing to me," Chenevert said.

"It's an interceptor ship," Sherrill said. "Small crew, fast, relatively heavily armed. It's designed to engage pirate and smuggler ships. And by 'engage' I mean destroy."

"So there's no doubt what it was here to do," Marce said.

"I think we already have the answer to that. Funny thing, when these ships are decommissioned, a lot of them get bought by pirate sorts. I think the reasoning there is they can outrun or fight the navy ships sent after them."

"Does that work?" Chenevert asked.

"The navy just sends bigger ships."

"More missiles," Hanton said.

This time the beehives launched their payloads early and one of the smaller missiles got within ten clicks of the *Auvergne* before Chenevert destroyed it.

"You're still toying with them, right?" Gamis asked.

"If it makes you more comfortable if I say yes, then yes," Chenevert said.

"It doesn't when you put it like that."

"I'm sorry."

When the *Auvergne* was two hundred klicks out the ship hit them with its own particle beams. They were on the *Auvergne* for a full tenth of a second before they were gone, and small puffs of debris were visible coming off the attacking ship.

"Oh, *nice,*" said Gamis.

"What just happened?" Marce asked Chenevert.

"I was waiting for the ship to open fire to confirm which features on the ship were the beam weapons. Once I knew, I took them out. And then also took out every other feature on the visible portion of the ship that resembled the beam weapons. Just to be safe."

"More missiles," Hanton said, pointing at the command screen.

"Mind you, that doesn't get rid of every defense they have," Chenevert said. "Excuse me for a moment."

Fifty klicks out and small details of the ship were clear to Marce and the rest of the crew on the command screen.

"Are we close enough?" Marce asked.

"Almost," Chenevert said.

Forty klicks.

"Anytime," Marce said.

"Getting there."

Thirty klicks, and the ship was visibly growing in the command screen without magnification.

"I'm getting a little nervous," Marce said.

"Soon," Chenevert said.

"Missiles," Hanton said.

"That was nervy," Chenevert said, a second later. There was a tinkling sound as the debris of one of the missiles collided with the *Auvergne.*

Ten klicks.

"Now," Chenevert said, and fired his beam, not at the engine itself, but at a small area up and to the right of it on the hull. The beam bored a hole into the hull, and lanced at the inside of the ship. Air and steam and a small amount of debris vomited out. Marce heard a thrumming inside *Auvergne,* a sign of adjustments being made so the *Auvergne* would be stationary relative to the other ship and not ram into it, destroying them both.

"That's it?" Gamis asked.

"That's enough," Chenevert said, and turned to Marce. "I needed to get close enough to get an idea of how energy routed through the ship," he said. "We assumed the engine was already damaged, so I didn't want to risk that. I sent the beam through what looked like a central energy exchange route. My guess is that it stops functioning, and the engines and power systems shut down to avoid an explosion, until it's repaired."

"How long until it's repaired?" Marce asked.

"Well, I destroyed it, so, never. At this point I assume they are running ship systems on their emergency power setup."

"That's enough to keep them alive for now, but not enough to run their field generator," Sherrill said. "If they go through the Flow shoal without a space-time bubble they're screwed."

"They're still on a glide path into the Flow shoal," Hanton said. "They'll hit it in nine hours, fifteen minutes."

"What do we do now?" Gamis said.

"Have a protein bar and wait for their call," Marce said.

The call came four hours ahead of the shoal.

"Unidentified ship, this is *The Princess Is in Another Castle,*" the voice said, over the radio connection. Hanton had given Chenevert the frequencies that were most likely to be used for communication, and Chenevert had set the *Auvergne* the task of cycling through them until something came through. "Captain Cav Ponsood speaking.

Please respond."

"Hello, *Princess,*" Marce said. "This is the *Auvergne.* Lord Marce Claremont here."

There was a long pause. "You said Lord Marce Claremont."

"That's right."

There was an even longer pause this time.

"What the hell?" Gamis said.

"Lord Marce, you have disabled our ship and we are adrift," Ponsood said when he returned. "We are without main power, and our emergency power is drawing down."

"Acknowledged," Marce said. "Also, your current path takes you directly into the Flow shoal in" — he looked at the command screen, where Chenevert had helpfully set a timer — "three hours, fifty-two minutes. Please be advised that if you enter the shoal in your present condition, without your field generator, you will be instantly rendered into nothingness."

"Uh, yes," Ponsood said. "We are aware of that information, and thank you for that."

"You're welcome."

"Lord Marce, it has come to our attention that despite disabling our ship, you have not elected to destroy us."

"That is correct, Captain Ponsood."

"We are wondering what your intentions are now, Lord Marce."

"Well, Captain, the answer to that rests entirely on you."

"Please explain."

"Why did you destroy the *Oliveer Bransid*?"

"We were hired to."

"Who hired you?"

"I don't know. We were hired by intermediaries who wouldn't tell me the identity of the primary contractor. I, uh, work in a very specialized contracted business field. I don't always know who is hiring me."

"Thank you, Captain Ponsood. Enjoy oblivion." Marce looked over to Chenevert, who nodded.

"The circuit is muted on this end," he said.

"You think he's lying about who contracted him," Sherrill said.

Marce nodded. "We'll find out soon enough."

Five minutes later Ponsood was back on the circuit, asking for Marce. Marce nodded to Chenevert, who opened up the circuit. "Yes?"

"Lord Marce, we were hired by an intermediary. A representative of the Wu family."

Marce frowned at this. "You were hired by the imperial family?"

"No, not by the royal family. By the Wus

that run the merchant house. Cousins of the emperox."

"Who were the Wus acting as an intermediary for?"

"I asked that of the representative. I've done business with the Wus before — it's why they contacted me in the first place — but never with them as the intermediary. They were always the primary client. Their representative didn't want to say, but I told him there was no way I would take the job without knowing. The job was time-sensitive and the Wus didn't really have any other option, so the rep swore me to secrecy and told me: the Countess Nohamapetan."

"How did the Nohamapetans know about the *Bransid* in the first place?"

"She heard about it from the Wus. The Wus heard it from an admiral, is what I was told. The navy is obviously close with the Wus. They get all their weapons and ships from them."

"That doesn't make sense. The Wus aren't close with the Nohamapetans."

"I don't know the relationships of the great families, Lord Marce. I don't have time to keep up with gossip. You asked who contracted me, and I'm telling you."

"Okay, but why would the Countess Nohamapetan want to attack the *Bransid*?"

"She didn't," Ponsood said, and an exasperated Marce was about to mute the line again, but Ponsood continued from there. "She didn't care about the ship one way or the other. It was a means to an end for her actual target."

"Who or what was that?"

There was a pause on the line. Then, "It was you, Lord Marce. The Countess Nohamapetan wanted you dead bad enough to send us to attack the *Bransid* to get to you."

Marce stared in disbelief. He looked around the bridge of the *Auvergne* to see every other set of eyes on him.

"Hello?" Ponsood said. Marce had been silent for nearly a full minute.

"Why?" Marce asked.

"I wasn't told that. Just that we were to make sure you were dead. I asked if that meant I could leave the *Bransid* crew alive if they surrendered you, and I was told that the *Bransid* could not be allowed to return to Hub, and I had a choice of destroying it, or destroying its field generator. That would have meant marooning the crew here to a slow death by starvation or suffocation. I opted for the faster way. It seemed more humane to me. You should know, Lord Marce, that the *Bransid* put up a hell of a fight. You wouldn't have captured us without the damage they did to us first."

"And the Dalasýslans?"

"The who, Lord Marce?"

"The people who inhabit this system, Captain."

"I don't know who you're talking about, sir. I was focused on the *Bransid,* which was keeping me busy enough. Are you saying that there are still people *alive* here? After eight hundred years?"

"Yes."

"It's just as well I didn't know about them. It wouldn't have done to leave anyone who could attest to what we did here."

"Except for the one person you came specifically to kill."

"The irony of this does not escape me, Lord Marce. I'm telling you because I have no other choice. Neither I nor my crew wants to die here, or like this."

"You're asking me to give you an option that you wouldn't give to the crew of the *Bransid.*"

"Lord Marce, if I didn't believe you would entertain the option, I wouldn't have opened my mouth."

"Hold on," Marce said, and looked at Chenevert, who nodded and muted the connection. Marce sat down heavily in a chair, put his face in his hands, and sobbed.

"It's —" Hanton began, but Marce held up a hand at him. Hanton stopped and looked uncomfortable. It was a common look around the room.

After a minute Marce nodded to Chenevert, who opened the connection again. "You're going to testify about all of this, Captain Ponsood."

"If that is what it takes to keep my crew alive, Lord Marce, I'll repeat everything I told you to any judge you pick."

"You're not going to tell it to a judge, Captain. You're going to tell it to the emperox. To her face. And I will be there as you do it."

There was a long silence. Then, "Understood, Lord Marce. With that said, I officially surrender the *Princess* to you. You are in command now."

Marce nodded, then realized that Ponsood would not be able to see that over an audio connection. "Thank you, Captain. My associate Mr. Chenevert will be discussing with you soon all the details of transferring yourselves over to the *Auvergne.* Be ready."

"I will. The sooner, the better."

"Understood." Marce nodded to Chenevert. "You can handle that?"

"I'm already talking to Captain Ponsood about it."

Marce was momentarily confused about this until he remembered that Chenevert was a virtual being. He supposed a virtual being could make as many versions of himself as he wanted. He nodded his understanding.

"Is there anything specific we want brought over from the *Princess*?" Chenevert asked. "Aside from the crew, of which I am informed there are seven."

"Small crew," Sherrill said.

"Ours is smaller."

"I want as many of their ship's records as possible," Marce said. "Plus any evidence Ponsood has for contracting with the Wus."

"I'm guessing this was a cash enterprise," Gamis said.

"It probably was, but I still want as much evidence as I can get."

"We need as much food as they can bring over," Gamis said to Chenevert. "Everything they have. I'm already sick of protein bars."

"Is there any way we can salvage that ship?" Marce said. "The Dalasýslans could probably scavenge everything from that."

"Captain Ponsood tells me the *Princess* has a small shuttle, which they will use to transport themselves and food over," Chenevert said. "Depending how much time we take bringing things over, and whether it's remotely pilotable, I can probably use it to nudge the *Princess* out of the path of the Flow shoal. Note it will likely damage both the shuttle and the *Princess.*"

"Better than nothing."

"Quite literally in this case," Chenevert agreed. "If after that time the shuttle is not too damaged, then I will see if I can program it to push the *Princess* along to the Dalasýslans. Then they can salvage both ships."

"I want to leave them the *Bransid* shuttle as well," Marce said. "No place for it here anyway. I don't want to leave it parked over Dalasýsla Prime."

"We have to go back and get Seve and Lyton," Sherrill said. "We can't leave them here."

"I can program our shuttle to fly itself to the Dalasýslans' ship," Hanton said. "Then pick up Seve and Lyton and the data from the *Bransid,* and back through the shoal to Hub."

"If the Wus knew where the *Bransid* was, then they know there's a possibility of it coming back," Sherrill said. "The *Bransid* could have fought off the *Princess.*"

"So you think they'll have someone waiting for us on the other end of the shoal," Marce said.

"I would," Sherrill said. "If I were them."

"We're not going to be in the *Bransid,*" Gamis said.

"No, but we'll be coming through the Flow shoal from Dalasýsla," Sherrill said. "If I were them I'd be blasting anything that came through that, including the *Princess.* The fewer witnesses the better."

Marce thought about that and turned to Chenevert. "Ask Captain Ponsood if he has any message drones."

"He does," Chenevert said a moment later. "He says they intended to send one after the *Bransid* was destroyed but forgot because they were too busy trying to get the ship to the Flow shoal and then fighting us off."

"Tell him to send one confirming my death and the destruction of the *Bransid,* and then say they are going to stay behind for a month to salvage the habitats. Give a specific date they plan to leave this space." Marce looked over to Sherrill. "If the Wus are planning to have someone blast them, they'll reschedule to match dates."

"Sneaky," Sherrill said.

"I don't want to be blasted to bits." He turned back to Chenevert. "And you finally will be able to visit the Interdependency."

"Wait, you want to use this ship to get back to the Interdependency?" Chenevert said. “I can’t do that. I don’t have a field generator.”

They all stared at him.

“I’m joking,” he said. “Of course I do.”

“We need to talk about your sense of humor,” Marce said, after he and every other human in the room recovered from their mini heart attacks. “Being semi-dead seems to have affected it.”

“It was like this before,” Chenevert said. “How do you think I died?”

Book Three

CHAPTER 19

Shortly before the *Bransid* was scheduled to return into Interdependency space, an appointment the ship and its crew would miss, two more Flow streams disappeared.

The first was the stream from Marlowe to Kealakekua. The two systems were lightly inhabited and direct trade between them was infrequent, as their direct Flow stream took a month to traverse, while routing through Beylagan cut ten days off the journey. It was a reminder that the time in a Flow stream was not necessarily related to the distance between two systems, and also the intricacies of the Flow were something only a few people understood to any extent.

As a consequence of this, the Flow stream between Marlowe and Kealakekua was only infrequently used for legitimate shipping and travel. It had instead become a favorite of smugglers, pirates and others who didn't mind taking a little extra time if it meant avoiding navy interceptors and local customs enforcement. When the Flow stream disappeared, no legitimate commerce or transportation was listed as lost. The eight ships and one thousand people who were lost were all on private, unlisted or illegal transports. There was no paperwork for their itineraries, no bills of lading and no record of their comings and goings. They were, simply, gone. Their customers, clients and loved ones would never know what had become of them, because they would not necessarily have known they had taken that route at all.

The second stream was not so obscure. It connected the systems of Guelph and Szeged, both systems considered part of the population and economic "core" of the Interdependency. Due to the nature of the Flow, the Count Claremont's work on its collapse and the estimated schedule of Flow disruptions had yet to make it to Guelph, and the commerce and travel between the two systems was in full flower when the Flow stream collapsed, unannounced and, to the people of Guelph, unpredicted.

The impact was immense. Tens of thousands of people disappeared, including two passenger ships, the *Allure of the Stars* and the *Oasis of the Stars,* which between them carried ten thousand souls. More than a billion marks of commerce evaporated. The journey from Guelph to Szegred, previously seven days and eight hours, would now be more than a month through alternate routes.

The return route from Szegred to Guelph remained open, but Szegred stopped all traffic outbound for fear of a similar collapse. Guelph stopped all its commercial traffic to its three other exiting Flow shoals until an explanation could be found. The explanation would arrive from Hub more than a month and billions of marks of lost commerce later. It was a wound on the cultural soul of Guelph that would never fully heal.

Along with the disappearance of these two Flow streams, the phenomenon of evanescence, sketched out to Grayland by Marce and Roynold, was having its effect as well, tearing open a Flow stream between Oecusse and Artibonite that lasted, unnoticed, a week before disappearing in as unheralded a fashion as it arrived. It was just as well that no enterprising ship had tried to enter its temporary shoal, as the transit time between the two systems would have been along the order of five weeks, longer than the stream itself would exist.

A stream of even shorter duration, between End and Neunkirchen, existed for fifteen minutes; a corresponding return stream would open up seven minutes later and disappear twenty minutes afterward. Like the stream between Oecusse and Artibonite, it would go unnoticed in either system. But briefly End, traditionally the most isolated system in the Interdependency, and recently even more isolated than usual, had a back door in and out of it. That no one knew it, or could have used it, didn't change the fact that it had been there.

In the Memory Room, Cardenia called up Rachela I, the first prophet-emperox, who stood before her, silent, waiting for her to ask something.

"Did you ever have doubts?" Cardenia asked.

"About what?" Rachela I said.

Cardenia laughed. Because of course that was the most Rachela answer possible. Cardenia had summoned up the memory of the first emperox numerous times now, to discuss the nature of visions, and how to sell them and how to make them stick, if not to the members of the nobility, then to the masses, to whom they were pitched in the first place. In all the time Cardenia had been talking to her great-great-great-ancestress, Rachela had never once projected (figuratively and literally, as her image was projected from clever lighting in the Memory Room's ceiling) anything other than serene confidence.

Some of that was probably because Cardenia's Rachela was not the real Rachela, just a bundle of memories and emotions animated by a heuristic-oriented AI that could tell you what Rachela was feeling at a particular moment in time, but couldn't feel that emotion itself. Or any of the emotions of any of eighty-seven previous emperoxs, including her father. Cardenia was aware that technically speaking, none of these emperoxs existed and she was merely talking to Jiyi, the Memory Room's avatar, who put on the former emperoxs like she might put on a new shirt. But when Rachela I or Attavio VI was standing in front of you, it was easy to forget you weren't speaking to the actual person.

But computer simulation or not, lack of actual emotion or not, it was still the case that at least some of the residue of every emperox's personality came through in conversation. Emperoxs who had been neurotic talked and answered questions like a neurotic person. The blustery, stupid ones gave blustery and stupid answers. The creepy ones — and there were a few — were made even creepier by the lack of overt emotion.

Rachela I's affect wasn't creepy, or blustery or neurotic. She was just . . . Rachela. Confident. A sort of confidence Grayland was getting good at pretending at, but still working on actually feeling.

Grayland considered Rachela I's question. "All right, did you ever have doubts about *anything*?"

"Of course. Only a sociopath lacks doubt, and I wasn't a sociopath when I was alive."

"Are you now?"

"If you brought a psychiatrist in here and had them give me an evaluation, I would probably come across as a sociopath. I currently fundamentally lack empathy, although I *can* pretend to it. Which may be a textbook definition of sociopathy. I don't have any doubts now, certainly."

"But you did when you were alive."

"Yes, many. Ranging from very small and trivial doubts about people, things, and incidents, to larger, existential doubts, for example, about whether we would be able to pull off founding the Interdependency."

"Why did you have doubts?"

"Leaving aside any of my own personality

quirks, because it made sense to have doubts. It made sense to worry that our plans were not complete and that there were contingencies we had not thought of, that I had not thought of, that would come back and affect how events would play out."

"And did they? Did your doubts come true?"

"Sometimes they did."

"How did you deal with that?"

"We made new plans as well as we could and put them into effect."

"You improvised."

"Yes. The one advantage we had, which is a thing I brought to the enterprise, was the understanding that the plan was not the goal. The goal was the goal, and we were going to get to it however we could. And if it meant changing our plans, sometimes in the middle of executing them, then we would."

"You sound proud of it," Cardenia observed.

"I was."

"I mean, you sound proud of it now. You, the simulation."

"I'm not, but Rachela was. And it makes sense to reflect that pride to you. It's why I became emperox. I was always meant to be emperox, I should clarify — the Wu family always knew they needed a front person who could balance both the state and church roles. A useful figurehead for both. But I was more than a figurehead because I was the one reminding the others, constantly, that the plan was not the goal. We succeeded because of it."

"Did you doubt that your prophecies would work?"

"Sometimes. Something we worked out between ourselves would go out in the world and fall flat, and I would have to spin it and sometimes abandon it altogether. I've told you before that the prophecies were aspirational, not predictive. It's only after we worked to make them come true that they had the appearance of inevitability. And we worked very hard on that."

"Making prophecies, and getting them across successfully, is much harder work than what I expected," Cardenia admitted.

"It's very hard work," Rachel agreed. "I retired them as soon as it was practically possible. I know no other emperox before you bothered to have any, because it made no sense to have them. They were already emperox, so much of the hard work of establishing a rule was already done. All they had to do was maintain that rule. We set it up so that would be easy to do through the tools of the state."

"So you're saying I shouldn't have bothered with prophecies."

"I didn't say that."

"Because you're not actually a human and have no interest in it outside of what I tell you."

"There is that. And also, your reign is unlike the reign of any of your predecessors, including mine. I worked hard to form the Interdependency, but I wasn't the emperox then. When I became the emperox, in most ways, my crisis — the formation of the Interdependency — was over. The House of Wu had succeeded. Your crisis is the dissolution of the Interdependency. You must prepare the systems of humanity to be alone. You have the tools of the state to do it, but the tools of the state will almost certainly not be enough. So now you must use the tools of the church as well. Which is why they were there for you. I put them there for you to use. Not you specifically. But any emperox who found themselves in this position."

Cardenia's eyes narrowed at this. "You anticipated the collapse of the Flow."

"No," Rachela I said. "I never really understood the Flow. It always looked like a lot of math, and I had people for that. But I did anticipate that there might be a time where an emperox might need more options than just being the emperox. That they might have to take on the mantle of prophet as well. You are the second prophet-emperox."

Cardenia recoiled. "Oh, I don't call myself that."

"I don't see why not."

"It's a little . . . arrogant. And also I don't think it's a title I can give myself. I think others have to use it first."

"From a marketing point of view I can tell you that you're wrong. If you want people to use the title, you should start using it yourself. Or at least start seeding it out there through your propagandists."

"We call them the Press Ministry now."

"Whatever. Have them start spreading it around. It will help more than you think it will."

"I have doubts," Cardenia said.

"I did marketing. I know."

"No," Cardenia said. "Not about that. I mean larger doubts. About everything."

"Of course you do. You're human."

"I'm glad you noticed."

"I can tell you are hoping for some wisdom from me right now."

"It ruins it a little when you put it like

that, just so you know."

"I will remember to approach it more organically the next time."

"Thank you."

"Would you like the wisdom anyway?"

"Yes," Cardenia said. "Yes I would."

"It's this: Confidence isn't about knowing you're right. Confidence is about knowing you can make it right. You have doubts because it makes sense for you to have doubts. Just like it made sense for me to have doubts. But remember the plan is not the goal. What is your goal?"

"To save as many lives as possible, through every means possible."

"Be confident in that, and everything else will follow."

"Thank you," Cardenia said, after a minute. "What you said about confidence makes sense to me."

"You're welcome," Rachela I said. "I read it in a book once."

Cardenia emerged from the Memory Room to find Obelees Atek waiting for her. Atek had a mildly apprehensive look on her face, in part because she was always uncomfortable coming into the emperox's private apartments, which she felt was an invasion of personal space, and in part because she didn't know what the Memory Room was and it disturbed her. Cardenia had explained to her that it was a relaxation chamber of sorts, which was occasionally accurate, but she didn't think that made Atek's apprehension any less acute.

Cardenia smiled at her assistant, took a breath, and became Grayland II again.

"Is my next appointment here?" Grayland asked.

"She is, ma'am, waiting for you in your office." Atek motioned with her hand for the emperox to lead the way.

In her office Lady Kiva Lagos waited, leaned way back in a chair, looking up at the ceiling, kicking one foot casually as she did so. Grayland was amused by this. Most visitors were overwhelmed by the office and its centuries of priceless cruft, but Kiva gave every impression of, *Yeah, you have a lot of shit in this place, so fucking what.* Which Grayland could definitely sympathize with.

Atek discreetly coughed. Grayland saw Kiva look over, see Atek giving her the *get the hell up* signal, and haul herself out of her chair for a bow.

"Lady Kiva, good to see you again," Grayland said, and excused Atek from the room. "Sit back down, please."

"I was staring at your ceiling, Your Majesty," Kiva said, sitting back down. "I don't think I've ever seen so much gold foil in one place."

"It's a lot, yes."

"One of the perks of being emperox."

"I suppose it is. I honestly don't think about it much. I rarely look up at the ceiling these days."

"Give it a try sometime, ma'am. It's pretty impressive."

"How is your friend doing? I'm sorry, her name escapes me at the moment."

"Senia Fundapellonan."

"It's a lot to remember."

"I told her the same thing when I first met her. She is doing much better, thank you, ma'am. And thank you again for sheltering her at Brighton Palace. It makes her feel a lot safer."

"Of course. And how are you? I know your friend was injured, but the bullet went through your window."

"I've replaced the window with something a little more bulletproof," Kiva said. "But other than that I'm still at my place. If someone wants to come find me, they know where I am."

"I don't know whether that's brave or foolish, Lady Kiva."

"It's definitely foolish, ma'am. But if

someone is going to make that much of an effort, then it doesn't matter where I sleep. So I might as well sleep at home. Besides, I have a good idea who did it. I've expressed my displeasure."

"I hear rumors that the same night your friend was shot, Countess Nohamapetan's chief of staff was assaulted in her bed."

"I wouldn't know anything about that, ma'am."

"No, I suppose you wouldn't." Grayland nodded over to Kiva's hand, which was bandaged. "What happened to your hand, Lady Kiva?"

"This?" Kiva held up her hand. "I broke it against something stupid."

"Was it worth it?"

"Absolutely, ma'am."

"Well, good. Keep it up."

"I have every intention of doing that. And on that note . . ." Kiva reached over, grabbed a pile of documents that were set to the side of her chair, and dropped them on the emperox's desk. "Let's talk about just what I've got on the fucking Nohamapetans."

Grayland raised an eyebrow at this.

"Oh, shit, I just swore out loud, didn't I?" Kiva said.

Grayland laughed.

"Sorry," Kiva said. "I've been trying to be on my best behavior, Your Majesty."

"I'd rather you just be you, Lady Kiva."

"Let's hope you don't regret saying that, ma'am."

"I'm pretty sure I won't. Especially after you show me what you have here."

"If you don't mind me asking, what do you plan to do with it?"

"The information? Nothing yet." Grayland caught Kiva's expression. "But I promise you, Lady Kiva, none of your work here is going to be in vain. I'll make use of it. Effectively."

"Then let's get into this," Kiva said, and pulled out the sheet. "And let's begin with these."

"What are they?"

"Nadashe Nohamapetan's secret bank accounts. As in, the ones she never expected anyone ever to find. They are very interesting."

"How so?"

"Because as of twelve hours ago, Your Majesty, someone was moving money around in them."

Chapter 20

"Are we ready for this?" Gennety Hanton asked as he looked around the bridge of the *Auvergne.* The ship was about exit the Flow shoal to Hub.

If there was to be any ambush it would be the moment the ship translated into regular space-time. Ships had no momentum coming out of the Flow; the *Auvergne* would be sitting in space, a motionless target for any missiles, beam weapons or harsh language thrown its way. Marce's plan to send a drone with dummy information had been followed, but whether it was successful was another story entirely. The ad hoc crew of the *Auvergne* was about to find out.

"I have my beam array on and ready to fire on anything that moves," Chenevert said.

Hanton nodded at this. "I'll be looking for incoming trouble over here."

"Thank you, Dr. Hanton," Chenevert

replied. “Be on a particular lookout for missiles.”

Marce thought that was a kind choice on Chenevert’s part. Chenevert was a computer and effectively the ship itself. He needed a human to inform him of incoming objects about as much as a parent working on a project needs a toddler to hand over tools. But Chenevert understood that Hanton needed to do something with himself in the moment and was happy to oblige him.

It made Marce wonder again who and what Chenevert had been in his non-computer, non–sentient ship days. In his conversations with Chenevert during the eight-day return trip, the virtual human had been garrulously vague on the subject, preferring to redirect Marce into discussions of the Interdependency instead. It was a subject Chenevert found endlessly fascinating, and to be fair, inasmuch as he and his ragtag company had basically dragooned Chenevert and the *Auvergne,* Marce thought it was only fair to get his virtual friend as much up to speed as he could.

What little Marce could get out of Chenevert in terms of this own personal specifics was that he’d been very wealthy, although whether from his own efforts or through family money was left unspecified; that one day he and a couple hundred of his closest friends decided to take a pleasure cruise on the *Auvergne,* along with a substantial percentage of each of their personal fortunes and possessions; and on that day they suddenly found themselves obliged to depart from Chenevert's home world in something of a rush, via the Flow, and eventually found themselves in Dalasýslan space, unable to return.

"You were refugees," Marce had suggested.

"We preferred to think of ourselves as temporary expatriates," Chenevert said. "We had every intention of returning one day, but then physics happened."

"The Flow stream you used to get to Dalasýsla collapsed."

"Yes." Chenevert frowned at this, and Marce was reminded again at how good the simulation of him being an actual human was. "We could have used having you around then, Lord Marce. You seem to understand all of this better than anyone else I've known."

"There was someone else who knew it as well as I do," Marce said.

"Of course. I'm very sorry about your friend Dr. Roynold, Lord Marce. I know you grieve for her. And for the entire lost crew of the *Bransid.*"

Marce nodded. "And you, Monsieur Chenevert? Do you miss the people who came with you on your journey?"

"Yes, certainly, although it was so long ago now."

"Not that long ago for you. You said you slept through the last three hundred years."

"Mostly slept, yes. A tiny bit of my brain woke up every now and again to check on the ship and keep it running. It's the virtual person equivalent of waking up briefly to scratch your nose when you have an itch, and then falling right back to sleep."

"Still."

"Yes. Well, the thing was, Lord Marce, when I left my fellow shipmates they had abandoned me. In the best way, because they had found a way to revivify Dalasýsla, and to invite the few remaining natives of the system to come live with them. They left me because they had a better place to be, and for that reason I was happy to see them go."

"How were they able to do that? Get Dalasýsla running again? It had been dead for centuries by that time."

Chenevert shook his head. "Not dead, Lord Marce. Dormant. Whatever collapse befell the habitat, the problem was not in its physical plant. Oh, the habitat had been damaged, and it had been scavenged, by the time we got to it. When I say my people got Dalasýsla running again, you should understand it was on a limited basis, relative to what it was before. But there was enough there that it could easily house my crew and the thousand or so Dalasýslans that still existed, spread across smaller habitats and ships."

"It's amazing that there were any at all for you to find. For people to survive that long isolation."

"Yes, remarkable. But also depressing, isn't it, Lord Marce? There were once millions of Dalasýslans, living rich and comfortable lives, and that number was winnowed down to a mere few hanging on by the proverbial fingernails. Not because they were cut off from the rest of the universe but because in the first few critical years after being cut off, they lost their collective minds. Or enough of them did that the others had to spend precious time dealing with them, and not the larger situation."

"People can be a problem," Marce acknowledged. "But your people didn't seem to have those issues."

"Not at first, at least," Chenevert said. "But then you told me that Dalasýsla was only made functional again for a few short decades. Whatever chaos visited the original Dalasýslans also seems to have visited them."

"You were asleep by then?"

"Yes. I was awake long enough to see them get the habitat up and running again, and then I put myself to sleep."

"When did you" — Marce motioned to Chenevert — "make the transition?"

"Almost as soon as we arrived," Chenevert said. "I was already dying when we left, Lord Marce. I used to like to joke that I was like Moses. I took my people out of Egypt and showed them the promised land, but wasn't able to go there myself. I was told I was being melodramatic, which was entirely correct. I like a bit of melodrama now and then. And also, I wasn't too worried about it. I knew when my body died, I had this to look forward to. It made death rather less traumatic."

"It's amazing."

"It's very old tech," Chenevert said. "Some improvements have been made to it, but it's basically a centuries-old design. Given your reaction I don't assume anything like it is very common in the Interdependency."

"Not at all."

"Well, it is also very expensive and fussy. You have to really want it. I did, and took it with me, and integrated it into the ship."

"Do you like being a ship?"

"It's mostly very pleasant," Chenevert said. "I miss certain physical things, like eating and sex. Sometimes I debate myself which I miss more. At the moment eating has the edge. But I like still being alive most of all."

"And yet you put yourself to sleep."

"Well, that was a practical decision. I was operating on the idea that one day the Flow streams that had trapped us at Dalasýsla might reopen, and whoever of my crew was left might want to go back to see if the situation had improved. Alternately that others might come, and if they weren't friendly for whatever reason, it would be useful to have a ship with weapons nearby. I had thought this might be in the twenty- or thirty-year window, rather than three hundred years."

"You could have woken yourself up."

"I enjoyed sleeping. I never did enough of it when I was human. I think I'm almost caught up now."

"The Dalasýslans — the ones now — remember you and your crew telling them that others would come. It's one reason they didn't seem all that surprised when we arrived. It was almost like prophecy for them."

"I don't know that we tried to make it sound like that," Chenevert said. "I think we had just made the point that more people might come if the Flow stream ever opened up again. Time has a funny way of distorting things, Lord Marce. But then, you did also arrive just as they needed you. And you bought them a considerable amount of time with your gifts."

"A wrecked spaceship and two shuttles that will run out of power soon," Marce said.

"Or perhaps they won't run out of power soon, because the Dalasýslans are exceedingly clever. No one can scavenge and make do like a Dalasýslan. That was certainly the case in my time, and it appears to be the case now. And while your arrival might not have actually been divinely ordained, the fact that you arrived when you did and gave them so many tools to survive must have looked miraculous to them. In which case the 'prophecy' came true for them. Or true enough, which in my experience is how prophecy works."

"You have much experience with prophecy?" Marce asked.

"Enough, in this case," Chenevert said. "Speaking of which, talk to me more about your Interdependent Church." And then the two of them went on, talking about everything possible except too much of Chenevert's life.

As they counted down the seconds until they arrived in Hub space, Marce decided whatever Chenevert had been in his previous life, in this one he seemed a pretty decent fellow.

"Here we go," Hanton said, watching his monitor. "Aaaaaaand . . . arrival. We're in Hub space."

"I'm not seeing anything being flung at us with murderous intent," Chenevert said to Hanton, after a few seconds. "You?"

"Nothing coming at us," Hanton agreed. "I do see three small objects floating by the Flow shoal."

"I see them too," Chenevert said. On the command monitor one of these objects appeared as the *Auvergne*'s cameras zoomed in on it.

"It's a monitoring craft," Sergeant Sherrill said. "They're at nearly every exit shoal. Records the ship and its arrival time against filed schedules."

"I can guarantee there were no filed schedules for this ship," Marce said. "Or this exit shoal."

"Is it an Interdependency monitor? Or

one from the Wus?" PFC Gamis asked.

"They're all made by the Wus no matter what," Hanton said. "Shipbuilding is their specialty."

"Regardless of whose it is, we're spotted," Sherrill said, and looked over to Marce. "What do you want to do?"

"I think we need to march right down the lane," Marce said.

"Sir?"

"Send a message to Xi'an traffic control to inform the emperox that her spy ship the *Samuel III* is back from her secret mission and ready to dock and report," Marce said. "And send it out in the open."

"Because spy ships do that," Gamis said.

"Spy ships that don't want to run the risk of being hit by long-range missiles from the Wus between here and Xi'an do, yes."

"The *Samuel III*?" Chenevert asked.

"It's an inside joke between me and the emperox," Marce told him. "I'll explain it later."

"I'm just impressed you know the emperox well enough to have inside jokes with her."

"Well, you know," Marce said, awkwardly. "She's pretty approachable."

"Indeed," murmured Chenevert, clearly reappraising Marce, who felt deeply uncomfortable being reappraised.

"Could you send that message, please?" he said, to change the subject.

"Already done, since we were already being hailed by Xi'an traffic control," Chenevert said.

"Are you sure it's Xi'an?" Gamis asked Chenevert. "You're new here."

"I'm monitoring other chatter from the same source," Chenevert said. "If your friends the Wus are planning to lure us in, they're doing so very elaborately."

"You never know," Gamis said, defensively.

"No, you never do," Chenevert said. "Although in this case, it seems unlikely, as we've just been directed to the private imperial docks. I've been told a detail has been detached to escort us in." He looked over at Marce. "You need to teach me your inside jokes."

The *Auvergne* was met at the private imperial docking area by a shuttle full of imperial guards, who went through the ship stem to stern, removing the crew of the *Princess,* who had been kept reasonably comfortably in three staterooms, as they did so. When the *Princess*'s crew had departed on the shuttle and a small contingent of imperial guards were left behind, a second shuttle arrived, this one carrying several other guards and the emperox.

"Lord Marce," Grayland said as she exited the shuttle. "It pleases us to see you again."

"Your Majesty," Marce said. He was aware that Grayland was using her royal "we" voice for the benefit of the Imperial Guard, and not as a distancing tactic, and in this very formal moment his brain flashed back to Cardenia and him naked in her bed, because brains were like that. He very much hated his brain for it. "It is likewise a pleasure to see you."

Grayland looked around and then returned her gaze to Marce. "The *Samuel III,* is it."

"Actually the *Auvergne,* ma'am."

"Lord Marce, this is not the ship you left on."

"No, ma'am."

"And while we are happy to know that we possess a spy ship so secret that even *we* were not aware that we possessed it, nevertheless we are concerned about the disposition of the *Oliveer Bransid* and her crew."

"The *Bransid* was attacked, and her crew lost, except for me and five others."

"By whom?"

"A ship that followed us from Hub space,

ma'am. We captured her crew and brought them with us. Your guards took them off the ship to be held more securely than here."

"And your friend, Dr. Roynold?"

Marce looked down and shook his head, silently.

"We are deeply sorry for you, Lord Marce," Grayland said.

"Thank you, ma'am."

"We have many matters we wish to discuss with you, but perhaps a shuttle bay receiving area is not the best place for that. Would you accompany us back to the palace for further discussion?"

"Yes, Your Majesty. But before that, I would ask you to come with me for a moment first."

"For what purpose, Lord Marce?"

"There's someone on the ship I think you should meet."

"They may accompany us to the palace, Lord Marce. As may the rest of your remaining crew."

"Thank you, ma'am. The thing is, it's not quite that simple."

A few minutes later, and after having been briefly introduced to the remainder of the crew, Grayland and Marce stepped into the bridge. A guard had entered with them, but Grayland dismissed him with a nod. The guard scowled but left.

"Marce, I really am sorry about Roynold," Grayland said, quietly. "I know she was important to you."

"Thank you —" Marce stopped and smiled. "I almost just called you 'Cardenia' in public."

"Don't do that. I don't mind that you almost did. I like it. Just, yeah. Don't do that."

"I'll remember."

Grayland looked around. "Aren't I supposed to be meeting someone?"

"Yes," Marce said. "Monsieur Chenevert, you can come out now."

Chenevert appeared, shimmering, which struck Marce as a very showoff-y way to do it. Grayland's eyes got wide as he did so. Chenevert walked over to Grayland and offered an elaborate bow. "Your Majesty," he said.

Grayland stared, and then smiled, and then did something that Marce was not expecting. She offered a similarly elaborate bow. "Your Majesty," she said, to Chenevert.

Who was *delighted.* "I am found out!" he exclaimed. "And so early. Your dear Lord Marce never suspected."

"He doesn't know what I know," Grayland said.

Chenevert turned to Marce. "I can see why you like her," he said. "I very much like her already."

"Uh . . . what?" Marce said, to both of them.

"Your friend here —" Grayland turned back to Chenevert. "I'm sorry, I didn't catch your name."

"Tomas Reynauld Chenevert."

"Your friend Tomas Reynauld Chenevert is royalty. A king? Emperor? Grand Duke?"

"Merely a king, Your Majesty."

"That's *all,*" Grayland mocked lightly.

"I'm not an empress like some. But it's not 'empress' here, is it?"

"Emperox. Not gender-specific."

Chenevert pointed to Marce. "And yet this one is a lord and his father a count."

"You're expecting logic from royal titles?"

"Point."

"You're a *king*?" Marce said, to Chenevert.

"Yes. Well." Chenevert made a motion with his hand. "*Was* a king. I'm dead now, and the executive power of the throne traditionally ceases on demise. Also, I was overthrown. So there was some argument whether I was still a king even when I was alive. I say yes, but then I would."

"I have some people here who would very much like to do that to me," Grayland said. "Overthrow me, I mean."

"I would recommend against it," Chenevert advised.

"Not a great career move?"

"It frees up your schedule, which is honestly fantastic. But the people who removed you then usually want to kill you too. And that's *inconvenient.* Any assassination attempts against you yet?"

"A couple."

"Aw. You're just a baby at this," Chenevert said.

"If I could jump in here," Marce said, and turned to Grayland. "*How* did you know he's a king? Was a king?"

Grayland waved at Chenevert. "Because he's *this.*"

"What does this have to do with him being a king?"

"You have a something like this too," Chenevert said to Grayland. "Equally impressive. Equally expensive. Equally invasive."

Grayland nodded. "I have something called a Memory Room. All of the previous emperoxs are there. Their memories are there, at least. But you're different. They have the memories and can tell you what the emperox was thinking or feeling at the time, but they don't have the emotions themselves. But you seem all there."

"I am all there. Or at least it feels that way on the inside. My family made improvements to the software over time. You may be running a very early build of it."

"I always assumed it was ordered made by Rachela. The first of our emperoxs."

Chenevert shook his head. "If it's the same as what we had, it's from much earlier than that. It originally dates back to Earth. Your people and my people got it just before the Rupture."

"The what?" Marce asked.

"The Rupture. It's what we called the event that isolated us from Earth and its network of Flow stream systems, and from you." He looked at Marce and Grayland, who were staring at him blankly. "Why? What do you call it?"

"*We* don't call it anything," Marce said. "We know we lost contact with Earth about fifteen hundred years ago, but we didn't know it had its own network of Flow streams."

"Or that there was another entirely separate group of systems, with its own set of Flow streams," Grayland said.

Chenevert looked at both of them, a dawning smile on his face. "How *interest-*

ing," he said. "You had an actual dark age. You lost everything about it. About the Rupture. And about us. And Earth and its systems, too."

"You knew about us?" Marce asked.

"Of course I did," Chenevert said. "That's how I got into your space in the first place. Technically it's a treaty violation that I'm here at all, but given that the option back home was being hanged, I was willing to take that chance. And I suppose if you don't remember you had a treaty with us, and with Earth, then I shouldn't worry about violating it."

"We have a treaty with you."

"Yes. Well, obviously not me specifically. But with the Assembly, of which my planet Ponthieu is part. Twenty systems in all. And then Earth's empire, of another fifteen systems. Your collection of systems, what you now called the Interdependency, was the Free Systems. More systems but fewer people than either the Assembly or Earth, because most of our systems had livable planets in them and yours mostly . . . didn't."

Marce and Grayland looked at each other again, dumbfounded.

"You really *don't* know, do you?" Chenevert said.

"This is entirely new to me," Grayland said. Marce nodded as well.

"There's irony to this, you know," Chenevert said. "Or actually, you don't."

"What's the irony?"

"It was the Free Systems that pushed for the treaty that broke up the systems into three partitions. And then created the Rupture when that wasn't enough isolation for it."

"Created the Rupture?" Marce said. "We *initiated* a Flow stream collapse?"

"You did. Or your ancestors did, anyway."

"That's not physically possible."

"You say that, and yet it happened."

"Do you know how to do it?" Grayland asked Chenevert.

"Me, definitely not. The scientists of Ponthieu and the Assembly? Not that I know of, as of three hundred years ago. It was something *you* had, and you didn't share it, I suspect because you didn't want to, you just wanted to be shut of *us*. And now it appears that you've lost the knowledge as well. I can't say I see this as a bad thing, Lord Marce, Your Majesty."

"You can verify this?" Marce said. "This history you're talking about."

"It's in our history books."

"And you brought those?" Grayland asked.

Chenevert smiled. "Your Majesty, when I left Ponthieu, I was leaving forever. I assure you, I have brought *everything.*"

Chapter 21

"What do you know about the Free Systems?" Cardenia asked Rachela I, in the Memory Room.

"They were one of the predecessors to the Interdependency," Rachela I said. "Although by the time we were forming the Interdependency, nobody called them that."

"Why not?"

"That loose alliance of systems had fallen apart centuries earlier."

"And why was that?"

"For the same reason many alliances fall apart — competing interests, lack of economic enthusiasm, stupid or venal rulers, and simple neglect, or some combination of each."

"I'm the emperox of the Interdependency," Cardenia said. "My mother was a historian. How do I not know about the Free Systems?"

"You did know about them, but you

weren't aware of that particular label. Pedagogy varies over time. It's possible that when and where you grew up, it wasn't considered important."

"That sounds evasive to me," Cardenia said.

"I'm aware that you are addressing me with some hostility in your voice," Rachela I said. "But I am not in any way trying to be evasive to you. Remember I have no ego to bruise and no need to justify either my actions or the actions of others. If I sound evasive to you, it's possible you're phrasing your questions in a way that sounds to you in your current emotional state as evasive."

"The problem is not you, it's me, is what you're saying," Cardenia said.

"Basically."

"You know, I met a computer simulation of a human today who could be evasive, if he wanted to."

"Okay," Rachela I said. "I, however, cannot."

Cardenia took a breath and tried to center herself because, damn it, Rachela was right; she was a little hostile at the moment and it was making her ask the wrong questions. After a minute, during which time the image of Rachela I stood quietly waiting, just like a computer simulation would, she tried again.

"Are you aware of any attempt in your time to stop teaching the time of our history in which the Free Systems existed?"

"No. It wasn't something that either I or my contemporaries considered."

"Did you ever try to censor or alter histories at all?"

"After I became emperox, my propagandists worked to sell the story of the creation of the Interdependency that we wanted to see propagated into the future, particularly with respect, as we've spoken before, about the prophecies. By the time I died, our angle on it, or something very close to it, was the generally accepted view of events. Of course there were alternate versions, but those tended to be less mainstream and their authors not tenured at the best schools. Additionally, we created blasphemy laws, which we used infrequently but that had the intended effect of further entrenching the official story."

"But you didn't actively work to change or alter the history of the period of time before the Interdependency."

"Not unless it was directly prior to the Interdependency — that is, during the period of time we were trying to create it."

"Have you ever heard of the Assembly?"

"That is a very vague question. 'The Assembly' could be any number of things."

Cardenia bit the inside of her cheek to avoid snapping at Rachela I, who would not be bothered by it, which would just make Cardenia angrier.

"Are you aware of a political entity called the Assembly, comprised of states in star systems that are not nor ever have been part of what is now the Interdependency," she asked, very specifically.

"No."

"Have you heard of the Tripartition Treaty?" Cardenia referred to the treaty by the specific name Chenevert had given her for it.

"No."

"Have you ever heard of an event called the Rupture, in which the Free Systems were cut off from other human states?"

"No."

"How did Earth become inaccessible to the Interdependency systems?"

"There was a collapse of the Flow streams to and from it."

"How did that collapse happen?"

"It was a natural event," Rachela I said.

"Are you lying to me right now?"

"I am not intentionally lying to you. It's

possible I am telling you information you either think or know to be wrong, but if so it's because the information of my own personal experience has been shown to be incorrect, not because I am dissembling."

"Did you wonder if there were other human systems out there? Besides Earth?"

"In a casual or idle way, yes. Given what I knew about Flow streams while I was alive, it seemed possible that new ones could open up and then people from Earth would visit them. One of the most popular entertainments of my reign had that as its plot. It was called *The Wizard of Oz.* But it was never something I gave much concern to. We were busy enough at the time."

Cardenia thought for a moment. "Are you the earliest person in the Memory Room? I mean, are there the memories and thoughts of anyone else in here besides emperoxs?"

"No," Rachela I said. "The Memory Room was specifically meant for emperoxs. The technology that operates this was banned by me for the use of anyone who is not an emperox. Not only this specific implementation of it, but any technological implementation that replicates its intent or effect."

"But the technology existed before you used it."

"Yes. It was very old technology dating back to Earth. I was looking to create a technology for this purpose, and one of the researchers checking various archives discovered it. It hadn't been used, as far as I can tell, because the implementation cost is prohibitive for anyone who is not a state, or does not have access to the wealth of a state."

"How much does it cost to run this room?" Cardenia asked.

"At this point very little, because the majority of the cost is in the past. The power and infrastructure for it are part of the carrying costs for the Xi'an habitat in general, which exists specifically for the purposes of the emperoxs. When extraordinary costs are incurred in its maintenance or upgrading, the imperial treasury simply creates the amount needed, increasing the money supply."

"That can't be legal."

"It's legal because I made it legal," Rachela I said. "And in a larger sense governments print money for their own purposes. This is one of them."

"So there are no other examples of this technology being used, prior to this room."

"Not that I am aware of, no."

"Did it bother you that so much of our

past is unknown?" Cardenia asked.

"It's not unknown," Rachela said. "But it's possible that large areas have been lost."

"How does that happen? We've been a highly technological, space-faring civilization from our beginning. It's not like the Interdependency is like Earth, where humans had to invent fire, and wheels, and rockets."

"Those are all technologies," Rachela I said. "History is not technology."

"You say that *in the Memory Room,*" Cardenia said, disbelieving.

"The Memory Room is not memory," Rachela said. "It is a means of preserving memory. A library is not information; it is a means of preserving information. In every case before memory or information can be stored, someone has to decide what must be stored. Someone must choose. Someone must curate."

"*Your* thoughts haven't been curated in here," Cardenia pointed out. "Every memory and thought and emotion you had, and that your successors had, is in here. That's how it works."

"Yes," Rachela I said. "All the memories and thoughts and emotions of only eighty-seven people to date, over the course of a thousand years, during which time countless billions have lived, each with memories and thoughts and emotions that no longer exist anywhere. They're gone. We're here. That's the curation."

"So someone *curated* away an entire era of our history."

"It doesn't have to have been intentional or malicious. As I mentioned before in reference to teaching, different eras have different priorities. They pick and choose and things fall to the wayside. When they fall away, whoever is next might not know how to find them to pick them up again."

"Or someone could have done it intentionally."

"Yes," Rachela said. "Although hiding the past never works as well as simply neglecting it."

"What do you mean?"

"When things are hidden, there will always be people who object, and who will then go out of their way to preserve and store what is being hidden, so that someone can find it later, either intentionally or by simply stumbling over it. This is why I never tried to hide alternative takes of history. It makes them more attractive to future historians when you do. I smothered them under strata of official history instead."

“Never hide, just overwhelm,” Cardenia joked.

“It worked for me,” Rachela I said.

Cardenia nodded at this and excused Rachela I, who winked out of existence. She sat there in the room, which was spare and unfurnished as always, and tried to think of where and how she might get the actual history of the time before the Interdependency. Of the time where the “Free Systems,” through their apparent stupidity and stubbornness, condemned their descendants to a terrifying free fall into chaos. Cardenia had to admit that if those people had been her immediate predecessors, she might want to bury their history too.

But she had to know. It wasn’t that she didn’t trust Chenevert, né King Tomas XII of Ponthieu, or his information. He had no particular reason to lie to her or to Marce. But extraordinary claims require extraordinary evidence, and what Chenevert was claiming was the most extraordinary thing that Cardenia had ever heard. It had to be substantiated.

And, well, how to do that? The Imperial Library at Hubfall had the single largest library in the Interdependency, with five hundred million volumes of work in print and electronic form dating back to the Racheline days. The Imperial Library at Xi'an — technically Cardenia's personal library as emperox, although open to visitors and researchers — had twenty million volumes, with a specific emphasis on the lives and administrations of the emperoxs. Trying to comb through even the smaller of these two, even in the significantly smaller numbers of the appropriate area of study, would take more time than Cardenia had, and would probably require more time than the Interdependency had before everything collapsed. And then there were the literally billions of other books and documents and theses around the Interdependency.

Never hide, just overwhelm, Cardenia thought. She thought about who it would be that would try to find the histories that had been hidden. And then she had another thought.

Well, I am in the Memory Room.

"Jiyi," Cardenia said, calling forth the Memory Room's default avatar, a creature without apparent age or gender. Jiyi appeared and stood before Cardenia, waiting.

"This room stores the memories and thoughts of all of the previous emperoxs," Cardenia said.

"That's correct," said Jiyi.

"What else does it store?"

"It would help if you were more specific."

"What do you have on the Rupture?"

"Are you asking about the notable third-century musical group, the motion picture from 877, or the pre-Interdependency historical event in which the Free Systems severed their connection with Earth and the Assembly?" Jiyi asked.

"So it's true," Marce said to Cardenia, that night, in bed.

"Not just true, but *hidden,*" Cardenia said. "Jiyi said that within fifty years of the Rupture it was the agreed-upon policy to refer to it as a natural event rather than instigated by the Free Systems. No one wanted to own it."

"Because it was a terrible use of technology?"

"Because the Free Systems almost starved. They were as economically dependent on the other systems in the Assembly and Earth's confederation as we all are with each other. Jiyi says numerous people pointed this out at the time, but the political will was to turn their backs on the other two unions. After they all got done congratulating each other, there were food and resource riots. Hundreds of thousands died and the Free Systems started raiding each other before everything got all straightened out."

"They saw the folly of their ways."

"No, the old guard died off and then the next generation decided never to speak of it again. And it worked, mostly."

"Then how did Jiyi find it?"

"You're not going to like the answer," Cardenia said.

"I mean, I just found out today that Jiyi exists and lives in a secret room where you have conversations with ancestors who have been dead for hundreds of years, so I don't know that anything you tell me will unsettle me more than that."

"Jiyi goes through people's stuff."

"Okay, you're right, I don't like that," Marce said. "How does that even work?"

"Jiyi is a thousand years old and has a mission to remember things. In that time it's found its way to have its agents access every network across the Interdependency and find all the nooks and crannies where people store or access information. But not all information. The information that people actively try to hide. It sends its little programs out, and they find it and bring it back to Jiyi. Who then sits on it. Forever."

"Why secret information?"

"Because non-secret information is already accessible. Jiyi's programming doesn't see the need to retrieve that. It only takes the information that's hidden. Rachela programmed it that way. Or had it programmed that way, since I don't think she was a programmer. I asked her about it today. She said, 'When things are hidden, there are always people who will object.' I guess she was the first."

"Why didn't she just tell you that Jiyi had been doing that for a thousand years?"

"Because she's not a person. She's a program and she only answers what you ask her. I didn't ask her if Jiyi had the information."

"That sounds evasive to me."

"It sounds that way to me too."

"So Jiyi knows everything."

"No, Jiyi knows everything *hidden.* If it's not hidden, Jiyi doesn't record it because Jiyi doesn't need to. It can just access that information like you or I do. But if it's hidden it can disappear. And Jiyi doesn't want that. It doesn't mean Jiyi *instantly* knows everything that's hidden. It's not magic. It's here and its agents are everywhere and it takes them time to come back. But Jiyi is patient like nothing else in the universe is patient. Sooner or later it finds everything it sets out to find. It may take decades or longer. But it finds it."

"I have so many questions about this," Marce said. "None of them good."

"I don't like it either," admitted Cardenia. "And yet without it I wouldn't know the truth about our past."

"That's not entirely true. The information was out there. Jiyi found it. *You* could have found it, eventually."

Cardenia shook her head. "The information was out there once upon a time. Who knows if it's still extant anywhere other than in Jiyi right now."

"It's creepy, Cardenia."

"It is, and you know what's weird about it is that, as far as I can tell, none of the other emperoxs besides Rachela knew that Jiyi was doing it at all. They just used it to talk to other emperoxs."

"Like you did, until just today," Marce pointed out. "Because that's what you were told the Memory Room does. Also, it's called the Memory Room, not the Hidden Information Room."

"It makes me curious how things would be different if other emperoxs had known."

"It would have been terrible," Marce said. "It's a form of absolute knowledge, on top of the absolute power you already have."

"I don't have absolute power," Cardenia protested.

"Of course not," Marce said. "That's why no one's worried at all that you are offering up mystical visions of the future of the Interdependency, or concerned that you are going to declare martial law when you address the parliament, which you can do at your whim, like any normal person without absolute power."

"I don't *feel* like I have absolute power," Cardenia amended.

"Just promise me that you will never tell your children that Jiyi can do that," Marce said. "You were almost married to a Nohamapetan. It terrifies me to think about what would happen if one of them ever knew what Jiyi could do."

"I have more bad news for you."

"Oh dear God."

Cardenia pointed to the back of her neck. "I have a network in my body and brain," she said. "Everything I think and feel and say and do is recorded. And when I die, all of that is going to be in the Memory Room too. So even if I never tell my kids, it doesn't mean they won't hear it from me. Just after I'm dead."

"That's got to be unsettling for you," Marce said, after a minute's consideration.

Cardenia shrugged and snuggled into Marce. "A little. But there are benefits. I didn't get to spend much time with my father growing up. I loved him and he loved me, but we didn't know each other at all. And now in the Memory Room I get to speak to him every day, if I want. It's like I get him back. And that's a blessing."

"It is," Marce agreed.

"If you like your parent, that is," Cardenia said. "I don't see Dad talking to his mother all that often. She was awful to him and the rest of the universe as I heard."

"Did you ever speak to her?"

"I brought her up once to ask her a specific question about a policy she made. After talking to her for five minutes I decided that I probably didn't ever have to speak to her again."

The two of them were silent for a moment.

"So . . . you're recording now?" Marce asked.

"I'm always recording," Cardenia murmured.

"So, uh —"

"No, it didn't record us having sex. I mean, it did," Cardenia qualified, and then watched the mild panic on Marce's face. "But it's not recording it that way. It's recording how I felt about it, and you, and this moment."

"And what will your ghost tell anyone who asks?"

"That all of the above are pretty great, actually."

"Just, you know. Don't go into detail."

"Maybe it'll be your kid too," Cardenia said, and then couldn't believe a thing like that had actually come out of her mouth, but it was too late, *fuck,* so she would just have to roll with it now.

"You can't marry me," Marce said, lightly. "I'm waaaay below your station. I'm barely even a lord. I'm a lord on a technicality."

Cardenia slapped his chest (lightly) in mock outrage. "Don't tell us what we can do, Lord Marce! We are the emperox! And we have absolute power! We shall marry you if we want."

"Yes ma'am," Marce said. "Sorry, ma'am. Reporting for marriage duty, ma'am."

"Not yet. We're still trying you out."

"Try me out all you like. But please stop using the royal 'we.' That's a little too kinky for me."

Cardenia laughed and climbed on top of Marce and started kissing him and was soon lost in everything that followed, except for that one practical part of her brain, which was saying, *You know, you really* do *have absolute power and absolute knowledge now.*

Maybe it's time to put them to use.

Fine, yes, I will think about it, Cardenia said. *Just shut up for right now. I'm busy.*

Cardenia's brain shut up.

But then woke her up a few hours later, and started talking to her again. She listened and after a time, stroked Marce's hair to wake him up. "I think I'm ready," she said.

"Oh, good," Marce said, sleepily. "Ready for what?"

"To move things forward," she said. "Will you help me?"

"Yes," Marce said. "But does it have to be *now*? I'd like to go back to sleep."

Cardenia let him go back to sleep, and then got up, walked over to the Memory Room, and let herself in.

CHAPTER 22

And just like that, everyone and all of their plans ran out of time.

Archbishop Gunda Korbijn was sitting in a small Xi'an Cathedral Complex courtyard, taking her morning tea, when the announcement came that the emperox would address the parliament that afternoon at 6 p.m. Korbijn read the announcement, nodded, finished her tea and then instructed Ubes Ici to make a call to Tinda Louentintu, chief of staff to the Countess Nohamapetan, and then to connect her in when he did.

Tinda Louentintu took the call, spoke very briefly to Archbishop Korbijn, no more than a few words, and then after an exchange of final pleasantries broke the connection and made a call to the Countess Nohamapetan, cloistered as she was in the *Blame.* Louentintu's voice was jubilant.

On the *Blame,* the Countess Nohamapetan also expressed jubilance and then gave her chief of staff instructions on whom to reach and in what order. Some of those people would have their own people to contact, so were to be contacted first, followed by other people of importance, followed by others who, while not as important, would offer safety in numbers and a quorum. That finished, the countess connected with Jasin Wu.

Jasin Wu by this time had already heard about the parliamentary address and was about to start his own round of coded messages and calls when the countess called and reminded him of everything he already knew, as if he was her lackey and not the actual Managing Director of the Actual Largest and Most Important House in the Interdependency, Thank You Very Much. But Jasin held his irritation in check because he understood the value of long-term alliances and planning. When the call was done, he then proceeded with his own list, which included Admiral Emblad of the Imperial Navy, and then he had his assistant call Deran Wu's assistant and invite his cousin to come to his office for a chat.

Deran Wu, also aware by this point of the announcement, went into his cousin's office at his invitation, and when the assistants were cleared out and the door shut, went over their own mutual set of plans and contacts, which were different but related to the plans and contacts that the Countess Nohamapetan was aware of. The House of Wu may have found itself in an alliance of convenience with the House of Nohamapetan, but one thing that would be essential is for it to be made clear, quietly but definitively, that this was not an alliance of equals and that the House of Wu, both in its incarnation as a noble house and its soon-to-be-remodeled incarnation as the imperial house, was and would always be the senior partner.

After leaving his cousin's office, Deran Wu did his own set of calls and messages as discussed, informed his assistant that he had an emergency meeting across town so to reschedule his meetings for the rest of the day, and then, when in the elevator down to his car, sent an encrypted message to Nadashe Nohamapetan, acknowledging that he was moving forward with their plan, and then, having done that, expressing in what he thought was a manner both jocular and sexy his own enthusiastic anticipation of how the two of them would celebrate their imminent success. Then he went to his meeting, with someone who didn't know he was coming.

Nadashe Nohamapetan read the second message from Deran Wu with mild disgust, then put the lesser Wu cousin out of her mind for the moment, because there were other more urgent things to worry about — namely, the transferring of close to a hundred million marks out of her secret accounts and into a secure and compact data crypt she had with her on the *Blame.* Nadashe had had a mild panic attack when a couple of her smaller secret accounts were locked and seized and decided now was the perfect time for her to get liquid.

A hundred million marks was nothing compared to her overall share of the House of Nohamapetan corporation, but seeing as she was temporarily and inconveniently meant to be dead, her ability to access her legitimate accounts had been severely compromised. Nadashe's mother was meant to repatriate those shares to her own holdings, but hadn't done so yet, and at this point a hundred million marks in liquidity was better than nothing.

Of course, if everything worked as planned, Nadashe would soon be back from the dead, for starters. But much of that depended on Deran, which is why Nadashe tolerated the appalling messages from him for now. The other part of it depended on another person entirely: Admiral Emblad of the Imperial Navy. Nadashe decided it was time to put in a call to him.

Admiral Lonsen Emblad was shocked to receive messages from a dead woman. But after her identity hash checked out and Emblad was sure it wasn't a prankster or an agent of either Naval Intelligence or the Ministry of Investigation, he and Nadashe had a long and fruitful discussion detailing promises made, payments received and plans already long set in motion, and Nadashe's expectation of those plans to continue apace. When Nadashe had hung up, Emblad mused on messages from the dead, and also on whom he would want to place his bet on: the House of Wu or the House of Nohamapetan. He had a few hours to decide. Admiral Emblad decided to do some of that thinking at the officers' club, with a drink.

Kiva Lagos, who had been the one to fuck with Nadashe's smaller accounts, just to see what whoever was withdrawing money would do about it, received notice of the parliamentary address while visiting with Senia Fundapellonan, who was celebrating having that fucking breathing tube removed from her throat. Kiva smiled at the announcement because she was aware that plans were now set in motion and it was going to be an absolute fucking delight to see how things played out.

In the meantime she caught Fundapellonan up on the events of the day, because these days Fundapellonan had no love left for the Nohamapetans, and it would give her joy to hear of their travails, and also because Kiva just liked talking to her. Kiva considered that she might be developing a thing for Fundapellonan, which on one hand would be a very not-Kiva thing to do, but on the other hand who gave a fuck if it was "not-Kiva," because she wasn't some fucking fictional character destined to do whatever some goddamn hack wanted her to do.

Fundapellonan smiled at Kiva, because she kind of liked her too.

Marce Claremont did not have to be informed about the parliamentary address because he had been there when the decision had been made, a fact that still stunned and amazed him. Not about being there when the decision was made so much as where the decision was made — the emperox's bed — and what he was doing there when it had been made, which was lying there naked after some really enjoyable morning sex. By now Marce was aware he was falling more than a little bit in love with Cardenia, not because she was the emperox (that part sort of scared the crap out of him, in point of fact) but because they were awkward in complementary ways.

And while he was now happy being a little in love with Cardenia, there was already a beginning melancholy background hum to Marce's emotions because he knew the relationship was doomed, not because they weren't compatible but because she was emperox, and he really was below her station. Emperoxs didn't marry for love, and they don't marry people who are lords basically by courtesy. Difficult times were coming, and Cardenia was going to be making some hard choices. Marce was, in a small and nearly subconscious way, preparing himself for when the hard choice Cardenia was going to have to make involved him.

Until then, however, he was doing what she asked of him: running the data he and Roynold (*Come on, it was pretty much* all *Roynold,* his brain said) had gathered from Dalasýsla, adding it to the data set she and he had already had, and then adding to that the frankly astounding amount of historical Flow stream data that Chenevert had in his possession for the Assembly and for Earth and even the Free Systems. All the data in question was no younger than three hundred and sometimes as much as fifteen hundred years old. But it meant that Marce's understanding of the general topography of the Flow was tripling, and with that information came more, newer and hopefully better understandings of how the Flow moved in their area of space. If Chenevert were something more than virtual, Marce would have hugged him.

Tomas Reynauld Chenevert, the former Tomas XII, who if he wanted to be truthful about it had not been entirely unjustly overthrown, was aware of the parliamentary address but was not particularly concerned about it because he did not see that it involved his current interests to any significant extent. At the moment he was more interested in the small agent program that he had sequestered in a virtual sandbox environment. The agent program had tried to access the *Auvergne* and had been flummoxed by its entirely different — and in this part of space, *unique* — processing environment. Chenevert had snagged it, pulled it apart momentarily to understand its code and its programming, and understood it to be an agent of the semiautonomous AI that Emperox Grayland II had mentioned.

Chenevert thought about everything that

could be done with the agent, decided at this point small steps were best, and sent the thing on its way with an invitation by Chenevert to its boss, to meet.

Jiyi, who had not received that invitation yet, knew about the parliamentary address because Emperox Grayland II had spent a significant part of the early morning discussing it with the imperial avatars in the Memory Room, most especially Rachela I and Attavio VI, and with Jiyi itself about information it had, outside of the realm of knowledge of the emperoxs themselves. Jiyi, which had no emotions or feelings in itself, outside of accessing the recorded thoughts and emotions of the emperoxs and having their avatars describe them to the current emperox, did not think anything in itself one way or another about the parliamentary address. If it had been asked to consider it, it would probably say it would have to wait until the current emperox, Grayland II, was dead and asked about it by her successor in order to give it any thought.

The current emperox, Grayland II, who was not dead yet, did not need to be informed about the parliamentary address since she was the one who was giving it, and the one who had informed everyone when it would be. And after sufficient time had passed for the announcement to diffuse into the world. Grayland II ordered something else: individual invitations to a special reception prior to the address, beginning at 4 p.m., at the imperial palace ballroom. The reception would be short, to allow for all assembled, including the emperox herself, to make their way from the imperial palace to the parliament, on the other end of the Xi'an habitat. But, the invitations said, it promised to be unforgettable.

Each invitation came with a small printed note from the emperox herself that said that the recipient was to be recognized for their achievements and service to the Interdependency. Regrets were not to be accepted, presence required by imperial command, arrivals no later than 4:10 p.m.

Grayland was not really worried about the attendance. She was certain no one invited would want to miss it.

Kiva had arrived, as requested, at 4 p.m. sharp, dressed in a ridiculous fucking pantsuit that was nevertheless somehow in fashion and therefore acceptable for an event like this, whatever the hell that was; Grayland's assistant was light on details but stressed that the emperox herself had requested Kiva's presence. Well, okay, fine. It looked like to Kiva that maybe the two of them might end up doing each other's hair and giggling about boys after all.

This prompted Kiva to look for Marce Claremont, whom Kiva was almost certain the emperox was now banging, and good for her. Kiva had liked Marce, who had been a solid if not especially imaginative lover and a decent human being in a universe that didn't put a premium on that. That made him probably a good match for the emperox, who also appeared fundamentally decent and was probably also a solid if not adventurous bang. Not everyone could be an adventurous bang. Not everyone needed to be an adventurous bang.

That said, Kiva didn't see Marce anywhere in the room. It was instead filled with the Interdependency's political and economic A-list: important members of parliament, the heads or directors of noble houses, a smattering of admirals and generals, even a few bishops, including Archbishop Korbijn. Everybody at the party who was not serving drinks or finger foods outranked Kiva by a significant margin, which confirmed to her that she was at the party because she and Grayland were now gal pals or something.

Something spangly caught Kiva's eye; she turned and saw the fucking Countess Nohamapetan on the floor, talking animatedly to Jasin Wu and Admiral Emblad, both of whom were politely attentive but also clearly didn't give a shit about whatever she was blabbering about. Kiva starting doing the calculus of just how much trouble she would be in if she tuned up the countess right there on the fucking ballroom floor. The calculus was not in her favor; Kiva decided to get a drink to see if that would change any variables.

Before she could flag down a drink mule, one of the side doors to the ballroom opened and the emperox was announced; everyone stood and clapped while Grayland II entered, accepted their applause and walked toward an ornate lectern at the front of the ballroom. The emperox was clearly poised to give some remarks, and possibly give out some pointless fucking awards. Kiva groaned inwardly. If she'd known it was going to be that kind of event, she might have skipped out. She looked around the room and saw a couple hundred really important people who were having roughly the same thought as she was.

"Come on," Kiva muttered under her breath, "let's just get to the address at parliament and go crack some fucking skulls."

As Grayland waited for the applause to die down, she acknowledged a few people in the room, waving or smiling or pointing. Grayland eventually found Kiva in the crowd and smiled, but as her eyes began to track away, she did something else.

Wait, did she just fucking wink *at me*? Kiva thought, and looked around the room again, to see if there was anyone else the wink might have been directed to. There was no one near Kiva that she thought Grayland would give a single real shit about. So, no, it had definitely been directed at her.

Kiva wished that she had gotten that drink earlier. Something was telling her she might be needing it soon.

"Hello, my dear friends," Grayland said, after the applause had died down. "So many of you here today. It is a delight to see you, you who represent what could be the very best the Interdependency has to offer, in leadership and in commitment to our union. I know you are all anxious to see how I will embarrass myself in front of parliament" — this line got dutiful chuckles — "but before I do that I have a few presentations to give. Please indulge me. First, will the Lady Kiva Lagos come up to the lectern?"

The fuck? Kiva thought, as she walked to the lectern to very polite applause.

"Lady Kiva, in a very short time you have shown yourself to be astute and extraordinarily competent in business," Grayland said. "When I thrust you into a custodial directorship at the House of Nohamapetan, no one would have expected that you would have done so much to clean up the house's finances and rebalance their books. You truly represent the best that the noble houses have to offer. As such, I am now appointing you to the vacant seat on the executive committee of the Interdependency. Congratulations, Lady Kiva."

There was applause to this, and then some woman walked up to Kiva with a fucking crystal thing, which Kiva took numbly in one arm, the other arm finding its way to Grayland, who stepped back from the lectern to shake Kiva's hand. Kiva leaned in close.

"I don't want this fucking job, Your Majesty," she said, quietly, in Grayland's ear.

"I know," Grayland said. "I need you there anyway. Sorry."

Kiva smirked at this and turned to go back into the crowd, but Grayland caught her by the elbow. "No," she said. "Stay up here, a little behind the lectern."

"Yes, ma'am."

"You're not going to want to miss this,"

Grayland said, and then stepped back to the lectern and called up Archbishop Korbijn.

The archbishop arrived at the lectern, dressed in archbishopric finery, or so Kiva supposed, since she didn't actually attend church with any regularity, although she had once had sex in a cathedral, which was great, if you like cold and echoey, which Kiva discovered she didn't so much.

"You said to me that you wanted to address an issue with me today, here," Grayland said to the archbishop. "Here's your chance, Archbishop."

Kiva watched the archbishop step up to the lectern and then noticed the look on a number of the faces in the crowd: uncertainty and confusion. A few were muttering to others. More just looked unhappy.

"Your Majesty, in the last month there have been grave and important concerns about your conduct," Archbishop Korbijn said. "Your visions of the future of the Interdependency, while comforting to many of our parishioners, have also generated legitimate apprehension among the powerful, in our church and outside of it, about your state of mind, and, yes, your sanity."

The muttering got suddenly louder —

"With that in mind, let me be absolutely

clear where the Interdependent Church stands on this matter."

— and just as quickly, silence, which lasted several seconds.

For fuck's sake, don't drag it out, Kiva thought. *Get on with it already.*

"The Interdependent Church confirms and celebrates the nature and manner of your visions as consistent with our doctrines and faith, and stands fully behind the power and majesty of their power of revelation," the archbishop said, and the uproar returned. "I likewise affirm that you are and remain the head of our church. We follow where you lead."

And with that the archbishop stepped back from the lectern, kneeled in front of Grayland II, and kissed her right hand.

The room erupted.

Grayland II bade the archbishop to rise and had her stand next to Kiva. Kiva glanced over to the archbishop, who didn't return the glance. Kiva noted she was sweating profusely.

I really wish I had gotten that drink sooner, thought Kiva. Kiva then noticed that all the serving staff had disappeared from the room, along with whatever woman had given her the fucking crystal thing she still had cradled in her left arm. Kiva decided to put the thing down.

By this time Grayland had returned to the lectern and was raising her hands to silence the room. Eventually she got her way.

"I know that last part came as a surprise to many of you," Grayland said. "As will this next part. Each of you who were invited today were told that your service to the Interdependency would be recognized. And now it will be. My dear friends, I will make this simple. In this room, right now, if you are standing in front of me, you are now under arrest for treason."

There was a bang as all the ballroom doors were kicked open and armed imperial guards flooded the perimeter of the room, and also formed a line directly in front of the lectern, just in case anyone was stupid enough to try to charge the emperox.

No one was. After a few initial shrieks and yells, the crowd of very impressive traitors fell into stony and stunned silence.

"Now, I know what you're thinking. How dare I accuse you? But it's not me who is accusing you, my friends." Grayland nodded toward a side door, which opened and disgorged Deran Wu. There were shouts and a surge toward Deran, which was quickly stanched when the imperial guards leveled their weapons. Deran stood impassively.

"Deran was good enough to detail the entire conspiracy for us," Grayland said. "And I have to say I was impressed with the theatricality of it. To have Archbishop Korbijn denounce me in front of the parliament as she was saying the benediction and to announce a schism in the church. To have the Countess Nohamapetan rise and accuse me of arranging the assassination of her daughter Nadashe."

"You did!" the countess shrieked. "She's dead because of you!"

"She was alive this morning when I messaged her," Deran Wu said, and there were gasps. "She's on your ship right now."

"Admiral Emblad," Grayland said. "You would stand and tell me that the Imperial Navy was no longer mine to command, and then, as the final blow" — Grayland shifted her gaze to the man standing next to the admiral — "you, Jasin Wu, would stand and announce that the House of Wu, my own house, could no longer support me as emperox, and that you were only one house among dozens. Those houses, as you can see, all represented here, now."

Holy shit, this is amazing, Kiva thought. The room fairly echoed with stunned silence.

"Which reminds me," Grayland said, and

nodded to the side door again.

"Oh God, what now," Archbishop Korbijn said.

A trim man came through, dressed in black, and stood in sight of the crowd.

"Cousin, you might remember Captain Cav Ponsood. You contracted his ship, on behalf of the Countess Nohamapetan here, to chase down and destroy the ship carrying Lord Marce Claremont of End. You did so because the countess believed Lord Marce was important to me, and by killing him, she would hurt me."

Kiva looked at the Countess Nohamapetan, who despite her every effort against it was smiling at the idea of Marce Claremont blasted to bits in space.

Fuck it, Kiva thought. *I'm kicking her ass in.*

Another man walked out of the side door. Marce Claremont. He looked over at the countess.

"You missed," he said. "But you killed nearly every other member of my crew. That's on you, Countess." He stepped back, behind Grayland. Kiva caught how he looked at her. Oh, yeah. They were definitely boning.

"Now," Grayland II said, from the lectern. "I know why I'm here today. Let's talk about why *you* are here today. You are all here because of what you think of me. You think I am weak. You think I am a naive child. You think my concerns about the collapse of the Flow streams stand in the way of your businesses and your own plans for power. You think because I claim visions I am unstable, or delusional, or cynical. You think because I am an accidental emperox that I should not be emperox at all. You think these things, some or all of them. And because you think them, you conspired to cast me aside. To raise my cousin Jasin in my place. To carry on the status quo as long as the Flow streams allow, and leave to others to worry about what happens next.

"Well, my friends, last night, I had a vision. A new vision. And in that vision, I saw all your plans. I saw all your schemes. I saw all your frauds, and your cheats, your secret affairs and your secret bank accounts. I saw every one of you as you are, not how you present yourself. And in that the vision, I saw you here, in front of me. Humbled. As you are, right now.

"Tell me, you who could be the very best the Interdependency has to offer, yet choose not to be: Who now is weak? Who has been naive? Who is cynical? And who is the emperox here?

"You have doubted me. Doubt me no longer. You have come to destroy me. I am not destroyed. You have come to burn me. *I* am the consuming fire. You will feel what it is to burn.

"That was my vision, and my prophecy. And now it is yours."

Grayland let that entire fucking masterpiece of a sermon linger in the air until Kiva felt the goose bumps on her arms.

And then just as suddenly, she clapped her hands. "Well, okay then. Now I have a parliament to address, so —"

"I killed him!" the Countess Nohamapetan screamed at Grayland.

"Pardon?" Grayland said.

"Your brother! Rennered! I had his car doctored!" The countess stepped forward, toward Grayland, who didn't move. "I am the reason he drove into that wall. I killed him. *I* am why you became emperox at all! You owe it to me!"

Grayland considered this as she came away from the lectern, walked to the countess and looked her in the eye.

"Lady, I don't owe you shit."

And then she walked out of the ballroom.

"Fucking best party *ever,*" Kiva said, to Marce.

EPILOGUE

"So you won," Attavio VI said to his daughter, in the Memory Room. "The great houses are in disarray because so many of them signed on for treason. The church is fully under your control. The military is purging itself of its rogue elements. And you have declared martial law."

"I have *not* declared martial law," Cardenia said. "I told parliament it has six months to create a plan to prepare the Interdependency for the collapse of the Flow. If they can't do it, then I will take it out of their hands. In six months another twenty Flow streams will have collapsed. It only gets worse from here."

"You said your friend Lord Marce thinks you can use the evanescent streams to buy the systems more time."

"Lord Marce can be optimistic in his thinking. I don't get to be. I have to assume the worst-case scenario. And the worst-case scenario is the Interdependency is unprepared because parliament can't figure itself out, and the one planet we have that can support life on its surface is blockaded by yet another Nohamapetan."

"It's still only the one ship sent to End," Attavio VI said.

"It was a *big* ship, Dad," Cardenia said. The *Prophecies of Rachela* featured a complement of ten thousand marines and more than enough firepower to blast anything it didn't like coming out of a Flow shoal into metal shavings.

"But still only one."

Cardenia shook her head. "Not anymore. A few smaller naval ships made a break to the Flow shoal when Admiral Emblad was arrested. They knew if they stayed they'd be arrested too. Four ships in all. Ghreni Nohamapetan just got reinforcements on End. And who knows? Now Nadashe may be there too." Nadashe, who had bounced from the *You Can Blame It All on Me* before she could be captured, with a hundred million marks in a data vault. The only thing she'd left behind was a note that said *Fuck you, Deran Wu.* Apparently Nadashe had been surprised by Deran announcing she was still alive.

Deran, who was going to get out of all of

this because he'd walked into the Ministry of Information with a data crypt filled with details on the conspiracy and asked for a deal, which the ministry gave him before Cardenia knew about it. She'd been annoyed because she didn't need Deran's information; everything he had she'd found with Jiyi. She'd have rather he be stuffed into the same jail cell as his cousin, because she knew he'd participated in contracting the ship that destroyed the *Oliveer Bransid* and nearly killed Marce. But she supposed it was better that she did not just magically appear with the data. Jiyi's collection methods weren't precisely legal. Deran's evidence would hold up in court.

Anyway, Deran was a hero now, with a story that he'd been participating to collect information to unmask the wider conspiracy against the emperox. It was a bullshit story, but it was a bullshit story that was going to propel him into the senior directorship chair at the House of Wu. Deran was going to be in the office Jasin used to sit in. Which was apparently all that Deran ever really wanted.

At least you know where he is, Cardenia's brain said to her. Nadashe, on the other hand, was still out there. She had no access to House of Nohamapetan funds — after the Countess Nohamapetan had completely lost it and admitted to assassinating Rennered, Cardenia had ordered every Nohamapetan account frozen and audited — but she could still do a lot of damage with a hundred million marks.

I hope you went to End, Cardenia thought. *Then you'd be out of my hair for a while.*

"I think I lost you," Attavio VI said, to Cardenia.

"I was just thinking about problems, sorry."

"I don't mind waiting," Attavio VI said.

"You don't mind anything at all," Cardenia pointed out, and then smiled. "Still, I very much like talking to you. I wish we had talked more like this when you were still alive. But this is still good."

"Thank you," Attavio VI said. "To the extent I can like anything, I like it too."

Cardenia emerged from the Memory Room and found Marce reading a message off his tablet.

"I was just talking about you," Cardenia said, coming up to him.

"To your imaginary friends, I see."

"They're not imaginary. They're just not real."

"Very subtle distinction."

"I suppose it is."

"What were you saying?"

"That you can afford to be optimistic about Flow dynamics and I can't."

"I don't know that I'm optimistic about the Flow," Marce said. "I can say I'm excited about it. We know so much more now than we did even a couple of months ago. I can tell you what I'm speculating about right now, if you want."

"Please," Cardenia said, fondly. She enjoyed watching Marce geek out.

"I have a pretty good feeling that the collapse of the Flow streams today is at least partially influenced by the Rupture," he said.

"What do you mean, 'influenced'?"

"I mean I think it did something to the stability of the Flow streams in local space. Rattled them. Shook them. I think the Rupture caused something like a pressure wave to course through the Flow, and we're seeing destabilization as a result."

"A pressure wave."

"Well, not *exactly* a pressure wave," Marce said. "It's something else entirely, in fact. But I can't really explain it in human languages. 'Pressure wave' is the closest I'm getting using words. If you could speak math I might be able to explain it to you."

"Hatide Roynold spoke math to you."

Marce nodded. "She did. Really well."

"I'm sorry she's gone."

"So am I. Anyway, this is all wild speculation on my part, because fundamentally I don't know how the Rupture worked. I can see the effect on the data Chenevert gave me from the time, but I don't know the process. I'm trying to work backward from the effect, but that's not really a great way to do things. Did you ever ask Jiyi if there was any record of the math behind the Rupture? Or what they made to make it happen?"

"There weren't any records," Cardenia lied.

"Well, that's inconvenient," Marce said, forging on. "But it makes the point that all along we've been thinking there's nothing we could be doing that would affect the Flow. But maybe we can after all. We know we found a way to close it off."

"Is there a way to open it up?"

"A Flow stream?"

"Yes."

Marce shook his head. "Closing off a Flow stream is easy, relatively speaking. You just have to snap it off at the Flow shoal."

" 'Just.' "

"I did say 'relatively,' " Marce pointed out. "Opening a Flow shoal is a lot harder because it requires accessing and moving through the Flow medium. It's like this: Closing off a Flow stream is like closing a door. Opening a Flow stream is like tunneling through a mountain."

"I like it when you use human languages," Cardenia said.

"They're my second-favorite type of languages."

Cardenia pointed at the tablet. "Is this stuff about Flow streams what you're looking at here?"

"No, it's something else entirely, from Sergeant Sherrill, who you met."

"I remember."

"She says that the retired fiver to Dalasýsla is on its way," he said, holding up his tablet to show the message. "Stuffed with food and seeds and hydroponics and technology and art and entertainment that's not eight hundred years old. It's amazing how quickly a fiver can get filled when the emperox tells someone to get something done."

"You said they needed it."

"They definitely did," he said, setting down his tablet. "You should have seen their ship."

"I told you I wished I had been able to come."

"I'm glad you didn't. It means you're still here."

Cardenia smiled at that. "Did you learn anything from the Dalasýslans that will help us?"

"I learned that survival is possible for longer than anyone would ever expect, when you have no other choice but to survive," Marce said. "I'm not sure that's a *great* lesson, but it's a lesson. But it only works for very small numbers of people. If we want to save millions, we need to think larger than that. And the only way we can do that realistically is to bring people to End."

"That will require sneaking past a large ship in rebellion," Cardenia said. "If you can find a way around that that doesn't involve just throwing ships at the Flow shoal until they run out of ammunition, I'll make you Duke of End."

"You don't need to do that."

"Are you telling me how to do my job, Lord Marce?" Cardenia joked.

"Sorry, ma'am."

"You better be. Also, come up with a way to sneak into End."

"Well, here's the thing about that," Marce said. He picked up his tablet and opened a document. "I think I may have found something."

ACKNOWLEDGMENTS

So, here's a true thing: The last few books have given me a deep and abiding appreciation for what the team at Tor does for and to my books. I've been turning them in more or less at the last possible moment, and still the people at Tor do a magnificent job turning my manuscript into a book that is worth buying and treasuring. I love that they do their job so well; it makes me want to do better for them.

So at Tor, many thanks to Patrick Nielsen Hayden, my editor; his assistant, Anita Okoye; art director Irene Gallo, who selected Nicolas Bouvier aka "Sparth" to do the spectacular cover art for the original publisher's edition (true story: because book production is often like that, Sparth's art was done before the book, and was so fabulous I made sure there were scenes in the book that could match the cover); book designer Heather Saunders; my publicist,

Alexis Saarela; and copy editor Deanna Hoak, whom I especially appreciate because I turned this in at the last possible moment and warned her it would be a hot mess from a copyediting point of view. She not only didn't murder me, she was totally great about it. Also thanks to Devi Pillai, Lucille Rettino, Fritz Foy, and Tom Doherty.

At Tor UK, many thanks to Bella Pagan and also Lisa Brewster for the deeply blue cover art.

At Audible, thank you as always to Steve Feldberg and his fabulous crew of awesome folks. Relatedly, thank you to Wil Wheaton, because, dude, Wil.

The mighty team of Ethan Ellenberg, Bibi Lewis, Joel Gotler, and Matt Sugarman handle all my agenting and lawyering needs, and I thank them humbly for it.

Thanks to Meg Frank, Olivia Ahl, and Ryvenna Lewis for checking in on me in the final stretch of writing to make sure I wasn't going completely bonkers. Likewise thank you to Kate Baker, Yanni Kuznia, Mary Robinette Kowal, and many other friends who encouraged me when I needed it.

Extra special thanks to Patty Garcia for her awesomeness over many years.

No thanks to Twitter and Facebook, who tried to suck me in on a daily basis when I needed to be writing.

(But thank you to all my friends and family on Twitter and Facebook, who are amazing.)

And as always thank you to Kristine and Athena Scalzi, wife and daughter respectively, who put up with me far more than I deserve. I would say more, but it's 7 a.m. and I was up all night finishing the book and now my brain is jelly. Anyway, they know I love them. I tell them every day, and write it in books, like this one, right now.

— John Scalzi, 6/18/18

ABOUT THE AUTHOR

John Scalzi is one of the most popular SF authors to emerge in the last decade. His debut *Old Man's War* won him the John W. Campbell Award for Best New Writer. His *New York Times* bestsellers include *The Last Colony, Fuzzy Nation,* and *Redshirts* (which won the 2013 Hugo Award for Best Novel.) Material from his blog, Whatever (whatever .scalzi.com), has also earned him two other Hugo Awards. Scalzi also serves as critic-at-large for the *Los Angeles Times.* He lives in Ohio with his wife and daughter.

The employees of Thorndike Press hope you have enjoyed this Large Print book. All our Thorndike, Wheeler, and Kennebec Large Print titles are designed for easy reading, and all our books are made to last. Other Thorndike Press Large Print books are available at your library, through selected bookstores, or directly from us.

For information about titles, please call:
(800) 223-1244

or visit our website at:
gale.com/thorndike

To share your comments, please write:
Publisher
Thorndike Press
10 Water St., Suite 310
Waterville, ME 04901